I0662993

When I Was Czar

Arthur W. Marchmont

When I Was Czar

Copyright © 2021 Bibliotech Press
All rights reserved

The present edition is a reproduction of previous publication of this classic work. Minor typographical errors may have been corrected without note; however, for an authentic reading experience the spelling, punctuation, and capitalization have been retained from the original text.

ISBN: 978-1-63637-646-2

CONTENTS

CHAPTER I

A LETTER HOME

MY Dear Miller,—

Your letter, which was as short as old Canfield's temper, reached me in Berlin as I was starting for here. I'm off to Khiva, this wise.

You'll remember my old yarn about the Czar having saved my life years ago in a pig-sticking do in Germany—he shoved or kicked me into a bush just in the nick of time when the brute made his rush—and how we then discovered the strong resemblance between us? Well, it's still true, and things have been happening in consequence.

I ran across Burnaby's book about Khiva a while back and resolved to go there. He says that three Tartars can eat a whole sheep at a single meal, and I want to see if it's true. Any old tag's good enough excuse for a globe-trotter, so I wrote to the Czar, reminded him of the pig incident, and asked permission to go East. As a result, I'm here as his guest; we've had a chat over the old time, and I'm to go where, when and how I like all over his dominions. He's an awfully decent sort, and I'm in for a real good time. But it's been a queer show.

There's a woman in it of course—and a glorious woman too. A tall, queenly creature, as handsome as a Greek, with the free carriage of one of our own American girls. I saw her on the train, or rather she saw me and seemed particularly interested in me, and it was suiting me very nicely when out came the reason. We stopped at a station some miles from the capital, and as the girl and I were separated from the rest of the people, she said in an undertone—

"Your Majesty does not count the risks of travelling incognito, alone?"

"There are pleasures to counterbalance any risks, mademoiselle," I answered. "Your solicitude is one of them." And I smiled, partly at her amazing mistake and partly because she was so pretty. Then to put myself right, I added: "But you mistake, I am no Majesty. I am an American, Harper C. Denver is my name." She lifted her eyebrows and smiled again, in obvious disbelief, and replied in French—

"An American who understands Russian, speaks French, and resembles His Majesty the Czar."

1

"An American who would gladly welcome an opportunity of seeing you again, mademoiselle."

"An American who does not desire it more fervently than I. Meanwhile, accept my warning, sire." She spoke with intense earnestness, and then left the train.

How's that for an adventure, eh? But that was only scene one. I sat thinking it over until the train ran into the station at Petersburg, and then came scene two.

The moment I stepped from the cars I saw that considerable preparations had been made to receive some one of importance, and while I stood looking about for him an old man, tightly bound in a somewhat rich uniform, with two or three companion volumes in attendance and a shelf of soldiers behind, came up to me. He waved everybody else out of earshot, and then with an almost reverential salute, said, in a low voice—

"Mr. Denver, I am sure."

"Yes, that's my name."

"Allow me to welcome you to the capital in my august master's name. I am Prince Kalkov, and His Majesty has instructed me to conduct you to the Palace. Will you accompany me?"

By this time the people on the platform had begun to show considerable interest in the proceedings, to my intense amusement, and came crowding around a bit.

"I shall be delighted," I replied; and accordingly the Prince gave a word of command to those in attendance, a guard of soldiers was formed, and I was in this way escorted to the first of a string of carriages in waiting.

"To the Palace at full gallop," cried the Prince in a tone loud enough to reach the by-standers. Some one raised a shout of "God save the Emperor," and in another minute we were off to the accompaniment of loud cries and ringing cheers from the crowd, which was by that time a pretty big one.

That was my sensational entrance into the capital. Here I am at the Czar's Palace, and from what I can judge there's a great deal more of the same kind to follow.

> "Which is why I remark,
> And my language is plain,
> That for ways that are dark
> And for tricks that are vain,
> The Russian at Home is peculiar.

And the same I shall hope to explain"—another time.

Comic opera with a dash of mysticism seems about a fair description of things up to now. More, when I've time to write.

By the way, couldn't you manage to leave Wall Street and the dollar raking process for a while and meet me on my return? I mean to go on from Khiva through India to China. Come and lunch with me, say in Pekin, and have a time among the pigtails. Wire me at our Legation and our people will forward to me. Seriously, you might do many things worse. Your old friend,

Harper C. Denver.

N.B.—I'm not monkeying about the Pekin business. Come and meet me like the good fellow you are, and hang Wall Street.

H. C. D.

CHAPTER II

PRINCE KALKOV'S PROPOSITION

"YOU mean seriously that I am to impersonate His Majesty?"

"For this purpose, M. Denver, that is my serious meaning."

"Well, it's a most extraordinary proposition."

"The occasion itself is quite an extraordinary one, of course. But I repeat, you will be doing His Majesty and his Ministers a service of extreme importance. I have asked you, of course, as I said before, only because I understand you deem yourself under a deep obligation to my master."

"You heard us speaking to-night of the incident. I owe him probably my life, and certainly an escape from serious injuries. We Americans don't go back on a call, and I admit it's up to him to call now. But this is such an odd thing."

"Think it over. It is a national characteristic of your countrymen to be prompt. Shall I return, say, in an hour?"

"Wait a minute, Prince," I said as he rose, and pushing my chair back I took a few turns up and down the room.

We were in the apartments which had been assigned to me in the Palace, and the Prince had interrupted me as I was planning out my projected journey to Khiva. It was nearly midnight, and my maps and papers lay open on the table.

"I am quite at your disposal, M. Denver," he replied courteously as he resumed his chair and watched me.

"Let me see that I've got the hang of the thing right," I said after a while. "You say this man, Boreski, is really dangerous; but I thought you had a quick method of dealing with dangerous men in Russia."

"It is not a case for ordinary methods, M. Denver, or I should not have come to you. I wish to deal with you with complete frankness, and have spoken unreservedly as to a personal friend of my master."

"We shan't pull very far together if you don't."

"To be candid, I am not sure what the man's secret object is—presuming, that is, he has one. We know little of him beyond the fact that he is an adventurer and a musician of exceptional brilliance, and that the Duchess Stephanie has conceived a great—I suppose, I should say—fondness for him. She declares she will marry him—in defiance of the Emperor's prohibition: a marriage of the kind being outside the pale of possibility, of course, owing to her relationship to the Imperial Family."

"You think he's after her money?"

"What other conclusion can one draw? The Duchess is twenty years older than he; she is the reverse of prepossessing in appearance; and he is young, handsome and certainly clever. Apart from other reasons the marriage would be a tragedy."

"And then there are these papers?"

"And then there are these papers, as you say. She is entirely dominated by him, and there is no doubt she acted at his instigation and—well, purloined them and carried them to him."

"He is certainly a daring fellow."

"A daring scoundrel, unquestionably," assented the Prince, accenting the "scoundrel."

"But knowing this, why not have arrested him?"

"I thought I had made that clear. I tried it, but he met me too cleverly. Indeed, I believe he actually angled for the arrest."

"Angled for it. How do you mean?"

"That he might get face to face with me and let me realize how far he could go, and would if pressed. It was then he told me of these papers, and that he had placed them in reliable hands to be given, if he were detained, to those who must of course never see them. Never, at any cost."

I smiled at the frank avowal.

"They are very awkward, then?"

"They might mean even war with the Powers chiefly concerned. They are extremely confidential documents. You understand, of course, M. Denver, that in diplomacy, any more than in poker, we cannot always lay the cards on the table."

"It was a fine bluff."

4

"Too dangerous for me to see him," returned the Prince with a smile, falling readily into the language of the pool room. "And the worst of it was he knew it and claimed the jack pot."

"He's a smart man. And his terms are?"

"Preposterous, absolutely; monstrous. The Imperial consent to his marriage; a special dowry of a million roubles; a patent of nobility; and a private interview with His Majesty. It was then I thought of you, His Majesty having told me you were coming here, and that you bore so striking a resemblance to him. I arranged the scene at the station this evening to test that."

"And you wish me to go to this interview, fool the man, and get the papers?"

"Precisely. Counting upon your obligation to the Emperor, I have indeed fixed the interview for to-morrow."

"The deuce you have. Isn't that rather sharp work?"

"The matter does not admit of delay; but it is of course open to you to decline."

"In which case?"

"I have not yet considered any alternative."

His coolness staggered me. But he was keen enough to see that I rather enjoyed the prospect of the adventure.

"Now as to the risks?" I asked after a pause.

"I cannot even pretend to gauge them, M. Denver. I don't think they should be considerable; but there is naturally the chance that the deception would be discovered. I don't think it is probable. Those who are constantly with His Majesty would know you in a moment of course; but these people only see my master on public occasions, and, as you have had evidence, are quite ready to be deceived."

"But the risk is there."

"Unquestionably," he assented. "The incident with the lady in the train which you described is, however, very promising. Still, as you say, the risk is there, and it is enough to make any ordinary man unwilling to run it."

"You flatter me, Prince."

"No, I try to judge you. An ordinary man would not be eager to rush off to Khiva. Besides, you are an American."

The appeal to my vanity was put astutely.

"If I were discovered I should have to get out the best way I could?"

"There might be some little trouble, but I don't think it would be really serious—to a man of resource, that is. You would be quite authorized to put the blame on me."

"And if the deception were not discovered?"

5

"It would be a short interview, and you would at the worst have to postpone your departure for one day."

"You don't anticipate any treachery? No assassination business, for instance?"

"Boreski has too much at stake. He would lose everything—including his worthless life, of course. About the strongest guarantee for your safety that you could have."

He put the amazing proposal bluntly and argued the case with as much coolness as if it had been little more than a simple conventional matter of almost everyday routine.

"You would naturally like to think it over," he said, after I had paced the room a while in thought.

"You have told me everything?"

"Yes, I think so, except, perhaps, that, of course, I don't for a moment believe Boreski made the proposition seriously."

"Yet it's an odd sort of joke, isn't it?"

"I don't mean that. I mean that no man in his senses would believe the Emperor would consent to his conditions for the interview—that my master should go to it absolutely unattended, that the place should be determined by Boreski and known to him alone, and that my master should meet a lady at the railway station, get into a strange carriage with her and be taken wherever they pleased to take him. Even in democratic countries monarchs don't act like that."

"Then what do you mean?" I asked, puzzled.

"That he intended to have his terms rejected in order that he might use the rejection to raise them. When I agreed—I only did so with you in my thoughts—I saw that his surprise amounted almost to embarrassment."

"There's this woman in it then, beside the Duchess Stephanie? Who is she?"

"I haven't an idea—some accomplice no doubt."

"Since the conditions are, as you say, so ridiculous, may he not be suspicious when we agree to them?"

"It is very possible. But on the other hand he knows that my master is as anxious as I am about those papers."

"And he may think the Emperor would take the risk. I see. Well, I guess I'll do it, Prince, but I should like to think it over."

Prince Kalkov rose at once.

"Naturally. I need only say, monsieur, that you will be doing His Majesty and Russia a service which we shall not forget. Shall I have your decision in the morning?"

"To-night, if you'll come back, say, in a couple of hours. You won't find me asleep after all you've said."

6

He smiled pleasantly, and as he went to the door, said—

"You are just the man I would have chosen for such a task, M. Denver."

"That remains to be seen," I replied; "but there's just one more question, by the by. Which are the countries concerned in those papers?"

He paused and gave me a sharp swift look, which broke to a smile.

"Not the United States, monsieur, but European Powers."

"That's the assurance I wished," said I, and then he went.

I had virtually made up my mind before the Prince left the room, and save for one consideration I should have consented right away. But I could not quite size up the Prince himself.

I was almost British in my distrust of certain classes of Russian officials. I had lived in Petersburg for some years as a boy, and my father, who was at the Embassy, had inculcated this prejudice.

I could never resist the feeling that they had some subtle undercurrent motive which made for duplicity; and I could not now shake myself free from the belief in regard to Prince Kalkov.

I had no tangible reason for it. He stood high in the confidence of the Czar; he had gone out of his way to make himself agreeable to me; he had treated me apparently with signal frankness; and had admitted the possible risks and complications of the very tangled business.

I had another slight qualm. My sympathies were rather with than against the man Boreski. I was not a Russian aristocrat; and from my American point of view I was disposed to admire the pluck of a man who was fighting single-handed against the powerful Russian Court, and giving that autocratic body a real bad time. His methods were not nice, but his adroit use of them was so smart that I could not help enjoying them. Whereas, if it came to a mere question of ethics, I couldn't see that, taking into account the shady episode of the secret papers, either side had much pull over the other.

What really decided me was my old obligation to the Czar. My inclinations were all on the side of going in for the thing; and probably I gave more weight to that consideration than it deserved. But anyway I convinced myself that I could wipe out the old debt by doing what was asked of me, and when the Prince came back, I met him with the statement that if the details of the thing could be fixed, I was his man.

He was manifestly delighted.

"I cannot tell you what pleasure your decision gives me. We

7

shall now circumvent him completely. This is Boreski," and he handed me a photograph.

The man was certainly handsome and distinguished-looking. Dark as a raven, with large, deep-set, thoughtful eyes under straight brows, a broad ample forehead, straight nose, very shapely mouth with curved mobile lips, and a narrowing chin.

"A handsome fellow, and that's the truth," I said.

"So the Duchess thinks," he returned drily, handing me her portrait.

"You said she was twenty years his senior. This is a young woman."

"It was taken last year: a Court photograph," and he smiled. "She's all but fifty."

"Love at fifty may be a very serious passion, Prince. Have you no scruples about blighting it? She might take it badly and pine away."

"She might do much worse, monsieur, and marry that rascal."

"Her fortune is her own, I presume?"

"She would forfeit much of it if she married without the Emperor's consent. Boreski knows that well enough, and trades on it. I do not think we shall find him a really strong man. He has the whip hand of us for the moment through those stolen documents; but when we once get those, we shall be able to frighten him, I am convinced."

"Ought I not to know the nature of the documents?"

"I have been expecting that question. Do you press it?"

"Not if it embarrasses you to answer. But how shall I know them when they are given up to me?"

"They are very confidential," he said, his face wrinkling in perplexed thought. He paused, and then with a sigh added, very slowly, the words seeming to be wrung from him almost: "I suppose there is no other way. They affect Germany and Austria. They include a secret treaty with Austria and a number of plans of fortresses, and the army mobilization schemes, etc., of our neighbours."

"I can understand your anxiety, Prince," I said drily.

"They must be recovered, M. Denver, at any cost or sacrifice," he answered with intense earnestness.

"I will do my best," I replied, and then we turned to discuss the details of the project. He told me his arrangements, the chief of which was his scheme to secure my safety.

"I shall take exactly the same precautions as if you were His Majesty himself," he said. "The carriage in which you travel will be followed; its description will be telephoned everywhere, so that it may be instantly recognized by our agents who to-morrow night will be stationed at the corner of every street of the capital. Within a minute of your entering the house, wherever it is, a large force will commence to converge upon it; and if there is any delay or treachery the place will be carried by force."

"Isn't that a breach of faith with Boreski?"

"Of course I gave him an official pledge the carriage should not be followed."

"Official? Rather a nice distinction, isn't it?"

He laughed. "One has to do these things officially."

"You mean you have to give a pledge and—break it."

He shrugged his shoulders. "We are dealing with a scoundrel."

"Does that justify unclean methods?"

"Unclean?" He caught at the word angrily.

"I said unclean. Please understand me. I am neither a courtier nor a diplomat, but just a plain American citizen; and when we Americans pledge our word we keep it, whether it be given to an honest man or a rogue. This pledge of yours must be kept, Prince Kalkov."

He grew excited for the first time, and gesticulated vehemently as he answered.

"It is impossible, impossible!" he cried. "You cannot appreciate the importance of those papers, M. Denver. Hitherto we have been unable to learn their whereabouts, but we know that to-morrow night they will be in the house to which Boreski will drive you; that is why this appointment is to be kept. And when we once know where they are, not this Boreski nor ten thousand Boreskis shall prevent my recovering them."

This cast a somewhat fresh light on the thing, and annoyed me.

"Then you must get some one else to keep the appointment, Prince Kalkov," I answered.

"But your promise," he cried, angry and embarrassed.

"My promise was to play the part of the Emperor in the matter, and I'll either be obeyed as Emperor or we'll call it off, and I'll remain plain Harper C. Denver. You can choose, right now."

He sat gnawing his moustache in perplexity, and wanted to expostulate and argue the point.

"But——"

"There are no buts in this. You can call it off or on—but on my terms. You can choose."

This was just what he did not wish to do, however.

"Your own safety——" he began again.

"You can leave that to me," I cut in. "Is it to be on or off?" And I looked him fair and square in the eyes.

He gave a deep-drawn sigh, twisted his moustache ends, made as if to expostulate, but stopped on meeting my looks, and then with a shrug of the shoulders gave way.

"It's an enormous responsibility, but if you insist I must yield."

"Good; then we'll be off to bed and leave the rest until to-morrow."

He rose and gave me his hand.

"Good-night, M. Denver. You are a strong man," he said.

"Good-night, Prince. We'll talk about strength when the job's finished. I'll do my best, as I said."

He paused by the door and turned.

"After all the whole thing is only tricking Boreski. I wish you'd let me do it my way."

"It's only a trick, of course; but the cards are on the table so far as the personation is concerned. I can't give in to the rest."

"As your Majesty pleases," he returned with a slow smile as he left the room.

CHAPTER III

THE EMPEROR STARTS

I   DID not leave my rooms on the following day, and passed the chief part of it preparing for the part I was to play in the evening, and discussing the details.

The Prince and I had several interviews, and his confidential attendant, a Frenchman named Pierre, waited on me. From him I had a number of hints as to little characteristics of the Emperor, gestures, movements, habits and so on, calculated to help out my rendering of the part.

We arranged that I should go in ordinary morning dress, and over this I was to wear a semi-military cloak borrowed from the Imperial wardrobe.

The papers I required were all prepared with scrupulous care. These were a patent of nobility making Boreski a Count—and I was instructed how to perform the little ceremony of investing him with it; a written consent to his marriage with the Duchess Stephanie;

and a draft upon the Imperial Treasury for the sum of a million roubles.

"The draft is post dated, as you see," said the Prince, "as the money is intended for the Duchess's dowry, and is not payable until the marriage. You can explain this."

"He'll probably look for the money down," I objected at once.

"He is dealing with an Emperor who would not break faith with him," returned the Prince with a grim smile reminiscent of our previous night's discussion.

"If these papers are so valuable, why not give the money at once and let me take it in bank notes?"

"When we have the papers we can deal with him for a tenth part of the sum. A million, indeed!"

"If your economic instincts lead to trouble, don't blame me," I returned a little sharply. "I repeat I think you should send notes."

"Your Majesty can promise him anything. If he raises any difficulty he can come to me," he added.

"There is nothing else I have to take?"

"Nothing except this ring of the Emperor's. You had better wear it, as it is well known; and perhaps had better take a revolver, although I don't think you will have any trouble calling for one."

"One never knows," said I, and decided to take his advice.

"You will, of course, be cautious not to attempt a word of Russian. Your accent would betray you in a moment. You can use French with absolute safety, as His Majesty's unfortunate preference for that language is well known. That is most important."

"I'm not likely to forget. I can understand everything in Russian, but I know my limitations."

"Then I will go and get ready to accompany you on the first part of the journey to the rendezvous at the Square of St. Peter."

Now that the time was so close I was a good deal excited and impatient for the curtain to go up.

"You have His Majesty's figure and walk remarkably, m'sieur," said the Prince's man watching me closely. "From behind I myself should be deceived even at so short a distance and in so good a light as this. It is wonderful."

"Unfortunately I can't keep my back turned to people all the time."

"That is true, m'sieur; but then it is always safer to turn the face to—dangers, is it not?" He put so much emphasis on the word that I turned and looked at him.

"You think a good deal of the dangers, then, Pierre?"

"There is always danger in this Russia;" and he grimaced to show his French dislike of it.

11

"Yet you stay here."

"I am only a valet, m'sieur, they pass over my head. But I have been fifteen years in the country and have seen many strange things."

"If the Emperor were really going on this business, you think he would run big risks?"

"It may be different with you, m'sieur; you may be discovered in time. But if it were the Emperor, I should rub my hands with pleasure to see him return."

"You take a cheerful view of things, Pierre. I expect you have a liver that troubles you."

He threw up his hands and shoulders.

"Americans and English are the same and like mad risks. But I would not do this—no, not for the crown of Russia. I know what I know."

"And I do it for the love of the thing, and I suppose that's about the difference between us."

"Monsieur is monsieur," he replied with a comical, lachrymose air. "But you will need to be very cautious. You have friends in Petersburg, probably?"

"No, indeed. No one knows of my presence here."

"That is strange—but perhaps—convenient. You would not be missed."

"No, not by a soul except here in the Palace."

He smiled mysteriously.

"If you are discovered, m'sieur, I should not let that fact be known. I should speak of many. A friendless man may be a helpless one."

"You have a pleasant imagination, Pierre."

"Russia is not France, m'sieur, nor America," he replied, cryptically, with so lugubrious an air that I smiled.

It was not a cheerful send-off, and in the carriage I told old Kalkov what his man had said.

"Pierre is a good valet but a fool," he answered with a grunt. "He had his nerves twisted once in a Nihilist row, and ever since has seen a Nihilist conspiracy in every trouble."

"You don't take these conspiracies seriously?"

"As a rule, no; occasionally they are dangerous of course; but generally little more than froth and wind—mere political dyspepsia from the soured stomach of sectional discontent."

"Is this Boreski a Nihilist?"

"Possibly. It is always possible. But I think not. We shall know much more when you return."

"If I do return, that is."

12

"Naturally;" and he smiled, not pleasantly.

I began to think how the cat must have felt when she had burnt her foot in drawing the chestnuts out of the fire and saw the monkey enjoying them. But it was too late to retreat now, even if I had been so minded. The Prince felt something of this, I fancy, for he gave me the opportunity.

"If you have any fear, M. Denver, and wish to draw back, we can return to the Palace."

"Not on any account."

"I want you to feel, whatever happens, that you have gone into the thing quite voluntarily. I wish to feel that too."

"I shall see it through, Prince."

"Spoken like an American," he replied promptly, and a minute afterwards the carriage stopped. "We have arrived."

We got out on the north side of a large square and looked about for the other carriage. None was in sight, but a hooded automobile stood in the shadow on the opposite side.

"Can that be it?" I asked the Prince.

"It would be very easily traced," he said.

"But not so easily followed. There is no other and we are already a few minutes behind time."

"We can cross and see."

His face was full of doubt.

"I had better go alone," I replied, detaining him.

"As you will. God send you may be successful for the sake of Russia."

His tone was intensely earnest, and with the words ringing in my ears I swung off into the road in the direction of the autocar, and when I turned once I saw him watching me intently and eagerly.

Now that the moment for action had really come, I was as cool as I could have wished. I took a mental note of everything and I was careful to assume so far as possible the swinging stride of the man I was personating.

As I neared the car a man stepped from inside it and touched his cap.

"Who is your master?" I asked, putting all the authority I could into my manner, and staring hard at the man. He was dressed like a chauffeur, and save for his black beard and moustache his face was almost hidden by the peak of his cap and a pair of hideous driving goggles.

"M. Boreski, m'sieur." His French was that of an educated man, I thought.

"What are your instructions?"

"We are waiting for some one from the Palace, m'sieur." The

13

"we" struck me as peculiar. I stopped by the car and looked harder at him.

"You speak French with a good accent, my man," I said, with some suspicion in my tone, and then the unexpected happened.

A girl, closely veiled, put her head out from the hood which covered the back seat, and with a dash of contempt said—

"The American will scarcely be afraid to trust himself with a woman."

I gave a start of genuine pleasure. It was the girl who had spoken to me on the train.

"With you, mademoiselle, I would trust myself anywhere;" and without hesitation I took the seat by her side.

The chauffeur got into his place and we were off at a smart pace into the darkness.

I looked back at old Kalkov and waved my hand to him, and as we whirled round the corner out of the square he drew himself up and gave me a military salute.

If I had any doubts before, they vanished the moment I was by the side of the girl. The adventure had taken just the turn I could have wished; and come what might, I was resolved to have a good time.

"That was Prince Kalkov, your Majesty?" she asked, speaking in Russian. I answered in French.

"Yes, my very faithful old friend and counsellor to whose planning I owe this—this excursion, shall we call it?"

"Your Majesty is——"

"Wait, please. This is a very unusual matter. I make one condition at the outset. My incognito must be strictly maintained by every one—by every one, if you please. I am not the Emperor, but as I told you yesterday, an American. My name is Harper C. Denver. I do not even speak the Russian language, although I can understand it, and I am travelling in Russia for pleasure."

She was undeniably as smart as she was pretty. She listened to me intently, and she asked in English.

"You speak and understand English then perfectly."

It was a pretty trap, but I was not to be drawn, so I replied in French—

"An American must necessarily speak his own language, mademoiselle;" and at that she laughed softly.

"You are doubtless staying at the Hotel Imperial, the favourite hotel with Americans?"

"No, I am staying at the Palace with my friend the Emperor;" a truth which sounded so ridiculous that she laughed again.

14

"We will be careful that a friend of our Emperor has his wishes regarded so far as possible."

We rode some distance after that without speaking until I broke the silence.

"There are three questions I should like to ask, mademoiselle. Have I your permission?"

"I cannot pledge myself to answer them, m'sieur."

"Where are we going?"

"That will depend upon whether you have kept faith with M. Boreski."

"In what way?"

"Are we being followed?"

"I gave express orders to the contrary."

"An American citizen can give orders to the police in Russia then, m'sieur," she put in.

"Under certain circumstances an American citizen can be master of the situation," I replied equivocally and with more truth than she could have any idea of. "Will you answer my question?"

"About ten miles, if all goes well—if your orders have been obeyed, that is. We shall soon know."

"You shall have any proof I can give you of my good faith in this respect. How shall we know?"

She appeared to think for a few moments, then turned and looked at me through her veil.

"If you mean that, there will be no difficulty."

"I give you my word of honour. Let me put my second question. Do you pledge yourself, you mademoiselle, personally, for my safety?"

"Unconditionally, and so will M. Boreski."

"I don't care about him. It is to you I trust."

I felt her start and her voice was unsteady as she replied—

"On my honour, your Majesty shall not regret that confidence."

"Then I will do anything and everything you ask. I put myself absolutely in your hands."

She rose then and spoke to the chauffeur.

"M. Boreski says your spies are dogging us and that the streets are alive with them."

"That is M. Boreski?" I asked indicating the chauffeur.

"Yes, that is M. Boreski. We anticipated there would be treachery of the kind." There was again a spice of contempt in her tone.

"So far as I am concerned your suspicions are unwarranted, mademoiselle. I have been badly served, and some one shall suffer for it. But what do you propose?"

15

"Will you change from this carriage into another with me, leaving this to be followed by your police?"

There was the same touch of scorn in her manner.

"Certainly I will not if you continue to doubt my personal good faith. I will return to the Palace and leave the thing to be arranged in some other way. Otherwise, I am, as I said, absolutely in your hands."

"I am convinced and ashamed of my doubts. Please forgive me." She spoke quickly and eagerly.

"Then let us make the change as soon as you will."

She spoke again to Boreski, and the machine gave a spurt forward as he increased the speed until we were flying along at a rate that made conversation almost impossible.

After some time we swung round a corner and stopped with a sudden jerk.

"Now," cried Boreski eagerly, and in a moment we two were on the ground and he had started again, while the girl drew me inside the gates of a house.

"You will see now how you have been obeyed," she said, and the words were scarcely out of her lips before a vehicle, driven at full gallop with a couple of mounted men close behind it, went dashing and clattering past us on the track of the automobile. "They are your police, monsieur, and have now a long ride before them."

She referred to them with a shrug of utter contempt.

"We have a short distance to go in the opposite direction, and shall then find a carriage."

Her coolness was admirable, and when we started to walk she could not have been more unconcerned if I had been merely seeing her home from a pink tea in New York.

We passed through two or three streets, meeting only a few loungers, and as we crossed a more important thoroughfare at the corner of which a man and a woman stood talking, my companion stopped and asked the woman where we could get a drosky. She spoke in broken Russian and added—

"We are Americans and have lost our way."

"You will find none about here," the man answered, and spoke in English.

"We are in a fix, it seems."

"Which is the way to St. Mark's Square?" I asked. "I know my way from there."

He gave us minute directions and we walked on.

"Those are police spies," said my companion quietly, "and if we had not spoken to them, they would probably have followed us. But no one suspects Americans."

16

"How well you speak English," I said, off my guard for a moment.

"No better than you, monsieur," she replied simply. "Your question in English was a great stroke!"

"You have been in England?"

"Yes, two or three times. I was educated there and in France. What a country of freedom is England. We shall get our carriage here," she said a little later, and presently it came rumbling along slowly and stopped at a signal from her.

"We shall not be more than a few minutes now," she said as we got in.

"You have not told me your name, mademoiselle?"

"I am Helga; and take the same surname as my cousin, M. Boreski—until my mission is accomplished."

"Your mission? What is that?"

"I will tell you some day—if you will grant me a hearing?"

"You may always depend on that, mademoiselle," I answered as earnestly as I felt, so earnestly indeed that she turned and looked at me in surprise.

"Pray God your Majesty means that."

And I was still pondering her reply when the carriage stopped and she told me we had reached our destination.

CHAPTER IV

WHEN I WAS CZAR

AS I sat in the sumptuously furnished drawing-room, waiting for Helga Boreski to join me, I felt both embarrassed and puzzled.

Who was she? What was the mysterious mission of which she had spoken? What was her connexion with this Boreski affair? What part was she playing in the serio-comic drama in which I had thus suddenly been involved?

I could see no answer to the questions. I had made as keen an observation of the house as a few rapid glances in the darkness would permit; but could see little more than that it was a large rambling building standing well secluded in extensive grounds.

17

Inside, the place contained all the evidences of considerable wealth, and it was clear somebody connected with it must have money.

Boreski had been described to me, however, as an adventurer, who was angling for his duchess in order to secure her private fortune. He was also unquestionably blackmailing the Government in the matter of the million roubles.

Yet the room I was in might have been the parlour of an American millionaire, so costly and precious were many of the pictures and ornaments.

Coffee was served to me by footmen who might have stepped straight from an English peer's household; and altogether, as I say, I was completely mystified.

My embarrassment came from a quite different cause. It was one thing to meet an adventurer like this Boreski with his own weapons and fool him into an appreciation of his own short-sightedness; but it was something very different to treat Helga in the same way. Rightly or wrongly I had come to the fixed conviction that, although I had met her in this very questionable association with Boreski's sordid scheme, she herself was as good as she was beautiful. And the idea of cheating her, of palming myself off for the Emperor, was more repugnant than I can say.

I was brooding over the problem with my coffee untasted when she came in, looking positively radiant. Her eyes were shining with excitement, her face was coloured with the glow of the ride; and she had gowned herself simply, but with exquisite taste, in subdued tones that set off her magnificent beauty of face and form to perfection.

Every action and gesture were full of grace, and as she moved across the room I followed her with a glance that she must have felt expressed my intense admiration. I was hopelessly bewitched by her ravishing beauty; and that is the truth.

"Are you still the American—as to ceremonial?" she asked.

"Oh, please;" and I motioned to a lounge, feeling abominably mean. She sank into it with a smile.

"Fresh coffee for—M. Denver," she said to the servant, pausing on the threshold of the name, and glancing at me she pointed to my untouched cup. "And cigarettes."

She lighted a cigarette and I did the same.

"You wished it all to be informal," she said when the servant had left the room. "It is also very extraordinary."

"And very delightful," I could not help saying.

"You have no longer any hesitation as to your own safety?"

"I have trusted you and am content."

18

"Would God it may always be so," she said earnestly under her breath.

"I should never doubt you," I returned with an emphasis. "But frankly I am completely mystified."

She laughed, and it was like the sound of sweet sleigh bells.

"This is my house; I live here with an old relative, Madame Korvata. She is what the Spaniards would call my duenna, and the English, Mrs. Grundy. But I am like the Americans—you Americans," she repeated with a glance; "in my love of personal freedom. I do as I like."

"That I can believe. And M. Boreski?"

"Is M. Boreski—that is all to me. He is my cousin, very distantly my cousin, and he has his plans."

She managed to suggest that these schemes were indifferent to her, and after a short pause added meaningly—

"We all have plans, haven't we? Little moves of the pawns on the chess board, leading to some great combination—perhaps, that is."

"M. Boreski is coming here?" I asked.

"You are already impatient to go."

The retort came quickly with just an accent of reproach and disappointment.

"On the contrary I am more than content to stay."

She gave me a sharp half-quizzical glance, with a smile in it, quickly suppressed save in her eyes.

"I wonder can that be true? What kind of test it would stand?"

"Any test you could choose."

"We shall see. I may remind you of that;" half challenge half banter this was. "But my concerns are nothing to you."

"Then let us make them something." Our eyes met as I said this with an earnestness that was personal if not Imperial, and she met my gaze openly and steadily. Hers were dangerous eyes for any man to look into, and especially for one who thought of her as I did.

"I wonder what you mean by that? What I ought to read behind your look and eager offer?"

"Nothing but goodwill to you. Believe that."

"You tempt me, monsieur—American," and she fell back in her chair with a half sigh and sat thinking intently. Presently she shook her head. "No, not yet, not yet. You know nothing of me."

"An ignorance you can easily correct. But no, you are right, it must not be yet," I exclaimed hastily.

I had no right to invite confidence from her until she knew who I really was. But my exclamation surprised her.

"Why not yet—from your side?"

19

"I cannot tell you. How long will M. Boreski be?"

She wrinkled her brow at the question.

"You mean you would first know what my connexion with his scheme is? A somewhat shallow trust yours, after all."

"It may seem so, but I did not mean that."

"Then what did you mean?"

Her eyes again sought mine as if to read my thoughts. I threw up a blockading smile.

"How long will he be?"

"You play with me," she exclaimed petulantly. "I do not make a pleasant plaything. M. Boreski will be here soon now. He will find some one to take his place and play hare to your police dogs—the dogs that were not to have been set upon us."

"'Us'?" I repeated with a lift of the eyebrows. "You do identify yourself with him then?"

She laughed.

"That is a man's retort. Suspicion for suspicion; and it serves me right. Now that the time has come, I am not myself. I am too anxious. I do not understand—Americans. You make me feel as no other man as ever yet made me feel."

Was this for the Emperor or for myself? I did not relish the problem and made no reply.

She sighed, and rising touched the bell, and remained standing while the servants came and removed the coffee-cups.

I was glad of the interval. It gave me time to remember my part and remember, too, how unstable was the ground I stood on.

When the servants had gone again she remained standing with one elbow resting upon an ebony column under a branch of electric lights, the soft shaded colours from which fell upon her, enhancing her beauty.

"In the train yesterday you said you wished to see me again," she said slowly in a low seductive voice. "You have had your wish, you see. It is good to be—an American. Will you have the same wish after to-night, I wonder. I wonder," she added musingly.

"It is a graver question whether you would grant the wish if I expressed it."

"Do you doubt it? You need not." And then quickly as if to get on to safer ground, "The wishes of such an American must be commands to—to Russian subjects."

I winced and my face clouded, and I wished my Imperial character at the bottom of the Black Sea. She was quick to notice the change.

"I have offended you. How?" There was eagerness in her eyes.

"No. I have offended myself, that's all," I returned with a little sigh of vexation.

"You are hard to understand," she murmured softly.

"Without the key to the riddle, yes;" and once more we lapsed into silence. During the pause she resumed her seat.

"M. Boreski should be here now, monsieur," she said at length, a notable difference in her tone. "You are going to grant his request?"

"I have come to obtain the papers he holds."

"I fear you will find him difficult to deal with after the police incident to-night. Police spies are to him an abomination. You had none yesterday. Why do you run such risks as to travel quite unattended?"

"I ran no risk. No one knew me," I answered, rather embarrassed.

"I knew you."

"Against what were you warning me?"

She read suspicion in the question.

"I am not a Nihilist; but Russia is Russia."

"You know something of these Nihilists?"

"I know many of them to be reckless desperate men."

"One has to take chances."

"Do you think this what you term a chance?"

"God forbid. But I am glad of your repudiation."

"Did you need it?" she asked, her eyes on mine again.

"I have told you I trust you, and I think have shown it. But you are an enigma."

She smiled and leaned forward until her face was near to mine.

"Do you think me worth the trouble of solving?" and she was still waiting for my answer and gazing at me when, to my chagrin, the door opened and Boreski entered.

I recognized him instantly from his photograph; an aristocrat to his finger-tips he appeared to me, with a perfect manner; as striking a personality in his way as Helga herself.

"M. Boreski," said Helga, rising, and he made a courtier-like bow.

"I am more honoured than I can say by the condescension of this interview, your Majesty," he said. "Pray pardon my lateness, but it is due to circumstances beyond my control."

As I knew he had been leading the police on a wild goose chase I had to restrain an inclination to smile.

"Mademoiselle here has already anticipated your explanation, monsieur," I said; and the two exchanged quick glances. "It was contrary to my express orders that you were followed."

"A very direct and precise pledge was given me, your Majesty, by His Highness Prince Kalkov."

His manner more than his words made me understand that he held he had been badly treated and resented strongly the breach of faith. This was the crossing of the weapons in the game of fence between us.

"It is not customary for me to explain my position twice, M. Boreski," I said with a lofty air. "Let us get to the business of the interview if you please. You will be seated," and I waved my hand to a chair.

"I thank your Majesty," he replied with a deferential bow as he sat down.

"We understand, of course, the peculiar nature of circumstances leading to the interview and the importance attached to the papers which you have. Where are they, if you please?"

"Ready to be produced the moment your Majesty has settled the preliminaries."

"You have named very high terms, monsieur."

"His Highness, in your Majesty's name, has already agreed to them," he returned quietly.

"But we are now face to face, monsieur, and we can re-open the whole matter. I propose to do that, and I invite you to tell me now precisely your ultimate object and your inner motives."

The question surprised him, and he pursed his lips and frowned in thought and looked across at Helga.

"I do not understand your Majesty."

"Come, come, monsieur, you must do that. You are young, you have a great career before you as a maestro, they tell me, a career which means ample rewards in money in these days—so that you cannot be seeking money only. What, then, is it?"

"Your Majesty is good enough——"

"Stay," I put in then. "I have explained to Mademoiselle Helga that I am strictly incognito. Regard me as no other than the American, Mr. Denver, and let us talk this out as man to man. Forget that there is any one present but a private individual who has influence with an absent Emperor. Now tell me frankly what is the real object you are seeking?"

"You are very gracious, but my object has already been explained—I desire to marry the Duchess Stephanie."

"As a means to what end?"

"Marriage is an end in itself," said Helga, speaking for the first time, and coming to his rescue.

"That would make M. Boreski a mere fortune-hunter, mademoiselle, an extremely distasteful and invidious part to play."

22

They were both surprised at the turn of things and were silent for some moments.

"I thought this part of the matter had been definitely settled," said Helga; and then for the first time a suspicion crossed my mind that the man was taking his cue from her.

He said quickly—

"So it has been."

"Are you tired of your art, monsieur? If you were to marry the Duchess Stephanie your career must of course end. What, then, do you expect to gain in its place? Money? What is a million roubles"— I only just avoided saying a hundred thousand dollars—"to a man with your gifts? Do you seek place, power, influence? Let me remind you, you are forcing your way into a circle which will never receive you as an equal. Political influence will be impossible for you—the Emperor himself would be inflexible on that point. If I read you aright, you are a man with ambition and individuality; and neither ambition nor individuality is content to be a mere adjunct to a wife."

"In America is not affection regarded as a possible basis of marriage, M. Denver?" asked Helga; and I turned with a smile to her.

"My kinswoman"—I made the slip intentionally and then corrected it—"the Duchess Stephanie is no longer so fascinating as in her youth, mademoiselle. I am only dealing with facts."

"M. Denver has no wish to insult me or the Duchess, I am sure," said Boreski, a suggestion of anger in his tone.

"Do I understand then that you are in love with the Duchess?"

"That is a point which, with all deference, I will not discuss," he returned firmly; but despite his firm tone I thought I could discern evidence that I had struck home.

"M. Boreski is irrevocably pledged to the Duchess," said Helga, "and in honour he could not draw back."

"The Emperor would find means to meet that difficulty," said I. "But be it so. I have come with the written consent to the marriage;" and I took out the papers which Prince Kalkov had given me, glanced at them and laid them on the table.

Boreski's face brightened. Then I added casually—

"I should have thought, indeed, that we might have torn up the consent to the marriage and made the draft here for two millions instead of one. A fortune and individual freedom would have seemed to me preferable—especially if coupled with it was a complete condonation of all other matters and—intrigues."

I paused before the word and watched him. The mention of the higher sum had brought a light of avarice into his eyes, which gave way abruptly to surprise and suspicion as I finished.

"Intrigues?"

It was Helga who put the question, and Boreski looked across at her so doubtfully as to suggest fear. Then he took out his handkerchief and wiped his lips.

"Intrigues, mademoiselle," I replied quietly. "M. Boreski knows my meaning." This forced him to speak, and his voice was nervous.

"I am at a loss to understand you, monsieur."

I paused and looked at him steadily until his eyes fell.

"Your sources of secret information are so many, monsieur, that I am sure you can ascertain that. Shall we say twice the amount and tear up this consent?"

He fidgetted with his handkerchief, and then making a great effort for self-possession he put it away and answered, with a spice of doggedness.

"I have named my terms and they have been agreed to."

"As you will. But of course you understand that without that condonation—or pardon—even one so highly placed as the husband of the Duchess Stephanie may be called upon to answer for his acts."

I waited to give him a last chance, and during the silence he was obviously embarrassed.

"You make grave accusations very lightly, M. Denver," said Helga, coming to the rescue again.

"Do you think we cannot prove them, mademoiselle?" I asked looking her straight in the face. The man's manner made me very sure. But she could act much better than he: women can as a rule. Her steady look changed to a winning smile.

"What do men do in America, monsieur, when they are so fortunate as to discover a mare's nest?"

"They console themselves if they find in it a woman's smile, mademoiselle," I replied lightly, "or take her assurance that it is nothing more serious."

"What can be more serious than a woman's smile, M. American?"

"A man's nihilism, mademoiselle, for one thing. But come, here are the papers, M. Boreski. I shall have the pleasure of addressing you as Count, I shall hand to you the consent to your unmercenary marriage, and shall give you the draft for a million roubles as the dowry conferred by a grateful Emperor. Where are the papers for me?"

He put his hand to his pocket.

"I——" he paused suddenly and then said hesitatingly, "I—I will get them. I have your permission to withdraw?"

He had himself in hand again.

"And to return—with the papers. Will you also see that a carriage is ready?"

As he rose I intercepted a very meaning glance between the two, and then once more Helga and I were alone.

All had gone smoothly so far; but there was clearly much that I did not yet understand, and I turned to Helga to question her.

CHAPTER V

A CZAR DEFIED

HELGA met my eyes readily with something like a challenge in her own, and as the first question was on my lips, a thought struck me. It was odd that coming to such an interview he had not brought the papers with him. I said so to her.

For answer she just looked at me and smiled. If she did not know the disarming power of her smile I felt it.

"You like to mystify me," I said.

"Why were you so hard on poor M. Boreski, and why"—she paused as if to calculate the effect of her words—"why do you suspect us of being Nihilists?"

"You? I did not say anything about you. It was M. Boreski."

"Is that quite candid, M. American?" It was an audacious stroke, considering whom she believed me to be.

"Your assurance would suffice to convince me."

"You put your sharp questions in flattering covers, monsieur. But your compliments have barbed points."

"Is it a barbed point that I would trust your word implicitly?"

"If I thought that, oh, if I could think it," she exclaimed with great earnestness, clasping her hands strenuously.

"Why should you doubt it?"

She turned full upon me.

"Because you do not know me; because——" she broke off and then said steadily, almost defiantly: "I am no Nihilist, nor is M. Boreski."

"And he has had no dealings with them?" I felt convinced that he had. "I mean to your knowledge?"

"You cross-examine like a lawyer." A flash of scorn was in her

25

eyes as she looked at me angrily. "If we have had what you term dealings with them, it was because it was necessary, and no other way was left to me."

"You are not afraid to handle edged tools, and I am sorry to hear what you say."

"I am not afraid of anything that can help my purpose."

"I never heard of Nihilism helping anything or anybody."

"I choose my own means, and go my own way," she said defiantly.

"I can believe that; but I am not accusing you, nor need you defend yourself—to me. I believe that whatever you have done, you have been driven to do, and have believed yourself justified in doing—for this great purpose you speak of. But others may think very differently."

"You do not ask what it is. You do not care, I suppose. Yet——" There was pain now in her voice, and a sigh finished the broken sentence.

"It is better that I should not ask," I said after a pause. She had made me forget for the moment, in my solicitude for her, that I must not have her confidence. "When will M. Boreski return?"

"My purpose is revenge," she cried with sudden vehemence, her face suddenly set and stern and her eyes bright. "Revenge for a cruel, cowardly crime, and wrongs as deep and bitter as ever weighed a woman to the earth and filled her heart with burning rage."

"I beg you, mademoiselle, to say no more," I protested.

"But I wish to tell you. I must, I must. It concerns the pampered villain who holds your confidence, Prince Kalkov, and"—she paused and looked at me, her face fevered with excitement and her eyes full of dread doubt, and then added in a low strenuous tone—"Prince Boris Lavalski."

I had never heard the name, of course, and could not understand her intense agitation. She searched my face as if hungry for some sign of recognition, and seeing none, her own clouded and then paled.

"Prince Boris Lavalski," I echoed.

"Oh, my God, my God, that it has come to this!" she cried in a passion of despair; and she hid her face in her hands, giving way to such uncontrollable emotion that my heart was wrung for her.

She remained some minutes in the stress of her whirlwind grief; most embarrassing minutes to me, for I knew not what to do or say, gladly as I would have said or done anything to soften her distress.

26

Suddenly she mastered her emotion, rose and faced me, her face worn, strained, and white to the very lips, which quivered.

"So be it, monsieur. You are still his enemy—and mine," she said in low measured tones. "Still the defender of that cruel monstrous infamy. We are then to fight on."

"I am utterly at a loss to understand you, mademoiselle. God knows I am no enemy of yours, and would only too gladly be your friend if——"

"That is impossible, monsieur," she interposed angrily, with the air of an empress. "Shall M. Boreski return?"

"I have been waiting for him," said I, still mystified.

"I sent him away that I might speak to you of this." She touched the bell as she spoke, and I noticed that she pushed it twice.

"I did not know that you were his principal," I said.

"There are many things you do not know yet: as many indeed as you seem quite unwilling to remember, or anxious to forget." She was very bitter.

"I assure you——"

"Is it necessary, monsieur?" she asked contemptuously, making one feel about as mean as a man could feel.

Until M. Boreski came in we said no more, and as he entered he shot a swift questioning glance at Helga.

"His Majesty is anxious to conclude the interview, M. Boreski."

He seemed to take his cue from her words and hostile manner.

It was clear that a considerable change was at hand, and I awaited the unfolding of it with interest.

Boreski treated me with the same deference as before, and having asked my permission, resumed his seat and produced the papers.

"The papers for the Emperor are here," he said.

"Give them me;" and I held out my hand for them.

But this he would not.

"With extreme deference I submit that I be allowed first to examine those which you bring, monsieur. If the request should appear strange, I beg you to remember that Prince Kalkov has already once broken faith with me this evening."

"You are cautious, Count Boreski." He started and flushed with pleasure as I thus addressed him by his new title. "But why should I trust them to you? If it comes to faith-breaking, are not those documents stolen? Surely there is a breach of more than faith behind your possession of them. Why then should I trust you?"

"I fear then we have reached an impasse," he said, with a courteous bow as he spread out his hands.

"Not a bit of it. Hand yours to Mademoiselle Helga." I turned to her. "You will hold them, mademoiselle, and give them to me when this cautious gentleman has satisfied himself that these are in order?"

"With your permission, the matter is no concern of mine," she replied coldly.

"It seems to me that you are both anxious to raise difficulties."

Helga shrugged her shoulders, and Boreski spread out his hands deprecatingly.

"With all deference, I submit I am not asking too much to be allowed to examine documents of such vital importance to me."

I thought for a moment. If I parted with the papers and did not get the others in exchange I should be pretty considerably euchred; but on the other hand his request was not unreasonable. Then I saw the way out. I remembered that I was armed.

"Very well. You can see them," and I pushed them across to him, and rising, stood between him and the door.

"Your confidence in our honour is very striking, monsieur," said Helga scornfully.

"Is that fair? I offered to trust them to you, and you replied it was no concern of yours. I am now dealing with the holder of stolen documents."

"And you judge M. Boreski by the standard of the persons who surround and advise you continually. No doubt you are right according to your experience," was her bitterly spoken retort.

"Your anger and injustice are too manifest to need a further reply from me, mademoiselle," I returned.

Boreski scrutinized the papers carefully, and presently I saw him start and lay one aside. I wondered if he could have discovered any forgery among them.

"There is one grave point here, and one of less importance," he said at length; and putting the papers together he handed them back to me, with the draft for the money on the top. "This draft is dated three days hence."

I took them and went back to my seat.

"The reason is obvious. This is in the nature of a dowry, and as such will be paid on your marriage, and not before it."

"With all submission, I cannot so regard it, and I cannot accept the draft as complying with the agreement."

It was just the hitch I had foreseen and pointed out to old Kalkov; but how to get over it I did not see.

"And the point of minor importance; what is that?"

"The consent to the marriage is dated, and if a date is to remain, it should be that of a week or a month ago."

"Why?"

At the quick question he looked across at Helga, who shrugged her shoulders.

"I do not see why you should not say. It concerns both the objections and accounts for them," she said.

"The Duchess Stephanie is already my wife, monsieur," said Boreski.

"The devil she is," I exclaimed in genuine astonishment. "That puts the whole thing on a totally different footing."

"It entails the consent being dated back, and makes the dowry payable at once, monsieur."

"It means also that you have put your head in a noose, and have forfeited the Duchess's fortune, since her marriage has taken place without my—without the Emperor's consent;" and I folded up the papers and put them back in my pocket.

"It certainly produces a quite interesting complication," said Helga, smiling.

"It does not affect the gravity of the papers I hold here," and Boreski tapped them slowly with his long white fingers.

For the life of me I couldn't see a way out of the maze. Had I been really the Emperor, I might have done it by sending instructions to old Kalkov to pay the million roubles; then by writing a fresh consent to the marriage I could have secured the papers, and so have made an end of the thing.

But I felt that Kalkov would only laugh at such a request from me, while of course I could not write a single word without the discrepancy of the handwriting being at once apparent.

I was loth to go back and admit my failure; but this I saw at length was the only resource. Every moment that I hesitated made the affair worse, so I put as bold a front on matters as I could and got up.

"This new admission of yours, M. Boreski," I said with an assumption of dignity, "is so serious as to require consideration. Be good enough to have a carriage brought for me at once. The interview is at an end."

He had risen with me and stood in indecision, when Helga interposed and took the lead in her own hands.

"You do not quite understand the position, I fear, monsieur," she said slowly.

"Do you mean I am not free to go—after your promise to me?"

"Oh no, no," she cried, with one of her smiles. "I myself will order your carriage." She rang the bell, and when the servant came she told him to order a carriage at once.

"I was sure of you, mademoiselle, and regret my hasty suspicion. You will pardon it?"

29

"It was a natural inference—for one accustomed to treachery," she replied, with soft sarcasm. "But we really are not traitors here. The way is open for you to leave—if you dare, monsieur?" And the challenge was in eyes, face, voice and manner alike.

"Dare? That is a strong word, mademoiselle."

"Intentionally strong," she retorted, with cutting deliberation. "Intentionally strong. I have been patient under injury, and have endured injustice, hoping, praying, and waiting for redress; living for the interview which I have had to-night—and had in vain. And now my patience is exhausted, and you have drained it to the dregs. Had there been a spark of just feeling left in your heart, a faint wan glimmer of desire to right the wrong done to mine and to me, and to wipe out the cruel stain of unmerited infamy, the name I mentioned to you to-night would have kindled the desire until, fanned by the remembrance of old and tried and dear friendship, it would have burned steadily with a bright avenging flame." She spoke without passion in slow level accents.

I had not the faintest suspicion of her meaning.

"What name was that?" I asked, having even forgotten it.

The question drew a smile of contempt from her.

"I will not insult myself by repeating it."

"The carriage is at the door, mademoiselle," announced the servant.

"You can go, monsieur," she said, when the man had left.

But she had startled as well as interested me, and I hesitated.

"I think you should speak more plainly. I am honest when I say I do not understand you."

Boreski had now passed out of consideration, and he stood back watching us two, as if acknowledging her leadership.

"You wish for plain speaking. You shall have it, monsieur—from the enemy you have made to-night. This is my work," she said proudly, pointing to the papers in Boreski's hands. "My work, only. I sought at first by all fair means to reach your—the Emperor's ear, believing, like the fool I was, that he would do me justice. But his minister was too powerful, too vigilant, too alarmed to let my complaint reach his ear. I knew why. God, how well I knew it! Then, and not until then, when I had failed by open means, I had recourse to these. I joined hands with another of Russia's victims, M. Boreski here, and with him, through the Duchess Stephanie, I found the means I sought. God knows Russian duplicity gives many chances, and one of them came my way, putting me in a position to gain by force the justice which was denied to mere pleading."

She paused again, but I did not speak.

"Those papers—but you know their purport well enough—mean

the exposure of Russian craft in every Court in Europe, with probably a war with the Powers that have been tricked and fooled. They know already that we have secret information, and we have been in negotiation with them. But I am a Russian, too, and planned this interview, hoping that when face to face with you I could touch the heart so long dead to the cries of friendship. I have failed; I see that. You will not remember; you cannot forget; even for you that would be impossible. You have denied me justice, but I thank my God you cannot take from me all my revenge."

Her passion was rising fast now under the stimulus of her remembered wrongs, and she went to the door and threw it open.

"Go, monsieur, go," she cried, with a magnificent gesture of defiance. "Cross the threshold in the mood you are, and as I live, those papers, proofs as they are of your ministers' infamous treachery, shall be in the hands already stretched out eagerly to receive them—the hands of Russia's enemies. That is what I mean. Go, monsieur, go—if you dare." She held the door open and stared at me in indignant defiance and challenge.

Was ever a man caught in a closer meshed net than that which held me at that moment?

I stood fumbling with the situation in sheer and desperate perplexity. I remembered old Kalkov's words that the papers might plunge the country into war, and that at any cost they must not be allowed to get into the hands of the Powers concerned. Yet if I left the house it was straight to those Powers they would go.

If, on the other hand, I remained, what could I do?

If I admitted to Helga that I was no Emperor, but a fraud, her anger would probably be increased, and she would carry out her purpose just the same. While if I went on playing at being Emperor, and listened to her story, I could do no good. It was out of my power to grant her the justice which she deemed had been denied. I should only be cheating her and emphasizing the lie which my presence as Emperor constituted.

To fall back on old Kalkov and curse him for having got me into the mess was comforting but unpractical; and I stood like a fool, probably looking the fool I felt, as I gnawed my moustache and twisted my beard in imbecile indecision.

31

CHAPTER VI

HIS MAJESTY A PRISONER

HOW long I stood there, hesitating and embarrassed, while Helga was holding the door open for me in that queenly pose of splendid indignation, I do not know, but realizing at last that I could not go and leave her to execute her threat, I turned back rather sheepishly and sat down again.

"You have put the thing on such a different and so unexpected a footing that we had better wait at least until you are calmer," I said.

But she was in the mood to push her triumph to the utmost.

"I shall never be calm on this subject. It is for you to say at once, monsieur, whether you decide to go."

"I don't see any such necessity," I answered curtly.

It is difficult to describe my condition of mind. The thing was really nothing to me. Whether Russia went to war with twenty other countries would not have troubled me. I had no concern whether her diplomatists had made fools of themselves, and that Helga should have them by the throat rather pleased than angered me. And yet I was as irritable as a millionaire when his digestion goes wrong. I suppose I was in a temper at having been beaten. No one cares to look small in the eyes of a woman he admires as I admired her. And small I certainly felt and must have looked.

Although I avoided her eyes, she stood holding the door still open, and looking at me as if to read my thoughts.

"Are you going, monsieur?" she asked, after a long pause.

"No, I'm not—yet." I spoke bluntly, almost rudely; and with a shrug and a lift of the eyebrows, she left the door and crossed the room to her former place.

"M. Boreski, will you see that the carriage is sent back to the stable, and is kept in readiness for M. Denver?"

Boreski understood her, and going out shut the door carefully behind him.

I made no attempt to speak, but sat staring moodily down on the ground and trying to think; and Helga on her side was resolutely silent. Several minutes passed in this dead silence until it got on my nerves. She forced me to break it.

"Well, what is it you want?" I asked, most ungraciously.

The way she met me was characteristic. She laughed softly and sweetly, and looked across at me.

"My mood has passed, monsieur," she said, quoting my words.

"Shall we wait for yours to pass also? Permit me?" and she rose and offered me a cigarette from a dainty gold case.

"I would rather smoke something stronger, with your leave." I took out a cigar, and she lighted a cigarette; and another long silence fell between us. She broke it this time.

"You have made me your enemy, and I have beaten you so far; but you will not find me ungenerous."

"Generous or ungenerous, I don't see any way out of the tangle. I won't listen to any more of your story; and you can't use those papers. I don't know what it is you want, and if I did, it would be no use, for I could not grant it. And there's the deadlock."

"Is it, after all, necessary that we should be enemies?"

"Apparently it is. There are certain things which I cannot tell you from my side, and certain others I will not hear from you. It is your own fault." This was very un-Imperial talk, but I was sick of the whole Emperor business, and still suffering from mortification.

The change in my manner appeared to strike her, for she looked at me sharply and replied as if with surprise—

"Have I ventured to ask you for your confidence about yourself, monsieur?"

"I did not mean to imply that you had. There is one thing," I added, as an idea occurred to me. "Shall I send for Prince Kalkov?"

"Under no circumstances shall he cross my door," she answered with prompt and unmistakable resolution.

"Will you postpone dealing with those papers then until I have had an opportunity of consulting him? That may prove a solution."

"I know Prince Kalkov too well. Within five minutes of your leaving my house those papers will be on their way to the destination I have indicated."

"Then in Heaven's name what are we to do?"

"If you will listen to my story you will see that Prince Kalkov is the man I accuse."

"But there are insuperable reasons why I cannot and will not listen."

"Then it is for you to find the solution."

"I can probably do that if I can communicate with him."

"Shall I order the carriage again?"

Checkmate again, and I tossed up my hands in hopeless perplexity.

She was obviously resolved that I should hear all she had to say, and I was equally determined, knowing the worse than futility of the thing, not to listen to her; and there we sat, in a contest of wills and wits, until the absurd side of the position began to appeal to me.

"It seems to me you are resolved to make me a prisoner."

"On the contrary, monsieur, the door is open, and a carriage ready at your instant command. If you remain, it is by your own desire, and of your own free will."

"Free will, when you place an impossible barrier in the way of my going? So long as I remain here you will not part with those papers?"

"So long as the hope remains that you will hear me and do me justice."

"The thing is so preposterous."

"The alternative is for you to choose."

It was then that I began to contemplate seriously the course of remaining in the house for the night. I should at least gain time; and time might bring a solution.

"It is a dainty prison, but still a prison, although the bars are invisible, and the gaoler yourself. You realize the responsibility of what you are doing?"

"I am prepared to face any responsibility, and you would be my most honoured guest."

She spoke very seriously, but there was a light in her eyes that told not only of triumph, but of laughter scarcely restrained. For all the seriousness behind the position, she saw the humour of it and enjoyed it. And so in truth did I; for nothing on earth would have pleased me better than to be in her company for any number of days, if I could only have divested myself of my confounded Imperial character. If she could have read my thoughts, what would her own have been!

I had to keep up the farce of assumed disinclination, however, and was meditating the best line to take when an interruption came.

The door was opened, and a servant announced—"M. Paul Drexel."

A flush of extreme annoyance mounted to Helga's face at the entrance of the new-comer, who was the reverse of a pleasant-looking man. He was about forty years of age; short, broad-shouldered, inclined to corpulence, awkward and ungainly in figure. His features were coarse and Jewish in character; he had beady, twinkling, stealthy eyes, and his manner suggested a mixture of truculence and cunning.

Altogether he looked entirely out of place in Helga's drawing-room, and I wondered what on earth could have brought him there, a wonderment which became genuine astonishment when he advanced with as much confidence as if he were the master of the house, and said in Russian—

"Good-evening, Helga. You see I have come after all. Is this the company you said would engage you?" He turned to me with a questioning, half suspicious, and rather insolent glance.

"If I had wished you to come I should have asked you," she replied, repressing her ill-humour. "Your visit is ill-timed."

I watched her very closely and detected something very much akin to repugnance in her glance.

"Possibly;" he laughed shortly. "But as I am here, introduce me."

There was a moment's indecision before she answered.

"This gentleman is an American, and does not speak Russian."

"American, is he? Well, I suppose I have a right to know the friends of my——"

This time she broke in quickly and interrupted him.

"I have already told you your visit is unwelcome."

"I heard you," he returned so rudely that I could have kicked him. "What language does he speak?"

"He understands Russian and speaks French."

"Why didn't you tell me? I speak French easily enough;" the second part of the sentence was in French. "Good-evening, monsieur," he said to me, "I am glad to meet you. Any friends of my——"

"M. Denver, this is M. Paul Drexel."

He started at this second interruption, and looked at her half angrily.

"Is that all you wish to say? Why?" Their eyes met for a moment, and he seemed to have the best of it, for Helga added—

"I am engaged to marry M. Drexel, monsieur." He smiled and rubbed his fat hands over his little triumph, and was so pleased with himself that my start of amazement escaped him.

"And I am of course pleased to know Helga's friends." He threw himself into a chair and continued to rub his podgy hands. If I had thought him a cad before, he was now positively hateful, and his vulgar assurance sickened me.

He took out a cigar, and as he turned away to light it I saw Helga wince, bite her lip, and clench her hands tightly. I could see that she was suffering; but this only added to my perplexity.

"So you are an American, M. Denver. A fine country yours; I was never there, but shall go some day."

"I am sure America will appreciate the honour," I said blandly. It was no concern of mine to conciliate the little cad; but he only chuckled.

"Good, very good. I suppose it did sound as if I thought I should be honouring the place. But I am content with Russia;" and he settled himself in his luxurious seat as if he were indeed very

35

content. "I shall enjoy a talk with you about your American Government some day, M. Denver."

I made no response to this approach; but it made no difference to him; no inroad upon the stockade of his self-complacency. He babbled on with remarks of the kind, and then let fall a question which seemed to have something behind it.

"I suppose you have lived much in America?" and his beady black eyes shot a swift sly glance at me.

"Even Americans are at home sometimes," I replied.

"Good again, good again," he laughed. "You are great travellers, globe-trotters, eh? And you yourself speak French so well; quite as well as most Russians indeed; and you understand Russian too, Helga tells me. Do many of your countrymen understand Russian?" and again the little sharp eyes came at me.

"My father was in the diplomatic service, M. Drexel, and as a child I was educated in Russia, Germany and France, and thus learnt all three languages."

Helga gave me a look of thanks which the man intercepted; and he stared at her, a cunning smile on his flabby face.

"Quite a linguist, you see, Helga," he said, and then assuming a casual tone—"By the way, the friend you were expecting did not come after all?" The tone did not deceive me. I saw that he knew who I was supposed to be, and that all this had merely been intentional monkeying.

Helga saw it as well, and answered calmly—

"M. Denver is the only friend I was expecting to-night."

"Then why try to fool me? Did you think I should not recognize—M. Denver? Haven't I a right——"

"No;" anger and resolution in the sharp monosyllable.

"Don't you consider me interested in your plans?"

"You will be glad to finish your cigar with M. Boreski, M. Drexel."

"No, thank you; I came to see you. I have nothing to say to Boreski to-night—unless, of course——" He left the sentence unfinished except for a look.

"Unless what, M. Drexel?" The anger she had carefully suppressed until now was getting the upper hand of her, and he saw it.

"Unless you drive me to it, I mean;" this doggedly.

"You are at liberty to say what you please to M. Boreski—or to any one else."

"You are providing me with an excellent opportunity," he retorted, beginning to get angry in his turn, and glancing at me.

"Use it. You may never have a better." The answer was crisp and supercilious—almost contemptuous.

A quarrel between an engaged couple must always be embarrassing for a third party, so I cut in—

"Pardon me, mademoiselle, may I withdraw?"

"Where?" she asked, with a bright, quick, challenging smile.

"I am in your hands," I said, smiling back.

"We will have M. Boreski in," and she rang the bell.

The little man fidgetted uncomfortably in his chair while we waited for the servant and then for Boreski. When he came Helga murmured an excuse and left the room.

For an instant the thought that some sinister move was intended flashed upon my mind, bred, no doubt, by my distrust of this unctuous little cad; but my trust in Helga dispelled it. I felt sure of her.

The two men eyed one another a moment, and it was easy to see that there was little love lost between them.

"Mademoiselle Helga is on stilts again to-night," said Drexel.

"You should not have come—unasked."

"Why am I kept out of this?" The question asked angrily.

"Because you have no part in it and are not wanted," returned Boreski deliberately.

"Nonsense. I shall do as I like. When you are tired of me you only have to say so. You know the alternative."

"I beg to tender you an unqualified apology, M. Denver, for M. Drexel's presence," said Boreski to me with his courtier-like air. "He has forced himself here."

"You should have told me then who your mysterious visitor was, instead of leaving me to fish it out for myself."

"I accept your apology, M. Boreski," I said, in my grand manner.

The little man flushed angrily and got up.

"Some of us may live to be sorry for this night's work," he said, with an unmistakable threat. It was clear that he held his position in the house by virtue of what he could threaten.

"I am sorry for it already," declared Boreski quietly. He had certainly the knack of putting a lot of sting into words which in themselves were innocent enough. "You should not have come, I repeat."

"I shall do as I like. I am not to be bullied or sneered at."

"You will drive me to do one day as I like, M. Drexel," said Boreski in his even suave tone; "and make me realize that there are less unpleasant things than your—your alternatives. As you ought not to have come, you had better go."

At this moment, to my relief, a servant entered and said to me—

"Your apartments are prepared, monsieur."

Both men started at this, and both displayed astonishment, Drexel giving vent to a laugh.

"I bid you good-evening, M. Boreski," I said; and then to Drexel: "Should I meet you or hear of you again, monsieur, this evening's experience will be in my memory;" and turning on my heel, I left the room.

As the door closed I heard Drexel's voice:

"My God! you play for high stakes, Boreski."

Helga was outside, and also caught the words.

"How I hate him!" she exclaimed vehemently, her eyes flashing, and her face set and strained.

"Then you have other enemies—beside me?" I said, with a smile.

The hard look passed away as she let her eyes rest on mine.

"You will not always be my enemy, I hope, M. American."

"I could never be anything but your friend—even prisoner as I am."

"Shall I order your carriage, monsieur?" with smiling audacious banter. "My guest has but to express his wishes here; my whole household is at his command."

"You know why I cannot go. I am afraid of the other—Helga." I paused before her name, and she flushed when I used it.

"All Helga could be such a friend, if you would let her."

"Well, she has a very willing captive—how willing, you do not seem to realize."

She lowered her eyes and stood with bent head for a moment in silence. Then she lifted it and looked frankly into my face.

"I should not have thought, now that I have seen you, that you could be so hard."

"Should I not rather say that to you? It is I who am the conquered, you the conqueror. And you laid claim to generosity."

"Am I not generous?"

"No; you take all—all."

"I don't understand you," she said, shrinking a little from my look.

"When the time comes you will."

"And when will it come?" The question was eager.

"I am almost afraid to think," I answered softly, out of my inmost thoughts.

"The sooner the better. The sooner the better," she cried. "You mystify me."

"And am I not mystified?" I glanced at the room where M. Drexel sat.

"Why can we not both speak plainly then?"

"We will see what to-morrow brings," I said, and held out my hand.

She made as if to carry it to her lips.

"I am really loyal," she murmured.

"It is I who am the subject to-night. I am only an American." And as I spoke I captured her hand and pressed my lips to it. "It is you, I say, who are conqueror."

I went up the broad stairway, leaving her looking after me, smiling, and I thought triumphant; and I hoped, pleased.

CHAPTER VII

"I AM NOT THE CZAR"

THE apartments to which I was shown were as luxurious in their way as the room in which I had been received, and as everything had obviously been ready in advance, I had a shrewd suspicion that Helga and Boreski had quite counted upon my remaining in the house.

It was a queer position in all truth; and dismissing the man who had been told to attend upon me, I lit a cigar and sat down to think it out.

One thing was quite plain. Old Kalkov had been fooled as to the objective of all the business. The marriage of Boreski with the Duchess Stephanie was a mere cover for the other scheme, and a very clever cover too, seeing that it had looked so amazingly like the sole end in view.

That was Helga's wit; and to a point it had succeeded. But where her plan had fallen to pieces was in believing that the Emperor would be so mad as to come and see her in his own august person. The thing was so monstrously absurd that I was surprised such sharp wits as hers had believed it possible and had not suspected some imposture.

That I had not been instantly detected for a fraud was indeed not the least curious feature: and I could only conclude that having once persuaded themselves to believe the thing possible, they were just in the frame of mind which helped the self-deception.

Probably my idea of playing at being myself had helped the deception, because it was naturally a part I could keep up consistently. I had been myself with occasional lapses into the Imperial imposture. And that was all there was to it. What would happen when the deception was discovered I could not even attempt to anticipate.

The evening had effected a great change in myself. The axis of everything had shifted. Helga's personality and plans had taken Boreski's place; and whereas I had been anxious to wipe out my old obligation to the Emperor and had had a languid, very languid, willingness to checkmate Boreski, my feelings now were keenly enlisted in Helga's behalf. Provided I could arrange the affair of the compromising papers, I was ready to throw myself heart and soul into her cause.

I had already thrown my heart, indeed. She was the most glorious woman I had ever met; and as I sat back dreaming under the spell of her grace and beauty and courage, I felt I would have given all I had in the world to gain her confidence and help her to win her end, whatever that might be.

Then I fell to wondering what could be the strange secret that had led to her betrothal to that fat, squalid, unctuous cad, Paul Drexel? What hold could he have over her and over Boreski? What could possibly have linked them together in that incongruous partnership?

"How I hate that man!"

Her words rang in my ears as the sight of her gloriously contemptuous indignation haunted my eyes. What could make a woman of Helga's courage and man of Boreski's daring—for daring he certainly had—so afraid of a paltry common scoundrel as to drive them to play at this betrothal?

Thank Heaven it was only playing. She would never stoop to become the wife of a brute whom she admitted she hated. Her heart was free if I could but touch it; she was to be won if only I—and there I sighed, recognizing the tremendous difficulties, and, like a wise man, tossed the end of my cigar away and got into bed, hoping that the night's rest would enable me to pick out the master thread of the strangely tangled skein.

I was up betimes and found my head clear on one point.

There must be no more Emperor business, let the result be what it would. I would tell Helga the truth, even if the heavens fell; and I went down with this purpose strong in me.

Then I would tell her of my friendship with the Czar and offer

40

my services as a direct intermediary to bring about an interview between them.

She was in the garden among her flowers, and in her simple morning costume, with the fresh colour in her cheeks, she looked even lovelier than on the previous night.

She welcomed me with a smile and held out some flowers.

"I am an early riser, you see. I love my garden. I have been out here more than an hour. You have slept?" she added, glancing at my face which was no doubt serious enough, for I rather dreaded what I had to say.

"Never better in my life," I answered. "But I wish to speak to you."

"And does that prospect make you so serious? I ought to apologize for exhaling such terrors." She laughed gaily and bent over a flower bush, and then glanced up half-coquettishly. "Let us wait a while. Be merciful, and do not spoil my morning."

"What I have to say cannot wait, mademoiselle."

"I make a very bad listener when I am bending from flower to flower, M. American. Unless it is that you are going."

"That will depend on how you take my news."

"Then you are not going at once," she said quickly. "Are not these lovely?" and she held up a bunch of flowers for me to admire, and looked laughingly at me over them.

"They are as lovely as——" I paused, looking into her eyes.

"Well?" she challenged.

"The hue of those blossoms rivals even that of your eyes."

"Is that an—an American form of compliment? I do not care for compliments."

"My compliment was for the flower, mademoiselle."

"Very pretty—but too Western to be Russian monsieur. But come, we will go in. I am always hungry in the mornings. Will you mind breakfasting with me alone? M. Boreski is coming afterwards."

"I shall be delighted."

"What, to see him?" This with a gay little laugh.

"No, to breakfast with you alone."

"Well, it will be practically alone. Madame Korvata, excellent guardian and good soul that she is, has reached the age which thinks more of what is on the table than of those who are at it."

"But I wish to speak to you alone."

"And keep me without my breakfast, monsieur! And is that— American, too? I am far—far too hungry to talk seriously or even to listen. Come;" and she led the way into the house, laughing as she went.

41

Thus at breakfast nothing could be said. Madame Korvata, a small woman well into the fifties, with large eyes and ample appetite, looked at me sharply when I was presented to her, said that she had met some pleasant Americans in her day and some very unpleasant ones, and then seemed to forget all about me in the more absorbing and profitable study of breakfast.

Helga appeared desirous of impressing even on the servants that I was an American, for she talked chiefly of my country, and seemed to take a delight in putting intricate and searching questions. That I answered them so easily caused her constant astonishment and some amusement.

"How well you know your country, monsieur," she said with a glance and a lift of the brows.

"It should not be surprising," said I.

"And yet it is—very. You appear to know it as well as—as Europe or even Russia."

"I explained last night that my father was a diplomatist, and I had advantages as a boy."

"And how deftly you turn things. You might have been trained in a Court and picked up the facility there."

The shooting of these little shafts amused her intensely, and the meal was punctuated with her laughter and sallies.

When it was over she led me to the garden, and then excused herself.

"I manage all my matters myself. I shall not be long, and then shall be at your service."

"I must see you as soon as possible," I said as she went off and Madame Korvata came out of the house smoking her cigarette. I lit a cigar, and the old lady waited and then said abruptly:

"I like your face, monsieur. You are like our Emperor. But how did you come to know Helga?"

The question was very simple, but yet embarrassing; and when I hesitated how to reply, she saw it and smiled.

"Don't answer unless you like. I hate bothersome questions myself, and never press them. I always pretend never to hear them, indeed. A deaf ear saves a lot of trouble. You think Helga pretty?"

"Mademoiselle is far more than pretty; she is beautiful."

The old lady smiled at my enthusiasm, and took a couple of puffs at her cigarette while she looked at me.

"Ah, they all say that, monsieur."

"All, madame?"

"And good, too," she continued, pretending not to hear my question. "Good, too. A big kind heart—and such a brain. Ah, she would be a great woman if she had her rights. She would make a

42

noble wife, monsieur, a noble wife; but—she will never marry—that is until she has them."

"You are very fond of her?"

"Everybody is. She is more than a daughter to me. Without her I should be—do you know the fate of destitute old women in Russia? God help them, for the Government don't. Helga does God's part for me."

"And you think she will never marry, madame?"

She glanced up with another of her slow, shrewd smiles.

"Get her her rights, and then——" She paused. "She is affianced, but I know what I think." She shook her head gravely. "But no one can do it. So they come and go—and always go at last, not to return."

I could not encourage her to talk about Helga's matters, and I smoked in silence, thinking over what had dropped from her; and when Helga returned, Madame Korvata went into the house.

"She has the sweetest nature," said Helga; "but I suppose she has been warning you. She always does."

"Warning me?"

"She has one regret—that I do not marry. She thinks that marriage is the only proper climax for a woman's life, and that whenever any one comes here, they come with that idea; and she always warns them that I shall never marry."

"She suggested you might be influenced by material reasons."

"I? How do you mean?"

"That if any man succeeded in getting you your rights, you would look upon him with very different eyes."

Her face changed on the instant from amused astonishment to thoughtful and intense earnestness.

"You speak of what you do not know, monsieur, and will not hear. There is nothing that could be demanded of me, no sacrifice however complete or ruinous, no danger however deadly, I would not face for that. That is my real life—all else is a mere setting and pretence."

"Can I speak to you now—without interruption?"

"Would you prefer to be here or in the house?"

"It is all one to me if you will listen seriously."

"Then let us speak here; it is my favourite walk." And we turned into the broad path circling a fountain and surrounded by flower beds abundantly filled and carefully tended. "Now, monsieur."

"In the night I thought over all the strange situation, and this morning came to a decision."

"There must be of course a decision one way or the other," she put in when I paused.

43

"You will understand that before I came here I had no idea I was to meet you. I expected to have to deal only with M. Boreski."

"That was part of my intention. In that I misled you, I know."

"It is nothing compared to the deception I have practised upon you; and I can only plead the excuse that I should not have done it under any inducements had I known of you. Please believe that."

"Deception? How do you mean?"

"I am not the Emperor, mademoiselle; I am only what I have asked you to regard me—a plain American citizen, Harper C. Denver."

If she was astonished at my confession or angry at it, she gave no sign of either feeling.

"That is a very serious confession," she said, speaking very slowly. "Very serious. When did you decide to make it?"

"This morning, realizing the present impasse."

"It is very ingenious, at any rate." Her tone was sarcastic now. "It did not occur to you to speak of such a—such a trifle last night."

There was still no anger in the glance she gave me.

"Frankly, I was too overwhelmed for the time by the possible consequences. But this morning I saw that the truth was at once the simplest and best way out."

"The necessity for the—truth was a little late in emphasizing itself, don't you think?"

"It seems so to you, no doubt; but I was on the horns of a very awkward dilemma."

"And Prince Kalkov?"

"Of course he knows it. I came at his instigation."

"And so you are really an American, and were in Russia as a boy, with your father a diplomatist; and you have been in Germany and France, and speak the languages without any of that horrible English accent; and you understand Russian; and you came here from the Palace; and were driven to the Palace the other evening, having been received with a guard of honour; and you are the living image of our Emperor. Do you know the Emperor, M. American?"

She said it all with such unmistakably good-humoured disbelief that when she had recourse to the term she had freely used the previous night, I could not refrain from smiling.

"The Emperor has done me the honour to make me his friend."

"You are very fortunate, M.—let me see, what is the name—M. Harper C. Denver," she replied with a gay laugh. "You are also an excellent actor, having picked up many little gestures of the Emperor himself. It is really a most wonderful coincidence."

"The reception at the railway station was planned by Prince

44

Kalkov, who knew of my coming and had heard from His Majesty of the strange resemblance between us."

"Really, Prince Kalkov is more subtle than I thought him. Well then, M. American, what do you propose to do?"

She stopped and looked me full in the face with a smiling challenge. It was plain as the Statue of Liberty that she didn't believe a word of my explanation.

"I wish to discuss the situation with you frankly. I wish you to believe that what I now say is absolutely true; and further, if you will accept them, to place my services for what they are worth entirely at your disposal. I would do anything to serve you and to atone in some way for this deception of mine."

"You ask me what is impossible," she answered readily.

"You decline my assistance?"

"No; I cannot believe your explanation—your confession, as you termed it. I cannot; oh, I cannot;" and she laughed and shook her head.

"I can only repeat it is the truth," I said seriously.

"I will be very frank with you and show you how it strikes me. You act it now quite as cleverly as you acted the Emperor last night. You will recall your little slips into the Imperial character; your manner in dealing with M. Boreski, and again with M. Drexel. Well, you find that to go away from here would compel me to deal with the compromising papers—and in that I was and am entirely in earnest; nothing can move me—and then you think by admitting this deception you can gain indirectly what you naturally want and cannot get directly—that is, time. I speak very bluntly, I fear, but this is so much to me that I must do so. And I tell you this second move has failed as signally as your first last night. I ask you to retract your—confession, monsieur."

"We seem to be getting deeper into the maze. What I have told you this morning is the truth, mademoiselle."

"I will put a test to you. Will you hear my story?"

"Yes, if you will pass me your word that you believe what I have said this morning. I could not hear you last night, because I could not accept your confidence in my false character of Emperor."

"You agree and then put an impossible condition. You have an intimate knowledge of the ways of the Russian Court and diplomacy. I ask again then, what do you propose to do?"

"My intention was to go to the Emperor and gain for you the audience you wish. I think I could do that."

"And meanwhile the papers?"

"I hoped you would hold your hand at least until I had tried."

45

"If the Emperor would not hear me in this house, what chance would there be of his doing so elsewhere?"

"But I am not the Emperor, mademoiselle."

"To me you are, monsieur, and will continue to be; so that if you leave here, I shall assuredly do what I said."

"Here we are at the impasse again, then."

"It is you who cause it," she retorted.

"I can see no other way out of it than that I have suggested;" and as she made no reply, we walked round and round the fountain in silence.

The silence was broken by the sound of a galloping horse, and presently a man, top-booted and travel-stained, hurried from the house towards us.

"From M. Boreski, mademoiselle," he said in Russian, handing her a letter.

She tore it open, and a newspaper cutting dropped from it, which I picked up and held out to her.

She read the letter quickly, started, paled slightly, and then glanced at me, her expression a mixture of excitement and amusement.

"Will you read what you have there? It is from a paper just issued."

I read it, and could not refrain from a smile on my part. It was very short and ran as follows:—

"Slight indisposition of the Emperor.—We regret to learn at the moment of going to press that His Majesty is suffering from a slight chill, and, acting under medical advice, will remain in his room to-day. We have the highest authority for saying that the indisposition is very slight indeed, and at most will keep him indoors for a couple of days. This announcement is necessary to allay any anxiety on the part of the public owing to his inability to review the troops in person to-day, as had been arranged. There is no doubt, however, that he will entirely have recovered by the time of the Crown Prince of Sweden's visit three days hence."

Helga was waiting for my eyes as I finished, and when she saw my smile, answered with a lift of the brows.

"A singular coincidence, M. American?"

"More probably cause and effect. Prince Kalkov has told His Majesty, and this is for your further mystification, and to prevent

46

the deception being discovered through the Emperor's presence at the review to-day."

"Yes, I think with you there is cause and effect," she answered. "Do you still keep to your—confession?"

"It is the truth, mademoiselle."

"I am afraid that you will find it as difficult to persuade others as to persuade me. And in that lies the danger."

Her face clouded, and she tapped the letter.

"Danger?"

"This is from M. Boreski, and concerns you closely. You must read it for yourself. It is a further complication."

A further complication it was in all seriousness, as a glance at the letter showed me.

It threatened indeed just a devil of a mess.

CHAPTER VIII

DEEPER IN

BORESKI'S letter ran thus:—

"I have just heard very disturbing news, and hasten to send it you, while I go to make inquiries. Drexel and I had a somewhat serious quarrel after leaving your house last night; very hot words passed between us on the subject of M. Denver's visit, and we parted after some vague threats on his side, to which I paid no very great heed. But this morning I learn from Vattel—whose information is, as you know, generally reliable—that Drexel saw Vastic and some of those with him, and has told them who M. Denver really is. You will understand what is likely to happen at any moment, therefore, if your visitor is not protected. I trust in God that all is well up to now. All sorts of consequences are possible, and you should act at once. It would be absolutely fatal to all concerned if anything were to happen at your house; and my advice to you is either to let M. Denver return home the instant you receive this or to leave the villa with him and go secretly to Brabinsk. Precautions can be much more easily taken there, and, more over, no one will then know where to look for you. But for God's sake act promptly.

"The enclosed is from the just issued Journal, and shows how the Court people are covering M. Denver's absence.

"I shall seek you as soon as I have definite news; but unfortunately there is little room to doubt the gravity of things."

"L. B."

"This means?" I asked when I had read it.

"The Nihilists, monsieur." Helga's tone was firm and deliberate. "Vastic is the name of one of the leaders of the extremists."

"You mean of the assassins?"

"Among the most reckless of them."

"What will you do?"

"My present scheme has failed," she replied, still calmly. "I must begin again; but I shall have proved my strength and I shall be revenged. M. Boreski is right. You had better leave at once. I would not have anything happen here for all the wealth of Russia."

"But I am not the Emperor," I protested.

"Need we play that sorry farce any longer? You had better go—and without an instant's delay, monsieur. Come, let us order the carriage;" and she started towards the house.

"And the papers?" I asked, following her.

"My hand is forced by this. I shall use them."

"My God, what a mess!" I cried involuntarily.

She paid no heed, but hurried me into the house, and gave orders for a carriage to be brought round at once.

"You are ready of course, monsieur," she said quickly.

But I had made up my mind. Her fear of "something happening" had given me a cue.

"I am not going, mademoiselle, without the papers."

"You will go, monsieur," she replied, her face setting.

"Then I take the papers with me, mademoiselle."

"On the contrary, monsieur, you will go without them."

"We shall see;" and I sat down with an intentional deliberation.

"I have pledged myself for your personal safety. You must go."

The purpose in her voice strengthened with every sentence.

"I will trust to my own right arm, mademoiselle. Without those papers, I do not leave the house, come what may."

"You are dealing with a desperate woman, monsieur. You must go."

"Then give me the papers to take with me."

She came and stood opposite me, her eyes aflame, and her hands clenched.

"You shall go if we have to use force to take you away;" and she moved away and laid her finger on the bell.

"You will not do that, mademoiselle."

"Why not?" she cried, turning round.

"Because the man who seeks to lay hands on me will touch nothing else in this life."

For a minute she stood silent in distracted hesitation.

The silence was broken by the sound of the carriage wheels.

"We will see," she cried, and pressed the bell.

"As you please;" and I rose and stepped back against the wall and drew my revolver.

At the sight of it she closed her eyes and threw up her hands with a cry of fear and anguish, and then clasped her hands to her head.

The servant came in then.

"Is the carriage there, Peter?"

"Yes, mademoiselle."

"Very well."

He went and closed the door.

"Your Majesty, I beg you for the love of God to go and save your life. Ah, do, do!" she cried distractedly.

"I am not the Emperor, mademoiselle; and without the papers I cannot and will not go."

She came nearer to me.

"I beg and entreat of you. If you are caught here, think what will happen to me."

"I have no discretion to think in such a case," I answered firmly, although the sight of her suffering wrung my heart.

Almost before the words were out of my mouth she sprang forward in a wild attempt to seize my revolver. But I had been in too many tight corners in my life to be taken unawares, totally unexpected though the manœuvre was, and I wrenched my hand away and held her harmless with the other.

"This is worse than madness, mademoiselle!" I cried.

She gave up the contest then, and drawing away, fell into a lounge in an attitude of despair.

I had won the victory, but the fruits were too bitter. I put the revolver away in my pocket and crossed to her.

"Will you give me the papers?" I asked.

"No, I will die first, and so shall you! Oh God, how hard you are! I wish I had never seen you."

49

"Then I will go with you to Brabinsk, and we can settle things there."

She rose at once and shook off her emotion.

"Do you mean that?"

"Where I go is of no consequence to any one. I have to convince you of your mistake. I will go to Brabinsk. I have to save you."

"You have no secret purpose in this?"

"Is that fair? If you need it, I give you my word of honour to act exactly as you wish—except in regard to those papers. I am resolved they shall not be used."

"But you will be missed. You cannot stay away. You—oh, this is madness, too, surely!"

"You are wasting time."

She thought quickly; then smiled bitterly and shook her head.

"No, monsieur, thank you. I do not walk open-eyed into a trap, however cleverly laid. You know I must take the papers with me, and reckon to get them by the way."

"That is a suspicion worthy perhaps of—M. Drexel. I do not thank you for it. I am not such a mean cad. But that you may feel safe, you can travel alone in the carriage and I will ride with, say, M. Boreski's messenger or any one you can trust to guide me."

"I am sorry for what I said. I do not think it; indeed I do not, monsieur."

"We have not much time for explanations, mademoiselle. We must act."

"It might not be safe for you to be with me."

"We will put it that way if you like," I said with a smile.

"How dare you make such a hateful insinuation when I repent and retract my words?"

"We seem fated to misunderstand each other. But shall we do as I say? Order saddle horses, and I will take steps to prevent any one believing they can recognize me."

"Ivan could guide you."

"Then send Peter at once to my room. I will be ready in a few minutes;" and without waiting for more I hurried away.

In less than ten minutes Peter had shaved off my beard and moustache, and had found me from somewhere a riding jacket. I ran down, and was fastening my cloak across the saddle of the horse that was to carry me, when Helga came out, dressed ready for the drive.

She started on seeing the change in me, and at first scarcely seemed to recognize me.

"I should not have thought so simple a thing would make such a difference in your looks," she said.

50

"I am ready to start, mademoiselle," was my answer; and I swung myself into the saddle.

"You have been very quick."

"It is for you I am anxious. Au revoir. Now Ivan;" and without waiting for more, I clapped the heels into my horse and cantered off. I looked back as I rounded a bend in the avenue, and saw that Madame Korvata had joined Helga, and that they were getting into the carriage.

Ivan rode up to me as we came out upon the road.

"To the right, if you please, your honour."

He looked along the road in the opposite direction somewhat anxiously, but his face cleared.

"Do you wish to travel fast?"

"I am in your hands."

"I think it would be best for a few miles, your honour," he said, and accordingly we whipped along at a smart pace until the suburbs of the city were left well behind. Then he struck through a number of by-roads, until I was utterly at sea as to our whereabouts, except that by the sun I could tell we were travelling north; and we fell into a walking pace on reaching a very steep zig-zag hill.

Ivan was a fine sturdy fellow, with a strong, very intelligent face, and he sat his horse with consummate skill. I liked his looks.

"You have been in the army?" I said, letting him come to my side as we mounted the hill.

"In a Cossack regiment, your honour."

"And prefer private service, no doubt?"

"I have a good mistress, your honour."

"Oh, I thought you were M. Boreski's servant."

"These are Mademoiselle Helga's animals, your honour."

I had noticed before that all about her spoke of her either as mademoiselle or Mademoiselle Helga, and never used any surname.

"They are two good horses and in magnificent condition."

"I am responsible for the stables, your honour," he said with a pleased smile at the remark.

"How far is Brabinsk?" I asked him next.

"Twenty versts by the road the carriage will take—about twenty-six by this road, your honour; but the horses could do twice the distance easily."

"So far is it? I did not know."

We rode on in silence, and I noticed him directing curious sidelong glances at me now and then, until at last he said—

"Your honour's pardon, but your honour is not Russian?"

I had been speaking Russian, and this had betrayed me.

"No, I am an American," I answered with a laugh.

51

"Then your honour has crossed the sea. I have never seen the sea. I have heard of America. And so you have political troubles there, too?"

"Yes. We call them Tammany there."

The word puzzled him greatly, and he repeated it several times gravely, shaking his head over the pronunciation.

"Is it the same as Nihilism?" he asked.

"No, indeed," I replied, and attempted a brief description of Tammany Hall and its methods. Either my description was vague or his understanding of it imperfect, for his face took on an expression of disgust.

"What an awful country, your honour; what tyranny! I am glad I am not an American. Yet after all one's own country is best, I suppose, and it must be sad to be an exile."

His tone and glance were quite pitying now. He regarded me apparently as an exile.

I began to be amused at him, and drew out some of his views on Russia. The result surprised me. He was an intense and indeed a passionate patriot, but he hated the Russian Government. The Czar, as the God-appointed head of Russia, was a quite sacred person, a sort of Fetish in his eyes; but the ministers round him were as the incarnation of evil. For the Little Father it was the heaven-ordained duty of every good Russian to lay down his life willingly and instantly; while he seemed to suggest that it would be almost equally meritorious to take the lives of those who did evil and ground the people in his name.

I looked for the key to this queer mixture of political faiths in the man's association with Helga, and knowledge of her wrongs.

"You are very devoted to Mademoiselle Helga?" I asked presently.

"My life is hers if ever she should need it, your honour," he answered readily, simply and very earnestly.

"You are a good fellow, Ivan," I said; and soon after that we rattled on again at the canter. As we rode, he evidently thought over what had passed between us, for when we drew rein again he came up and said—

"I crave your honour's pardon, but was it your honour who came last night to mademoiselle's villa?"

"Yes. Why do you ask?"

"I am mystified, your honour. It was you then whom M. Boreski bound me by all I hold sacred to guard with my life. And yet you are an American—a stranger—an exile. He told me——"

He stopped and shook his head in perplexity.

"What did he tell you?"

"That I was to serve your honour as if you were the Little Father himself; God keep him; that there was danger from the desperado Vastic; that I should probably have to guide you by by-ways to the Palace from the villa. And yet you are an American. I am filled with wonder."

"Don't I look like an American, Ivan?" I asked, smiling.

"Your honour has shaved since I first saw you. Then I thought you were the—— I trembled at your look, my lord."

"Had I been what you thought, you looked for danger then?"

"God would have given me strength to protect His Majesty. I am mystified; but it is not for me to ask questions."

"You know this Vastic, then?" I asked next.

"He is a good man, absolutely sincere, your—your honour," he fumbled now over the way he should address me, and his manner had changed from frankness to nervous excitement. "Quite sincere; but a madman on one point; and his madness makes him dangerous and reckless."

"A fanatic you mean against the Government?"

"Against the Emperor. We have fought once for that, and he nearly killed me. But we shall fight again, and then I shall win."

"How do you know that?"

"It is fate, your honour; and, besides, I have practised."

The combination of fatalism and deliberate preparation tickled me, and I smiled.

"And you were afraid for my life then?"

"Not yours only, your honour, not yours only; but mademoiselle and M. Boreski's also."

"Mademoiselle's?" I cried with a start. "How and why?"

"I crave your—your honour's pardon, but I may not speak of my mistress's affairs."

"I am her friend as staunchly as you can be, Ivan; and if you can tell me anything without speaking of her private affairs, do so."

He thought for a while.

"It is only what I myself fear."

"Then you can surely tell me," I said eagerly.

"If your—your honour had been what I thought, and not an American only, Vastic's anger and that of those with him would have fallen on mademoiselle herself."

"Why?"

"It is so plain, your honour. He would have held it such treachery for—for such a one to have been at the villa and to have left it unharmed."

"My God!" I cried as the light burst upon me. "You mean they

53

would condemn the mademoiselle and M. Boreski for not having taken my life when apparently they had the chance?"

"Your honour can surely see that clearly."

As the full danger and possible horror of the thing rushed upon me, I dashed my heels into my horse.

"Come, then, for God's sake! Let us get to her and see that she is safe," I cried, and we covered the remaining miles as fast as the gallant beasts under us could travel. And gallantly they carried us; up hill and down, without let or stop we rattled along, Ivan to the full as eager and urgent as I, until we reached Brabinsk and drew up before the door of a secluded house lying away from any road. I dismounted from my sweating, panting horse, and asked for Helga.

She had not arrived, and we were quite unexpected; but at a few words from Ivan I was admitted, and he led the horses away to the stables.

I was too anxious to remain in the house, and as soon as I had washed and removed the traces of the reckless ride from my clothes, I went out to the gate and waited with a feverish impatience for signs of her coming.

The thought of the danger into which she had plunged maddened me; and I breathed a fervent thanksgiving when at length I caught sight of the carriage.

CHAPTER IX

HELGA SPEAKS

"THANK God, you are safe," I cried as I assisted Helga from the carriage, my pent-up anxiety making my tone intensely earnest.

"Safe? I?" and she looked at me in astonishment. "Why, has anything happened?"

"I am excited. Ivan has told me of your danger."

"Then Ivan must be taught how to hold his tongue."

"I drew it from him, mademoiselle. I made him tell me."

"Could you not have asked me about my own affairs?"

"I did not question him about your affairs, of course."

"Then my supposed danger is not my affair?"

"Why play with words? You must explain everything to me. I must know all."

"Must?" with a lift of the brows. "Your ride seems to have made you strangely impatient. Can you restrain it while I take off my hat, monsieur? I am hungry, too, after my ride. Are not you?"

"I am in a fever to know all, and that's the truth."

"I must lecture Ivan for exciting you."

"I beg you to say nothing to that good fellow."

"You know that you look much more American now that you are clean shaven, and seem to act up better to the part! But you must not take my breath away;" and with a laugh she left me.

If there was really the danger of which Ivan had spoken, Helga certainly took it very calmly. But I could not be calm, and I paced up and down the room fuming and imagining many evil possibilities for half an hour, until a servant came to usher me to another room, where a meal was laid and Helga with Madame Korvata were awaiting me.

"Even if we are all going to die in ten minutes, we may as well have something to eat first," said Helga.

"Considering the surprise and no notice, they haven't done badly, Helga," declared Madame Korvata critically, looking at the well-spread table. "What a blessing it is that when one reaches the age which appreciates the importance of food, one has good food to eat."

I sighed, and Helga smiled at my impatience.

"As you invited yourself to Brabinsk, monsieur, I will not apologize for so impromptu a meal," she said.

"A crust of bread and a glass of water would be more than enough for me in my present mood," I answered restlessly.

"Is your digestion bad, monsieur?" inquired Madame Korvata sympathetically. "At your age you ought to be able to eat anything. You look well and strong too; I should never have thought it."

"Thank you, I enjoy excellent health, madame."

"That's made a great change in your looks, monsieur. You are not so much like the Emperor now."

"Have you ever seen the Emperor without his beard, Aunt Korvata?" asked Helga, with a glance at me.

"No, my dear. I've only seen him once. I was judging, like most people, by his portraits. You have never seen him very close, have you?"

"I have often wished to," returned Helga, with another glance. But my restlessness was so insistent that this lightness jarred upon me, and I remained almost moodily silent until the end of a meal that seemed unendurably wearisome. I was consumed with my

55

anxiety to question Helga about Vastic—her Nihilistic associates and her connexion with them.

"Can I speak to you alone, at once, mademoiselle?" I said as we rose from the table.

"Yes." The answer came after a pause which made me think she was going to put me off. We went into the room where I had first been shown. "I have not been at Brabinsk for some time and wish to see to certain things."

"I am sorry to detain you, but I cannot wait. I wish you to tell me the nature of your and M. Boreski's relations with this man Vastic and his associates."

"So, then, you are interested in part of my story—that part which you think might bring me under suspicion?"

"For God's sake don't let us fence with words. I am too anxious. You know that you are doing me a gross injustice in saying such a thing, and that my sole motive is concern for you—you yourself, and the danger which may threaten you."

The earnestness of my manner made her earnest too.

"How should I know that?"

"Because I swear it; because you can read it in my acts. You must feel it; I am sure you do."

She met my eyes, and seemed to understand some of the passion that I felt was glowing in them.

"You are incomprehensible, monsieur," and her eyes fell.

"You must see how I feel. Is it true that because you harboured last night a man whom you believed to be the Emperor, you are likely to be in danger from these reckless fanatics? That question has been burning in my brain ever since the suggestion was prompted by Ivan's words. Is that to be the terrible consequence of this hapless, ill-conceived visit?"

"It was I who planned the visit, monsieur. Do you think I should not foresee any possible consequences?"

"My God, it's true then!" I exclaimed. "How could you be so mad, so blind, so reckless?"

"Blind I was not; reckless you have made me."

"I?"

"Well, Prince Kalkov and your advisers, monsieur, if you prefer that."

"But I am not the Emperor, mademoiselle," I cried angrily. "That is what I mean. You have incurred this fearful risk for nothing."

"You have said so already, many times, monsieur."

I tossed up my hands in despair and began to stride up and down the room.

56

"There must be an end to this," I cried sharply. "I must find some means of making you believe the truth."

She rose and came to me.

"If I were in such danger as you think, would you help me?"

"Show me how and test me." She looked long and anxiously in my face.

"Those are sweet words to hear," she said, with a smile and a note of triumph.

I took her hands, and she left them in mine.

"Tell me all about these men, and let us together see what is best to do. The thought of your danger maddens me, Helga."

"You will listen to me now—hear all I have to say; and then help me in the one purpose of my life?"

"I will help you, God knows, loyally in everything—in everything; but I cannot give you the kind of help you seek, because I am not the man you believe. You must not give me your confidence while you hold to that mistaken belief."

She was going to protest again—I read it in her eyes—but, instead, she paused, and then asked—

"If I care not what you are, will you listen?"

"Readily, readily."

"I will tell you then," she said in a low tone, as she withdrew her hands from mine gently. "I am Helga Lavalski." She looked for some token of recognition of the name from me, as she had on the previous night, and when she saw none her face clouded, and she passed her hand across her eyes as if in pain.

"If I do not recognize the name, it is for the reason I have given you. Until you spoke it last night, I had never heard of it."

"It is not possible," she said in low accents of pain. Then, after a pause, she lifted her eyes and continued: "If it must be so, we will pretend that; but the time was when Boris Lavalski was the chosen friend of—of His Majesty, and when the name was oftenest on his lips. They were almost as brothers."

"You had better tell me all in your own way," I said.

"It is barely seven years ago that the change came which parted them—a change due to the man I will name presently. My father stood in that man's path: the one was honest, the other a villain: and by villainous, underhand, infamous methods a charge of treason was laid and proved by perjured liars suborned by the arch-conspirator. You will remember the Nihilist plot at the time?"

I did not, but it was no use interrupting her to repeat my ignorance of the whole affair.

"Well?"

"A truer and more loyal servant the Emperor never had, but his

57

ears were poisoned; the apparent proofs of an assassination plot were laid before him; a trap had been set for my father, and by it he was ruined. He was kidnapped and held a secret prisoner; the tale being spread that he had fled the country; and in his absence the decree of banishment was signed. As foul a crime as was ever committed."

"You have the proofs of this?"

"That is not the worst. By an even fouler stroke an order for his execution as a Nihilist was obtained. Many men were put to death at that fearful time, and one of the orders with a name written in pencil was signed by the Emperor. This name was afterwards erased and my father's substituted; and then another lying tale was carried to the Emperor that a mistake had been made and my father had been put to death."

"By Heaven, what consummate infamy!" I exclaimed. "But the proofs of this! What and where are they?"

"I was scarcely more than a child at the time, barely eighteen, but I was included in the scheme. I should have been arrested had not my friends hidden me and then hurried me from the country. Otherwise, I should have gone to Siberia. As it was, I was proscribed and banished, and all our possessions were seized in the name of the Emperor. Do you wonder if I live but for revenge?"

She paused, but I made no comment.

"I took up the task eagerly. Two years afterwards I returned to Russia in another name, and, girl as I was, I set myself patiently to hunt down the powerful minister who had planned this crime and risen upon it to higher honours. Bit by bit, a fraction here, a fraction there, I collected the proofs, working always secretly, until a stroke of fortune came my way, and a witness, who had been first a tool and then a victim of the same powerful villain, laid the whole truth bare to me. Meanwhile, by the death of a relative, I had become once more rich, and could pay well all who helped me and promise them protection. It was a terrible life for a young girl, monsieur, and in those few years I lived a lifetime. But I had gained what I sought, the proofs and witnesses to support me."

Triumph as well as anger was in the look she gave me.

"I set myself then to gain your—to gain the Emperor's ear and to get my father's case re-opened. But there I was baffled by the man who stood between me and him. I had to fly the country, or my fate would have been as my father's had been; and those who worked for me were no match for this man's power and vigilance and cunning. I would not accept failure, and I returned to Russia secretly to seek some other avenue, and at that crisis I met M. Boreski."

"Had you better tell me his affairs?" I asked warningly, but she waved the warning aside.

"I am telling you everything. He is an exiled Pole—Count Primus Noveschkoff—and for his part in a Polish plot he was exiled and beggared. He is a great violinist, and I saw my way when I learnt that the Duchess Stephanie had become enamoured of him and he of her, strange as that may seem to you, who know her age and lack of personal charms. I helped him to secure her for his wife for I knew the Court would eventually pardon and ennoble him, and that through her I could eventually gain the Emperor's ear. The obstacles to such a match were of course countless, but I was not daunted, and you know the scheme that I laid—to gain the papers we have obtained—and how it has fared."

"And M. Paul Drexel?" Her face clouded at the question, and she paused.

"I have told you once before I would do anything to gain my end."

"But how comes such a man to be on the scene at all?"

"You are interested then in the story I have had to force upon you?" she asked with one of her searching, half-triumphant, half-defiant glances.

"I am intensely interested in this part of your story," I answered earnestly. "What is he really to you? How comes he here? Do you mean that you would marry such a man, despising him as you do, to gain your purpose?"

My string of questions, and the vehemence with which I asked them, seemed to please her, for she smiled.

"I would do even that—if it were necessary. He has forced himself upon us, and his silence on certain things—why should I not tell you, I have told you all," she broke off. "I have trusted you."

"I know that."

"He knew M. Boreski's real character and past, and it was in his power to checkmate everything by denouncing him to the Government. He had to be silenced, and his price was—the promise of my hand. I paid it, only thankful he made it so light and did not insist on an immediate marriage. I should have married him—then;" she dropped her voice at the last word and paused before it.

"And now?" I asked, my own voice a fraction unsteady.

She waited before replying, and then looking up frankly said, after an interval, in her usual calm tone—

"It will not now be necessary. You know my story."

The silence that followed was very embarrassing to me. It was clear she still insisted upon believing I was the Czar. It was in that belief she had spoken, and it was because of that same belief that she and Boreski had been led to break with the man on the previous night. She was so confident the mere recital of her wrongs to me—as the Emperor—would secure the justice, to obtain which was the passionate desire of her life, that I knew how bitter the truth would be when it was forced upon her. It was just an awful mess, and I sighed involuntarily. She looked up in quick questioning perplexity.

"I am looking for some sign from you," she said anxiously.

"You have not told me of this man Vastic and his friends."

"I am no Nihilist, monsieur, but I have not hesitated to ally myself with them and to use them. They could obtain certain kinds of information which I was helpless to gain without them, and I was glad to have their help. Indeed, I was compelled to have it."

"Good God! and didn't you see the danger?"

"Has my life been so even that I need fear an added risk or two? I have helped them in my turn with money—thousands and thousands of roubles I have given them." Then, with a quick change to fierceness: "Why did the Government make me an enemy? Why deny me my justice? Why destroy my father and seek to destroy me? Why refuse to hear me? If it was to be war between us, was I to be tender-handed in the weapons I used? Place yourself in my position, monsieur, and say what you would have done."

"I would not have turned Nihilist," I answered firmly.

"Nor did I. I am as loyal to the Throne as any woman in Russia. If I were a Nihilist, would you be alive now?"

"I am not accusing you. I am thinking of your present danger."

"Danger!" she cried contemptuously. "I should despise myself if I sat down to count every shadow of danger that crossed my path. Live a life such as mine and you will come to laugh at dangers as I do. Nothing, no not even the instant prospect of death itself, should stand, or ever has stood, between me and my purpose. Could I have done what I have had I been one of your timid mouse-scared women?"

She looked glorious in her proud repudiation.

"Still, we may as well sound the depths of it," I said practically. "Does Vastic know who you are?"

"No."

"Has this Drexel any suspicion?"

"He may have;" the reply was given with a contemptuous shrug.

"To repeat my former question, if Vastic believes you had the Emperor in your house and allowed him to leave, would he be likely to regard that as an offence against the brotherhood?"

"Probably."

"And punishable—how?"

"They might decree my death."

"My God, and you speak of danger so calmly," I cried.

"Danger can always be faced, and generally met and overcome, monsieur."

Her courage was dauntless.

"Does Drexel know of this place—Brabinsk?"

"I think not. But he is a spy by nature, and may have found it out."

"He would surely tell Vastic and the rest?"

"Surely, no; probably, or possibly, yes. There are limits even to the courage of his baseness." She paused, and then added, "If he thought you were here, he might do anything."

I sat thinking intently, distressed and baffled by the knowledge of the dangers among which she moved. She waited for me to speak, and gradually an expression of dismay and pain clouded her features. She was looking for some sign from me, as Emperor, that I would help her to the object always foremost in her thoughts. And receiving none, the belief that she had got her story to me and had yet failed to gain the Imperial protection, chilled and hardened her. And well it might, forsooth.

I was too stunned by the enormous difficulties on all sides to see what to do or say.

Suddenly she rose, her manner half-anxious appeal and half-veiled threat as she said—

"The man who ruined my father was your confidential adviser and his former friend, Prince Kalkov. If you feel that he is too valuable to you, you will probably do nothing and leave me to deal with those papers as I will. But I beg your—I beg you, monsieur, to think, if not of my father and my wrongs, at least to consider what it may mean to Russia. In an hour doubtless you will be able to decide and leave Brabinsk. And remember, oh remember, how I have trusted you and how much I have built upon this interview."

And without waiting to hear the protest that sprang to my lips she left the room.

CHAPTER X

VASTIC

IT was dusk when our interview ended, and lighting a cigar I stepped out through the window into the gardens to think.

The tragic and unutterably sorrowful story which Helga had told me had filled the cup of my sympathy with her to overflowing, and help her I vowed I would in some way. But she herself made that help extremely difficult to plan. If I left the place without giving her some pledge in my false character as Emperor, she would instantly make use of those papers, and thus shut the last door upon the chance of his doing anything.

There was the possibility that if I were to give her some such pledge I might afterwards be able to get her the interview with the real Emperor that she desired. But so much further deceit and lying would be involved that I ruled out the idea at once.

There was also one other feeble way—to get some communication to the Emperor, telling him the whole thing, and leaving him to act. But while such a plan might possibly do good, it was much more likely to do harm. Prince Kalkov would be immediately consulted—and then the deluge. It was more than probable, indeed, that any message or communication from me would be intercepted by him. So that notion had to go after the other.

Helga's stubborn refusal to believe that I was no more than just a private individual was of course the bed rock of the mess, and nothing that I had said or done had shaken her belief in the least. Nothing seemed likely to do it, moreover, short of getting the Emperor to stand shoulder to shoulder with me so that she might see us together.

There was, further, the to me unendurable risk of leaving her alone at Brabinsk to face the danger from these wretched Nihilist fanatics. Had the other parts of the problem been capable of solution, that alone would have kept me by her side.

Of all the tests to which a man's nerve may be subjected, few can be more terrible than the fear of secret assassination. But there is one, and I ran up against it there. To know that there are a number of human wild beasts planning to put a bullet in your head or a knife in your heart is bad enough, but it is infinitely worse when you feel, as I did, that if they failed to do that for me they would probably endeavour to do it for the woman I loved.

And thus I paced the lawn in a mood of intense embarrassment, complicated with a double fear for my own life and for Helga's.

With that thought in my mind I had a good look round the house. It was, as Boreski had said in his letter, a good place for taking precautions. A square solid stone building, with all the lower windows protected by bars or heavy shutters, and it would be as difficult to break into it as to get out of it.

In my mood then I had a keen appreciation of its strength, and I came back to the front again feeling very thankful to the man who had planned and built it.

It was a dead still evening. The twilight had faded very quickly, and when I had been smoking and worrying myself for about an hour, without getting an inch nearer to any solution of the problem Helga had set me, my ears, which are very keen, caught a sound in the distance.

It was very faint, but before it ceased I recognized the beat of a horse's hoofs.

I was in a nervously high strung condition, and as I knew that there was no house near enough for me to be able to hear any one who might be driving or riding up to it, I tossed my cigar away and drew back into some bushes to wait for what might be to come.

It might be just a messenger from Boreski, or even Boreski himself; or, on the other hand, I persuaded myself very easily, it might spell danger. In either case I could do no harm by keeping a watch.

Clearly it was not Boreski, or any one from him, as in that case he would have ridden right up to the house. My ears might have deceived me, of course; but I was conscious of what some people term a creepy sensation as I accepted the other conclusion—that the matter did bode danger of some kind.

I was right too. I stood as still as a statue on my sentry go, and after some minutes I heard a light crunch of gravel under stealthily treading feet and saw a man creeping warily toward the house.

At the same moment I caught a glimpse of Helga. I could see from my place through the open window of the room where we had sat. I saw her enter the room, glance about her in surprise at not finding me there, and then cross to the window and peer into the dark garden.

The man at the gate saw her too, and drew back quickly. A very significant indication.

Helga stood a moment at the window, and then stepped out on to the verandah that ran along the house and looked about her as if seeking me. But I gave no sign of my presence, of course; and after a

63

while she went back through the window, leaving it open, crossed the room with a quick step, and passed out of my line of sight.

Soon afterwards the man crept very cautiously and almost silently a short distance up the gravel walk, pausing at every step and looking about him as if to make certain he was unobserved.

When he was quite close to me he stopped, and I recognized him. It was Paul Drexel. For a moment a hundred possibilities connected with his visit at such a time and in such fashion rushed into my mind, and I was on the point of darting from my hiding-place and seizing him, when he turned and made a signal.

Following his gaze, I saw that two other men had entered the grounds and stood mute and motionless until he waved to them, when they crept up to his side. Then all three got on to the grass, well in the shadow of the trees, and held a whispered consultation.

I could not, of course, catch a word they said, but I saw them point to the open window; and when the consultation ended two of them stole like shadows round the skirt of the lawn under cover of the trees to the window, in front of which both lay flat on the ground.

Then Drexel crept back a short distance, paused, turned and walked up the gravel, with intentionally noisy and heavy steps, to the house door.

It did not require the instincts of a Vidocq to know that some very ugly business was on foot; and while Drexel was getting admitted to the house, I was trying to consider what the thing boded and what I had best do.

In point of fact I did nothing—about the wisest course, as it turned out. To have moved from my hiding-place would only have scared away the two men lying prone by the verandah, and so long as I knew of their presence and they were ignorant of mine, I had the best end of the stick.

I made a pretty cute guess at the meaning of the visit. Drexel had no doubt gone to the villa with the men in the hope of finding me still there, and had learnt by some means of my coming to Brabinsk.

The stroke was aimed at me I felt, and there was less alarm for me in that thought than if it had been directed against Helga. For the time, at any rate, there would be no danger to her, and as I was thus forewarned I could take my own measures.

It is a somewhat skeary thing to have to think out plans to circumvent men who mean to assassinate you, and to realize, as I did, very clearly, how much must hang upon your not making a false step.

As I stood like a statue in the shadows of the trees, I had time to think things out a bit. I had my revolver in my pocket, and I came to the conclusion quite deliberately that if there was any shooting to be done I would let no one get the drop on me, and I would certainly shoot to kill. I had twice in my life had very narrow escapes from death through hesitating in the face of a crisis, and this was not going to be a third time. Some minutes—ten perhaps—lapsed after Drexel was admitted to the house before anything happened, and all the while the men by the house lay as still as death. Although I knew just about where they were, I could not see their dark forms on the ground.

Then Helga entered the room into which I could see, and Drexel followed her. The instant he was inside he shut the door and put his back against it.

Helga seemed perfectly calm and self-possessed, and when he spoke with much gesture, as if excusing himself, she replied with contemptuous indifference, mingled with little shafts of indignation.

The conversation lasted some time, until one of the two men outside lifted his head, so that it came between me and the light from the window, and listened. Then he and his companion, still lying prone, drew themselves cautiously up on to the verandah and lay close to the open window.

Themselves unseen, they were watching intently what passed within the room, and listening to every syllable that was spoken by Helga and Drexel.

So absorbed were the two spies, and so utterly unsuspicious of my presence, that I might have risked closing in upon them, had it not been that the broad drive lay between me and them and the slightest sound of the gravel under my footsteps would have spoilt everything.

I chafed at the enforced inaction, but the issues were those of life and death, and I dared not take such a risk. Helga's life, as well as mine, was in the balance.

At last the minutes of inaction were at an end.

Both men, as if at some signal from Drexel, sprang to their feet and stepped into the room, and I saw the flashing look of anger from Helga at their entrance.

The noise they made in entering gave me the chance I wanted. Two or three light springing tiptoe leaps put me across the drive, and I hurried over the smooth lawn with eager feet, drawing out my revolver as I ran, until, imitating their tactics, I lay full length on the ground in full sight and within earshot of all that went on in the room.

I soon had evidence then of the deadly business on which the men had come.

"I tell you he is not in the house."

It was Helga's voice, of course, and she was facing the three men with dauntless courage in voice, look, and manner.

"It is useless to say that, mademoiselle. We know he is here, and call upon you in the name of the brotherhood to give him up to us. It is more than your life is worth to refuse."

The speaker was seemingly the leader, and his deep vibrating bass voice rolled through the room in tones of intense earnestness.

"Have you ever known me tell you a lie, M. Vastic?" This, then, was the reckless Nihilist himself.

"Do you deny he has been here?"

"An American, M. Denver, has been here; but left this house more than an hour since."

"To go where?" The question came like a sharp stern command.

"I do not know."

"He is the man we seek. You know that. Do you dare to trifle with us?"

"I allow no one to address me in that tone," said Helga proudly. "I have told you the truth."

The man turned to Drexel, who I saw was very pale.

"You are sure this man who calls himself Denver is the Emperor. If you have lied, you will answer to me."

"Ask mademoiselle," said the cowardly cur.

"Mademoiselle, what say you?"

"That the man this—this carrion spy speaks of"—and she turned such a look on Drexel that he winced—"is Mr. Denver, an American. And if he were the Emperor, M. Vastic, and I knew where he was at this moment, you are the last man on earth I would tell."

"I need no other evidence," was the threatening reply. "I give you two minutes in which to tell me where to find him. If you refuse, you will suffer the consequences. You know the penalty of shielding one whom the brotherhood has sentenced. Say when the time is passed," he ordered his comrade, and to enforce his threat he drew a revolver.

Helga gave no sign of flinching, but met his stern gaze with one to the full, as steady and resolute.

"You can murder me if you will. I do not know," she said firmly. Not a change of colour, no quiver of the lip, nor tremor of a finger showed her courage to be shaken, or her purpose weakened by the ordeal.

But it was different with me and I made ready to take up my part in the scene. I calculated precisely what to do. The second man was near enough to the window for me to strike him down as I entered, and I drew myself to my feet in readiness.

66

But at that moment he moved to speak to Vastic. He spoke in a whisper and seemed to expostulate. But the leader remained unmoved by what he said, and the second man with a shrug of the shoulders stepped back to his former place.

Helga watched the short whispered conference closely, but gave no sign of any feeling, momentous as the import was to her.

Drexel was, however, growing deeply agitated. His face was as white as salt, great beads of perspiration were on his forehead, his lips were quivering, and he clenched and unclenched his hands with quick nervous movements.

The turn of affairs had appalled him.

"M. Vastic," he began in low hoarse trembling voice.

"Silence, M. Drexel," thundered the leader. "This is now my affair. It is your part to obey. Now, mademoiselle, the time is run out. I give you a last chance to be——"

The sentence was never finished, for as he spoke Helga gave a great cry, and I dashed through the window, dealt the man near me a blow on the head with my revolver which felled him, and the next moment I had Vastic covered.

"Hands up, you. I've heard what you said," I cried.

"M. Denver," exclaimed Drexel.

Vastic turned on me instantly, full of fight, and with the quickness of light raised his revolver to take aim.

It was his life or mine, and without a second's hesitation I fired and shot him.

The fraction of a second decided it. His pistol went off almost simultaneously. But the bullet went wide, for mine was in his brain, and he was already staggering.

There was a scuffle behind me, and another shot was fired by the man I had knocked down. I turned on him, but he was too quick for me and with a cry sprang out into the darkness.

Drexel meanwhile had opened the room door to fly.

"Come back, you, Drexel, or I'll fire," I cried, covering him. He came back trembling like the cur he was. "Close the window, Helga, and have some help here."

She was shutting the window when the servants, with Ivan at their head, came in, having heard the pistol shots.

"Have that man held, Ivan," I said, pointing to Drexel, who indeed was in a state bordering on collapse, "and go instantly in search of a man who has just fled. Quick, as you care for your mistress's life."

I bent over Vastic and laid my hand on his heart.

When I looked up Helga was standing by me.

"He is dead," I said in reply to her glance.

67

"My God!" The cry forced itself between her pressed lips.

"Have the body taken somewhere for the present," I ordered one of the servants, "and then see that every door and window in the house is safely bolted. I will speak to you presently," I added to Helga, who was now trembling. "I must question this man," and laying a heavy hand on Drexel's shoulder, I led him into another room.

CHAPTER XI

CONVICTION AT LAST

EVENTS had so crowded the few minutes that I had not had time to think, except in those flashes of decision necessary in a crisis. My instinct in such times is to act first and think afterwards. Do something, whether right or wrong; but do it. And I have often found that the wrong thing done quickly may be less dangerous than the right thing done after a too careful deliberation.

The moment the man Vastic lay dead before my eyes, I regretted having shot him: a regret due not only to a naturally intense repugnance to take a fellow-creature's life, but also to reasons of policy. So far as ethical considerations were concerned, I felt I was justified. He was going to kill me; and you cannot argue with a six shooter. It would have been just too soft to have asked him to put his gun down while we discussed the question of my identity. The positions would have been reversed. I should have been dead when he realized his mistake, instead of his being dead when I realized mine; and of the two, I preferred vastly the present sequence.

What I felt I ought to have done was to have winged and disabled him. He would have been just as effectually incapable of mischief, and we should all have been spared the embarrassment of having to deal with his dead body.

I did not anticipate any serious trouble with the authorities, for I had no doubt that old Kalkov would be able to arrange the matter. Vastic was in all probability known to the police; he had been killed in an attempt upon the life of the man he believed to be the

Emperor; and his death was not unlikely to be welcome enough to the Government.

But there were his comrades to consider; and that they would set about avenging him there was no room to doubt. There had been an eye-witness who, unless Ivan caught him, would carry the news straight to them; and their anger was as certain to fall upon Helga as to be directed against me.

This prompted a number of disquieting and perplexing considerations.

My first thought was for Helga's safety; and obviously the only thing to do was to get her away to some hiding-place where these men would be unable to find her. To induce her to leave would, however, be so difficult, that I could think of but one means of influencing her—and that was to encourage her mistaken belief that I was the Emperor. It meant deceit on my part; but in such a case the end must justify the means. She must be saved; and if no other way was open, I must be content with that.

There was another consideration, moreover. My own safety depended to a great extent upon these members of the Nihilist brotherhood continuing to regard me as the Emperor. It was true I should probably be the object of attack so long as they believed I was virtually at their mercy at Brabinsk, and divorced from the usual safeguards and precautions which fenced off the Emperor in the Palace. But that danger was temporary, and would cease the moment I got back to the Palace, and resumed my own character.

With the temporary danger I could trust myself to deal, now that I was forewarned. But if they once got an inkling of the truth, I should be the object of their vengeance every minute I remained in Russia, and very possibly afterwards. And I had the greatest possible repugnance against playing the part of quarry for Nihilist bloodhounds to hunt all over Europe.

These considerations and many others wove themselves rapidly into the web of my anxious perplexity as I paced up and down the room, followed by the staring, fright-filled eyes of the despicable Drexel, whose cowardly treachery had caused all the trouble. He was so frightened indeed, that every time I chanced to look at him he would shrink and cower and hang his head in fear.

"You may well be frightened," I said at length, turning on him; "for I'm thinking whether the safest thing to do is not to put a bullet in your head. Dead men carry no tales." I spoke with intentional brutality.

"For the love of God don't do that, your Majesty. It's not my fault; indeed, indeed it isn't. Oh, God have mercy on me;" and he shuddered in a veritable paroxysm of terror.

"Are you armed? Turn your pockets out. Quick!" I cried.

The haste with which he complied was almost ludicrous.

"I only carried this for self-protection, your Majesty. You know I have made no attempt to use it," he said, as he brought a revolver out of an inner pocket.

"Not even to try and protect the woman you were to have married. I know that because I was watching you."

"Then your Majesty knows I had no chance. I should only have been killed on the spot."

"Well, and if you had been? Is that a worse death than at the hands of the executioner?"

"Oh God, oh God, have mercy on me," he moaned, covering his craven face with trembling fingers. It has always disgusted me to see how readily this type of mangy cur turns his thoughts to the Deity when some specially infamous act has been followed by discovery.

"Do you think your God likes your kind of work? Get together what little of a man there is in you, and face the thing. Don't slobber and whine like that. You make me sick with disgust."

He seemed to make such effort as was possible, and after a few moments ventured to look at me.

"Will your Majesty graciously hear me? I am really innocent. I am indeed."

"Prove it. Tell me all you've done since last night."

"I can give your Majesty valuable information."

"Informer now as well as spy, eh? Answer my question."

Whether he thought he could read some hope in these words I don't know, but he began to show less abject terror.

"I know the secrets of all the people here—M. Boreski and Mademoiselle Helga. Will your Majesty spare my life if I tell you?"

"Do you think I would make a compact with a thing like you?" I cried in disgust. "You can tell me nothing I do not already know, except how you brought Vastic and the other on my track. Tell me that?"

"M. Boreski is a Polish conspirator, and mademoiselle——"

"Stop!" I interposed sternly. "Speak of yourself and your part."

"It is information your Majesty should have," he said.

"Damn you, keep to your own part," I cried furiously, "or to the police you go under guard at once."

He shrank back from my fierce words, and his flabby face turned grey with renewed terror.

"As your Majesty wishes," he said, when he had recovered sufficiently to speak. "They have cheated me and lied to me; they made me promises to buy my silence, and last night quarrelled with me and set me at defiance. They told me I was free to go and do as I

70

liked. No man can bear to be cheated. I was mad in my anger, and I went to Vastic and told him."

"Told him what?" I demanded, when he paused.

"I was sorry the moment I had spoken, and repented my anger."

"To the devil with your feelings. What did you do and say?"

"I said that Boreski was false to his oath to the brotherhood."

The cunning with which he thus got out his charge against Boreski of being a sworn Nihilist and at the same time coloured the description of his own act, did not escape me.

"How?" I asked; and he fumbled with the question in dire doubt.

"By failing to report a matter of grave importance to the brotherhood, your Majesty," he answered at length.

"What matter?"

"Particulars of your Majesty's movements."

"In other words, you told them I was at mademoiselle's villa, and that M. Boreski knew it."

"Not that you were, your Majesty—I am no traitor—but that you had been." He made the distinction eagerly. "I intended to punish Boreski for his insult to me, not, as God is my judge, to bring any danger upon your Majesty."

"You are a bad liar. You brought the men here."

"No, no, no! your Majesty. On my soul, not in search of you. Besides, I was in imminent fear of my life. I saw then the mistake I had made in ever saying a word. They made me accompany them to the villa, and when we heard Boreski was not there, nor Mademoiselle Helga, they forced me at the pistol point to seek them here."

"You knew I had come here?" and I searched his face with angry eyes.

"I—I did not know. How could I know?"

"I do know it," I said, putting up a bluff. It told. The despair in his eyes showed me this.

"Vastic would have killed me," he murmured.

"And you preferred he should kill me. I see."

"Oh, don't say that; don't think it, your Majesty. I am innocent. Indeed, indeed, I am. Oh, my God, that this should be thought of me;" and he set up his whining again.

"One more question, and I've done with you. How many men came with this Vastic?"

He showed such unnecessary agitation at the question that I saw he had still some hidden motive or hope, and I had threatened it.

"Only one, your Majesty; only the man you saw, as I am a living man."

He was lying, of course; and equally, of course, I must have out of him the truth on a point of such vital import to us all at Brabinsk. I thought round his possible motive, and then hit on it.

He was trusting that Vastic's associates would return to accomplish the task in which he had failed, and in that case they would of course rescue the spy who had served them so well.

"You are quite sure that there was only one?" I asked, in an ordinary tone, as if merely needing a repetition of his statement.

"I could not be mistaken. I swear it. I would not lie to your Majesty in such a matter," he asserted eagerly.

"Very well," I said, and rang the bell. "I have yet to decide what to do with you for the present."

When the servant came, I told him to wait and guard Drexel until my return; and going out, I asked for Ivan, and inquired whether he had caught the man he had gone after. Unfortunately he had not. Not a trace of him had he seen, but he had heard the sound of wheels, and concluded that the man had dashed for the vehicle in which the three had come, and had galloped off.

This seemed to lend colour to Drexel's statement; but I had been so sure of his lying that I went back, resolved to put him to a pretty severe ordeal.

I sent the servant out of the room, and then looked sternly at the prisoner, who was staring eagerly at me as if to read his fate in my face.

"I have made up my mind in regard to you. If you had told me the truth in answer to my last question, I might have spared you. But you lied—and that lie will cost you your life."

I drew my revolver again, and made pretence to examine the cartridge.

"You led these men here in search of me. I know that. I saw you when you first entered the grounds here, and watched you. For aiding an attempt on my life the penalty is death, and rightly so. I intend to inflict the penalty myself. Stand up;" and I levelled the pistol at his face.

Stand up he could not; he lacked the actual physical strength. He sat grasping the arms of the chair, staring at me, his eyes wide open and mouth agape, his lips quivering and his colour dull grey.

"I cannot die; I cannot die. For the love of Almighty God, spare my life, your Majesty. Oh God, oh God!"

"Stand up," I thundered; and he winced and shrank and quivered at my voice. An abject, terror-struck craven, he was at once pitiable and hateful even to look at. His very voice refused to obey him as he gasped and gurgled in his effort to speak; but at length he stammered—

"I have lied to you; but spare my life, and I will tell the truth now. I will, I will, as God is my judge."

"Quick then, for my finger itches with impatience."

"We three came alone, as I said, your Majesty; but a number of the others were to follow us as soon as possible, in case of the scheme failing and help being needed."

"How many?"

"I—I don't know. Eight or ten, or twelve perhaps."

I laid the pistol down.

"You have saved your life for the while," I said. "As for the rest, it will depend upon what occurs here."

The rush of relief at my words was too great for his overstrung nerves, and he fainted. I called the servants and ordered them to restore him, and then bind him and put him in a place of safety.

This done, I hurried in search of Helga, to consult with her upon the new developments.

I found that she had had Vastic's body removed to one of the cellars of the house, and she had entirely recovered her self-composure.

"Your nerve is splendid," I said admiringly.

"Such a life as mine trains one to face emergencies. What does your Majesty wish to do?"

"There is a good deal to settle," I answered, accepting without protest her method of address. She intended me to understand that her conviction was firmer than ever; and as I believed I could influence her with much less difficulty if she held to it, I appeared to acquiesce.

"You have formed some plan, monsieur?"

"Yes. In my view, the sooner we are all away from this place, the better;" and I told her briefly what I had forced from Drexel.

"They could do no harm to us here, even if there were a dozen of them," she said.

"True, but we should have much more chance of escaping their notice if we were to travel to the city by night rather than by day."

She was perplexed by this, and questioned me with her eyes.

"You yourself are now in imminent personal danger, and must lose no time in getting to a place of safety."

"Where can we go?"

"To the Palace," I answered, speaking on the spur of necessity to give some definite answer; and in truth that seemed the best thing to do.

She started and caught her breath.

73

"You mean——" She was all anxious eagerness now.

I paused a second, and then took the plunge and answered with deliberate significance—

"After what has passed here, your safety is now my concern and your desires are mine."

She read my words in the way I intended. She turned slightly pale, and in her agitation caught at the back of the chair by which she stood.

"Thank God," I heard her whisper under her breath.

I felt pretty mean at the trick I was playing, when I saw how she took it; but I had persuaded myself there was no other way, and held firm.

"I have not trusted you in vain," she said, after the pause. "Your Majesty has but to speak your wishes; it is for me to obey;" and she gave me one of her sweet, frank smiles.

I felt meaner than ever; but I was in up to the neck, and deliberately plunged deeper. Under an impulse I could not control, for her smile and words of trust carried me away, I took her hand.

"Is it the Emperor you trust, Helga, or the man?" I asked, in a voice low with passion.

"It is you, monsieur;" and again she lifted her glorious eyes to my face, and then withdrew them on meeting my look.

"May God deal with me as I merit, if I desert you."

We stood thus for a moment, when, at the sound of some one approaching the room, she drew away from me, with a glance and a sigh.

It was Ivan with news.

"We have heard the sound of some one driving furiously toward the house, my lord. What shall we do?"

"I will come," I answered, and he hurried away.

"You will run no risks, monsieur?" cried Helga swiftly and anxiously.

"I have too much at stake—now," I answered, out of the earnestness of my heart. "God send we may all get out of this safely. I will arrange with Ivan for our leaving. Will you get ready?"

"I will do everything you wish."

The words were in my ears as I hurried out and up the staircase to the room where Ivan was keeping watch. I had my plan. I would take Helga with me back to the Palace at all risks, get an audience with the Emperor, and lay the whole affair, her story and all, before him, and ask his protection. In truth, I was mad enough just then to venture anything.

These things rushed through my head as I ran up to Ivan.

"All is well, my lord," he said, coming to meet me. "It is M. Boreski."

"Good," I exclaimed. "Now we shall know more of the truth." A remark far more disastrously true than I could have anticipated.

When I went downstairs again, Boreski had already been admitted, and was with Helga. All impatience for his news I entered the room; and opening the door, started.

A third person was there: a tall woman in black, heavily veiled.

"Good-evening, M. Boreski; you are welcome. What news do you bring?"

"Good-evening, monsieur," he replied, and I noticed restraint in his tone and manner.

Helga too was looking at me curiously. I smiled to her, but, instead of replying, she looked to the woman in black.

"Well?" she asked. I began to scent mischief.

The woman threw up her veil, and I saw she was well on in years, pale and plain, but had an air of distinction.

"Do you know me, monsieur?"

"No, madame. To the best of my knowledge, I have never had the pleasure of seeing you in my life."

She shrugged her shoulders and Boreski threw up his hands.

A pale shadow crept over Helga's face.

"Are you quite sure, monsieur?"

"I am positive, mademoiselle."

"And so am I," said the new-comer, with a touch of scorn. "That is no more the Emperor than I am."

I saw things then. There was a moment's critical silence. Then Helga broke it, speaking in a chill, cutting tone.

"This is the Duchess Stephanie—M. Boreski's wife."

"Exactly," I answered; and for the life of me, acute as the situation had suddenly become, I could not for the time get out another word to redeem it.

The cold, hard look in Helga's eyes as she faced me was for the time unendurable, and I turned my head away in sheer tongue-tied embarrassment.

CHAPTER XII

HELGA'S ANGER

IT was certainly one of the most untimely kicks which Fate could have dealt me; and it took all my reserved strength to brace myself and shake off my first feeling of dismay in order to put any sort of face on the thing. But I have a good deal of india-rubber in me.

So I pulled myself together, and surprised them all by turning on Boreski and saying, in a very sharp tone—

"Why didn't you get here a quarter of an hour sooner, and have saved half this embarrassment?" It is generally a safe tactic when something goes wrong to attack the other fellow. Boreski started, and I followed up the attack. "If you loiter and fool away the time at such a crisis, what is it but just opening the door and inviting trouble to walk in?"

"I have not wasted a single minute, monsieur," he replied. "Besides, I cannot see what that has to do with it."

"Mademoiselle can tell you," and I looked at Helga. I think she saw the drift, but she said nothing. Poor girl, she was too overwhelmed by the fiasco of her plans.

"The question is not whether I came soon or late, monsieur," said Boreski with slow precision, "but who and what you are."

"That's exactly what I mean. The very pith of it."

"I do not understand you, monsieur."

"That does not trouble me very much; but mademoiselle does." I was resolved to force her to speak. Besides, my temper was beginning to be tried by Boreski's manner.

"This is a matter for us as men to settle without bringing Mademoiselle Helga, or any other woman, into it."

"Rubbish and nonsense," I said irritably.

"Monsieur!" he exclaimed angrily, "I do not permit any one to address such words to me. You will not explain your imposture by insulting me."

"Keep your temper with me, if you please, monsieur, or you will only render a bad situation worse."

"This is monstrous," said the Duchess Stephanie. "He is Prince Kalkov's spy, of course, and seeks to cover the infamy of his imposture with this amazing insolence."

This gave me an excellent cue, for I saw Helga wince; and I hoped she resented alike the charge, and the way it was made. What the other two thought of me I cared not a five-cent piece: and with Helga herself I had only to explain away my last act of implied confirmation of her mistake as to my identity. It would not be easy, of course, because the disappointment to her must inevitably cause her to exaggerate its meanness.

"I am neither a criminal nor a spy, madame," I said.

"I will have an explanation," cried Boreski insistently.

"I have no explanation to give, except that if you had arrived a quarter of an hour earlier all this—this excitement would have been unnecessary. For what occurred in that quarter of an hour I am profoundly sorry;" and I looked again at Helga.

"You are right, Stephanie; this is a monstrous thing," cried Boreski. He rose and came toward me, and said, with a sort of fierce contemptuousness: "You do not explain because you have no explanation. You are a spy; some new and zealous member of the secret police, no doubt. You will be kept here until I find means to make you speak."

"Good," exclaimed the Duchess, "very good. The only way, of course."

I contented myself with a shrug of the shoulders, and met his angry look with one of complete indifference.

"I have seen that kind of mood before with other impostors and spies of the same type."

"Your opinion of me, M. Boreski, is a matter of absolute indifference." I said this calmly and deliberately, and added: "And I repeat, you are only making a bad situation much worse."

"Such effrontery!" exclaimed the Duchess, with another of her angry comments.

"I give you a last chance to tell the whole truth about yourself, before I send for the men and hand you over to them."

"It's very good of you, monsieur," I answered flippantly; and then turning to Helga: "It occurs to me, mademoiselle, that while we are quarrelling here, we are wasting invaluable time."

"Why don't you speak?" she replied, breaking her long silence.

The Duchess Stephanie, not understanding what lay beneath the words, shrugged her shoulders and gave an audible sniff of contempt.

Boreski, on the other hand, crossed to the bell.

"We will have no more of this. I will have the men in."

"Stay." This from Helga, in an unmistakable tone of command.

The other two stared at her for an explanation.

"We cannot detain M. Denver. You are at liberty to leave the house, monsieur," she said, turning to me.

"But that is just what I will not do—at any rate, yet. When I know you are safe, I will do whatever you wish."

"I do not need your further assistance, monsieur." This very proudly.

"Can't you see that you are just a little unjust?"

"You have deceived me grossly, monsieur."

"Only because you would not let me undeceive you; and I saw, or thought, the only way left was to let you believe what I saw you persisted in believing."

"You saw it, then, and acted intentionally?" she said, very bitterly.

"Yes; I don't deny that with regard to what passed between us last. But I thought—I hoped you felt you could trust me."

She lowered her eyes and avoided the earnest look I directed on her; and there was a pause of some length. Then, without looking at me, she said—

"I can only say now, you are free to go, monsieur."

"While you are threatened by the dangers I have all unintentionally brought upon you, I will not go."

"It is impossible for you to remain, monsieur."

"I have said my last word on that point, mademoiselle."

Boreski had fidgetted uneasily as we spoke, and now intervened.

"You have heard, monsieur, what——"

"Silence, if you please, M. Boreski," I cried with heat. "You do not understand. If I cannot comply with mademoiselle's wishes, do you think I shall heed what you say? It is you, with your hot-headed quarrel with Drexel last night, who have brought about all this mess. And Heaven knows it is bad enough to satisfy any ordinary blunderer."

Boreski fell back before my hot words and looks, but his wife was quick to take offence. She got up pale and angry.

"Either that spy is driven from the house, Helga, or I do not stay in it. I will not hear my husband insulted."

It was like a woman of her type, of course, to put her oar in with such a silly splash and make things much worse. But it had the effect I wished. It forced Helga to defend me.

"You do not understand, Duchess. M. Denver is no spy. He came to us yesterday under equivocal circumstances, but this morning took the first moment to tell me he was not the—was no other than M. Denver, an American; and I in my blindness could not and did not believe it. It is I who am responsible. It is all a terrible tangle, but I will answer for him."

"I thank you for that, mademoiselle. I was sure you would do

78

me justice." I was so happy at her words that I could easily afford to ignore the sneer with which the Duchess resumed her seat.

"It is all very extraordinary," she said hastily. "But you are right in one thing, Helga, I do not in the least understand it."

Helga did not appear at all anxious to explain, so I took the opportunity to make my own position clearer, not for the Duchess's benefit, but for Helga's.

"It is as simple as disastrous, madame," I said. "M. Boreski, having quarrelled last night with this Drexel, the latter went to M. Vastic, one of the leaders of the Nihilist Brotherhood, and told him he would find the Emperor at mademoiselle's villa. He went there, and finding we had come on here, he and others followed us, and he attempted my life. I shot him, and I have since dragged from Drexel the admission that many of his associates are coming here, and it is extremely probable they will make some attack upon us to avenge him. Their vengeance would of course include both M. Boreski and Mademoiselle Helga, as well as myself. That is why I cannot leave until she is safe."

"Drexel is here, then?" said Boreski quickly.

"If you wish him to confirm what I have said, monsieur, you can question him. But I think we ought to be seeing to things."

"It is horrible," exclaimed the Duchess, intensely frightened. "If I am discovered here everything will be ruined. Loris, you must take me back to the city at once." One excuses a woman for thinking first of herself, of course, and I quite appreciated the awkwardness of her position. But Helga was not so tolerant. She looked at the Duchess coldly and a little scornfully.

"M. Boreski had better take you away at once, Duchess," she said.

"I had better go," said Boreski. "What must be done is to explain to Vastic's friends the manner in which we have all been duped."

It was my cue, of course, and I saw my way instantly. But it struck Helga from quite a different point of view.

"That would be only to turn this into a private feud against M. Denver for the death of Vastic. That is as impossible as it would be dishonourable."

"Cannot this gentleman defend himself? He came of his own will surely, and should not shirk the consequences," said the Duchess.

"M. Boreski is right," I put in, "and I think I see a way." I got up as I spoke.

"What are you going to do, monsieur?" asked Helga quickly, in some concern.

"I am going to obey your wishes, mademoiselle, and leave the house," I answered with a smile.

"I should not let him go. If these men come here it will be in search of him; and if you give him up to them, it will show them they have nothing against Loris and you, Helga."

But Helga was thinking closely, and seemed not to hear this admirable advice. Boreski looked from one to the other in doubt what to do. For a few moments there was silence.

Then an ominous interruption came from outside. A sound of a pistol shot, followed by running footsteps along the verandah, and the violent slamming of a door somewhere.

The Duchess jumped to her feet in fear and great agitation.

"What can that be?" she cried.

"I fear it means you must delay your flight, Duchess," said Helga with scarcely veiled disdain.

"Have I your permission to go and see what has occurred, mademoiselle?" I asked; and without waiting for it, I turned to the door.

As I opened it, Ivan reached it.

"Can I speak to you a moment, my lord?" he asked, looking very set and determined, and breathing quickly.

"I will come with you," said Helga. We went out and left Boreski and his excited, panic-stricken wife alone. "What has happened, Ivan?" asked Helga. "That shot; is any one hurt?"

"No, mademoiselle. I was outside looking round, thinking it best to keep a watch, and two men who had concealed themselves in the shrubbery rushed upon me. I fired the shot more to give the alarm than thinking to harm them, and then ran back indoors."

"What do you think it means, Ivan?" I asked.

"I think there is only one explanation, my lord. There must have been some of M. Vastic's friends in the district, and they have come because of his death."

"Do you know how many?"

"I cannot say for certain, my lord. I saw several as I ran to the house door."

"You have done very well to find this out and give us warning. But we must devise means to avoid a conflict of any kind. They may be merely watching the house; I should think that's most probable, indeed. They would scarcely attempt to force an entrance."

"They attacked me, your honour," said Ivan.

"Merely to get from you who was inside, I expect. So keep as vigilant a watch as you can, while I think what to do. Of course they must be kept out—at any rate, for a time."

I had my purpose fixed already, and when Ivan had gone I

turned to Helga, and found her eyes fixed upon my face steadily. I did not wish her to read my thoughts, and forced up a smile.

"I think Ivan has unnecessarily alarmed us, mademoiselle."

"I am trying to guess what is in your thoughts, monsieur."

"I shall be very happy to tell you. I think these men have come to watch the house, as their habit is," I replied briefly.

"What an actor you are!"

"A man who has knocked about the world as I have picks up the knack, more or less, I suppose. I seem to have played the part with you a bit too well, I am afraid. I should like you to know that I'm horribly sorry and horribly ashamed."

"To-night when you spoke of my leaving here with you, you allowed me to deceive myself. You allowed it intentionally."

"Yes; I did more. I encouraged the deception. I suppose you can't think a man would do a mean thing for any but a mean motive, yet I——" I broke off, and threw up my hands. "It's no use trying to explain all I felt. I can't do it." We were standing in the large square hall, and I walked to one end and stood by the great stove. "When I look at you and think of it, I feel like what they said of me in there—a spy. I was one when I came to you."

"You spoke of taking me to the Palace?"

"I meant to do it, too. I would have got you to the Emperor. I should have had some claim on him for this business, and I'd have got you a hearing. But I suppose it looks to you like treachery."

"And you made me think that, as the Emperor, you were taking me there to do me justice. I should never trust you again."

"Don't rub it in. I feel quite mean enough already. You might be sorry, too. I'm not going to ask you to trust me again."

"And you could listen as you did to all my story! To think I should have put myself in the power of such a man."

I winced under this punishment as a dog under the lash.

"Do you think I should betray you?"

"How can I tell, after what has happened?"

"True. There is that, of course." I paused with a frown of pain. "Is it any good for me to say I should not? I wish you could say you don't think it."

"What are your wishes to me?" she cried, flashing her eyes at me.

"Nothing, of course; or less than nothing—just spurs to your contempt, it seems. Well, I don't suppose there's anything else to be said."

"If I have made you feel how dishonourably you have acted, and how cruelly your conduct has crushed and ruined everything I hold dear, it may perhaps make you pause when you find your next victim."

"I'm not likely to forget even without these lashes of yours to remind me." I could endure no more of this merciless injustice. "I will go and see what Ivan is doing," I added, recrossing the hall.

"Stop, if you please. I have faithful servants who will protect me if I am in any danger. I will not be beholden for my safety to you, M. Denver."

I turned and looked at her scornful, angry face. I had rather she had struck me.

"My God!" I cried, "Even that;" and I sat on a lounge and put my hand to my head. There was a rustle of skirts, and when I looked up she had gone, and left me to my belated remorse and my new purpose.

I would have given anything for a single word of forgiveness, or even for a glance of some feeling less bitter than her contempt and anger. Well, it would have to come afterwards, when I had saved her, despite her repudiation of my help; and I rose to carry out my plan.

I went to Ivan and asked him what he had seen. He told me a number of men were round the house. He noticed that I was pale—for the interview with Helga had shaken me badly—and asked if I was ill.

"No, I am not ill, Ivan, but strange things have happened. Listen to me and help me. I am not what you have thought, but what I told you during the ride—M. Denver, an American. All unwillingly I have brought your mistress into great danger, and I am going to get her out of it. I am going to those men outside to convince them I am only what I have told you."

"But——" he began excitedly.

"Don't interrupt me and don't look like a madman. This must be done, otherwise they will never believe that mademoiselle has not been guilty of treachery to them, and her life will always be in danger at their hands. Now, don't be a fool and make a fuss. I caused the trouble, and I must find the way out of it. And the only way is this."

"Great Lord of the Earth, they will kill you before you can get time for a word. It is madness, monsieur, stark, staring madness."

"Don't waste time in this way. I know the risk you speak of as well as you, and I am content to face it. If that happens, what you have to do is to make them know the truth after they've done it. It will be easier then; but, easy or difficult, you must make them understand it somehow; for only so can we save your mistress's life. She told Vastic in the other man's hearing that I was not the

Emperor; remember that, and rub it into them well; and make them understand that Vastic's death was my act and mine only. Of course, if they don't pot me off-hand, I may be able to open their eyes myself."

"I must tell the mademoiselle, monsieur," he protested.

"You'll do nothing of the sort. If you do, I'll—I'll thrash you. Just lead me to a door I can get out by quietly, and leave the rest to me."

He looked at me so long and earnestly that I thought he was going to protest again. But he did not. Instead, he seized my hand and pressed it to his forehead.

"Let me go with you, monsieur," he cried, almost hoarsely.

"Don't be a fool," I said roughly, although his devotion touched me very nearly. "Show me the way out. You'd be no use to me out there, and your mistress can't spare us both at such a time."

"Come then, monsieur," and he led the way down a long corridor. "Wait, monsieur, while I see if they are near the door," he muttered, and then left me. He was gone so long that I grew irritable, and when he came back I spoke very sharply.

"This will be the best way, monsieur," and taking me to the front door of the house, he left me again.

"Come here, and be ready to shut and bolt it after me, Ivan," I said angrily, as I drew back two of the heavy bolts.

As I did so, I felt a light touch on my arm, and turned quickly to find Helga, white and agitated, by my side.

Then I knew why Ivan had run away. If he had not, I would have made my threat good.

CHAPTER XIII

THE ATTACK

"WHAT are you doing, M. Denver?" asked Helga.

Her inopportune arrival took me so completely by surprise that for the moment I could think of no plausible answer.

"I—I was seeing to the security of the door," I said very lamely.

"Making it secure by drawing back the bolts, do you mean?"

Her voice had still the hard steely tone that had so hurt me before, and her glance was coldly penetrating.

"One must first draw back a bolt before shooting it again to see that it is in order."

"You had already drawn back two and were on the third when I stopped you. You were going to open the door."

"You know so well what I was doing that I suppose you know also I was going to open the door to let the men in. I am a spy and was acting like you no doubt think a spy would. Why should I try to hide things any longer? You know me so well." I spoke as if now reckless.

"Ivan has told me everything you said to him, monsieur."

"Then Ivan's a fool and ought to have his head punched. You told me before that means must be found to stop his chattering tongue. Of course he only knows what I chose to tell him."

"You were going out to these men in a forlorn hope of making them see you are not the Emperor."

I laughed and shrugged my shoulders.

"That's what I told him. But you know me better than to think me such a fool. You know I was going out as one spy to other spies."

"Then you were really going out to them?"

"My capacity to harm you in here being checkmated, it was natural enough I should look for some other means. Surely you can see this." And after a short pause I added with another laugh, "You have made me your enemy, you see, and must take the consequences."

For a moment or two she said nothing, keeping her eyes fixed intently on my face, with an expression that baffled me.

"How were you going to do what you said to Ivan?"

"Isn't that just a ridiculous question? I had to make up some sort of yarn for him. But you know how good I am at acting. I said what came first, of course; but I tell you I was going out to give these men the chance of getting at you easily—to set them on you, that is."

Her eyes clouded and she frowned.

"Can you never tell me the truth, never be candid with me?"

"Surely you are unreasonable. How could I make a more perfectly candid declaration of war?"

"Do you wish me to think you utterly vile, that you paint yourself in these colours?" The cold steel tone gave place to a note of passion.

"I know what you think of me. You told me to-night; and I don't see that anything could make it much worse."

"Yet you have forgotten." Her voice was cold steel again.

"Perhaps. Of course a spy must have unpleasant things said to him, and have to learn to forget quickly. It's a happy gift at times I assure you." I spoke as indifferently as I could.

"There is not a true note in your voice. You do remember that I said I would not owe my safety to you. I repeat it, I will not."

"Is that any reason you should object to my going out to betray you?"

"Do you wish to insult as well as humiliate me, monsieur?"

The pendulum of her mood was swinging over to passion again.

"Have you spared me?" I asked sharply. "When the lash of your contemptuous words is burning and scorching like fire strokes now? Had you not deemed me utterly base and mean, would you have said what you did? If you thought it then, you must think it now; and you may as well think I am foul and cowardly enough to go out and betray you? It would be no great effort of imagination for you. I beg your pardon," I said, thrusting my momentary anger away. "I did not mean to lose my temper. I have been sorely tried, but I will not do that. No, I do not wish to humiliate or insult you. I thought perhaps I could help you a bit out of this mess I have got you into."

"I should regard your help as a humiliation, monsieur."

"Knowing that, I did not mean you to hear of it. That's Ivan's fault."

"You shall not go out to them, monsieur."

"Very well, mademoiselle."

I bowed, and she stamped her foot angrily at the gesture.

"You know your life would not be worth a moment's purchase."

"You have done me the honour to show how worthless it is."

"You twist everything I say to you," she cried impatiently. "You will give me your word of honour that you will not go out."

"You are very inconsistent. At one moment you all but order me out of your house; at the next you prevent my going. It is absurd."

"When I told you you could leave, we did not know of the danger."

"What is my life to you?" I took a leaf out of her book and asked the question in a tone as cold and hard as she had used, while I looked at her very steadily. She met my look but did not answer my question. "You think me a spy, what then——"

"I do not think you a spy, monsieur. You know that. You heard me tell M. Boreski that I would answer for you. You can be bitterly unjust."

So there was some feeling after all under her cold manner.

"We will not speak of injustice, mademoiselle," I said, in the same tone. "But I had forgotten Boreski. I owe this to him even more than to you perhaps; so that I cannot pass my word not to go out. He would not object—nor his Duchess either."

85

"You will drive me mad, monsieur," she cried impetuously.

"Because I use the tone you have taught me?"

"I say you shall not do this insane thing."

Her passion mounted fast enough now, and I was not unwilling to feed the fire. Anything rather than her contempt.

"Very well. Then shall we go in and play a hand at cards while these gentlemen outside complete their plans? Allow me," and I made a mocking pretence to offer my arm.

She drew back and trembled with anger.

"How dare you!" she cried.

I flung up my hands.

"You are difficult to please, mademoiselle," I said, smiling airily.

"Will you give me your word?"

"Can you suggest any other way out of the thing? That is much more to the point."

"You shall not risk your life in this mad way."

"Hush!" I held up my hand. My ear had caught the sound of grating steps on the stone outside the door. We stood and listened, and the sound came again, followed by a gentle knock at the door.

I led her a few paces away.

"I'm going to answer that knock myself. Trust me. I will not betray you. Go into the room to Boreski."

"Not for a thousand worlds," she answered vehemently.

"Let this misunderstanding cease. I will run no unnecessary risks."

There are moments when many things are made plain; and that was one of them for Helga and me.

"I cannot trust you—to run no risks, I mean. I cannot."

"In other things?" She was silent. "Helga?"

She started as I used her name, and drew a deep breath which escaped in a tremulous sigh.

"You know," she whispered.

My heart gave a great leap.

"Thank God!"

The knock at the door was repeated.

"Do as I ask and leave me to deal with this. I shall run no risks—now."

"I—I cannot."

Ivan had heard the second knock and now came to us asking for instructions.

"Can you ascertain how many there are at the door here, Ivan? Try and make out from some upper window."

"You will not venture out?" said Helga as soon as he had gone.

"Everything is altered now. I go back to my former plan. We can stay here until it is safe to leave—since we know these men are dogging us, daylight will probably be the safest; and we will get to the Emperor when you are safely concealed in the city."

I had too much to live for now to care about putting my life to the hazard in the way I had purposed in my mood of desperation. It was once more my desire now to make the men believe that I was indeed the Emperor, so that the pursuit of me should cease the instant I could get back to the Palace.

But my plans were still fated to be thwarted.

"I can only make out two men, monsieur; but there may be many others hidden close by," said Ivan, returning.

"We can at any rate speak to them. Call a couple of the men to be ready at hand in case of need," I told him; and in that way like a fool played into their hands.

Ivan at my bidding went to the door and called through it—

"Who is there?"

"We are police. Open."

This was either a very ugly new development or a lie. I chose to regard it as the latter.

"What do you want?" was Ivan's next question.

"We seek M. Vastic. Open at once."

"There is nobody here of that name. We open the door to no one at this time of night."

"We shall break it in," said the voice. "Open, in the name of the Emperor."

"Tell them to break it in if they can," said I, and Ivan gave the reply; whereupon they commenced to hammer and bang at the door with such a clatter that the mere noise itself ought to have roused my suspicions. But my wits were as dull as a dunce's to their ruse; and I had not a thought of their trick until a loud noise with a great smashing of glass at the back of the house told us their object had been merely to distract our attention downstairs while the real attack was delivered on an upper floor.

"Go to Boreski, mademoiselle," I cried as I dashed up the broad stairway, followed by Ivan and the men. The others had rushed up by a back staircase and met us on the landing.

"Where have they got in?" I asked.

"That room," said one of them, pointing to a door. A glance at it showed me the key was outside, and in a moment I had turned it upon those within. Not a second too soon. As the lock shot home the handle was rattled by some one inside.

Ivan had seen me and immediately rushed through into an adjoining room where I heard him lock and bolt the door.

87

"The room leads into this dressing-room, monsieur," he said as he came out. "But the door is only a slight one and will not keep them back."

I went in and examined it, and, coming to the same conclusion, promptly abandoned it as a point of defence. I then sent Ivan to fetch Boreski, and while he was away thought out an impromptu scheme for defending the landing place.

It lent itself well enough to such a purpose. It formed a square, on one side of which were the stairs; and it was thus possible to place men so that they could command the doors by which the men must come out; and my simple plan was to form a sort of barricade with some heavy pieces of furniture from behind which we could operate.

With Boreski came Helga full of pluck, resource and ideas. I explained my plan to them and sent two men downstairs to keep watch against a further surprise.

"We can keep the watch, the Duchess and I," said Helga instantly; "and thus leave you much stronger." But the Duchess as promptly declared she had no nerve for work of the kind and further tried to induce Boreski to stay with her.

He was no coward, however, and when Helga vetoed the suggestion with great indignation and I joined with her, he sided with us and she had to give way, doing so with great reluctance.

Helga then went downstairs and our preparations were soon complete.

Meanwhile the men in the room were suspiciously quiet. Probably they realized, as we did, that they had gained very little by getting into the house by the way they had chosen and were really caught in a kind of trap, from which further progress into the house would be attended with more danger than they cared to face.

A glance at my watch showed me, to my surprise, it was nearly eleven o'clock. The hours had flown very quickly.

"At what hour is it daylight?" I asked Boreski.

"About half-past three," he said.

"Then we shall have four or five hours of this. They'll clear off when the light comes."

"Hadn't we better speak to them?"

"By all means if you can do any good. You know them, I don't."

He climbed over the barricade and rapped at the door.

"Who is there?" he asked. "I am Boreski." No reply was made, and he knocked and called again. "I don't believe any one is in there," he said to me in a whisper. "I can't hear a sound."

"Let's hope they've gone then, but I doubt it," I replied, and then as a suspicion flashed on me, I turned to Ivan. "What about the upper storey. Are there any ladders about the place long enough to reach it?"

"Yes, monsieur, at the stables."

"That explains the silence then. Come with me quickly;" and climbing the barricade I rushed up, followed closely by Ivan. We were in the nick of time.

They had already planted a long ladder reaching to the window of one of the front rooms and three of them were more than half-way up. I threw the window open.

"Come, gentlemen, quicker please. You keep us waiting," I called.

The result was almost comical. The man at the top muttered something to those below him, and in an instant all three went sliding helter-skelter to the ground, and picking themselves up scurried off in the darkness to cover.

"They won't be in a hurry to try that again," I said as I closed the window; "but we must watch them. Let one of the men come up here and keep a lookout;" and I went down again to Boreski.

Another long wait followed during which we heard plenty of movement in the room close at hand.

"Something's doing," I said. "I wish to Heaven we knew what."

"I'll try to speak to them again," he replied, and made a second attempt with no better result.

Later, Helga sent for me. I found she had got the women-servants well in hand and all were engaged in keeping a vigilant watch.

"We can see them going up and down that ladder, and each man seems to carry something up and come down empty handed. See," and she led me to a small barred window from which I could see the ladder.

What I saw made me catch my breath. A couple of men went up with an armful of straw and a third followed with a bundle of small wood. They were going to set fire to the house. I did not speak this thought to Helga.

"What does it mean?" she asked.

"I'll try to find out."

"You think I'm afraid, I suppose? You know that they mean to set the house on fire, and you won't say it."

"I mean that I'll find the way to stop that. Call to me the moment those three men come down again."

I returned to Boreski and told him.

"We must enter that room and stop it."

"Yes, I'm with you."

"You go in by the dressing-room door and take Ivan. I'll take

89

this man. When I call to you, get in as fast as you can. Turn out all the lights here or they'll see us enter."

Out they went promptly and we stood in the darkness waiting for Helga's voice.

"They've come down, monsieur," she called a few minutes later, and in a trice I had turned the key and burst into the room.

The luck was ours. The room was empty. Never dreaming that we should venture in, they had left it unguarded. All round the sides were piled heaps of straw and dry wood, ready to be fired, and the evidence of their dastardly trick lay plain to our eyes.

Had it not been for Helga's quickness the infernal plan would have been successful.

"We have them now," I said eagerly to Boreski. "We'll trap them here. They'll be back in a moment. We'll wait and give them an unexpected welcome."

We hid in the darkness, the four of us, and presently heard the sound of heavy feet mounting the ladder.

"No shooting," I whispered. "Just seize them. We may catch more by-and-by in the same trap. And wait until all are in the room. Silence like death, till I move."

Not a sound escaped us, and for my part I held my breath when the head and shoulders of the first man appeared at the open window, and he stepped all unsuspecting into the room; and a second and then a third followed, each with his bundle of straw or wood as fuel.

One of the men came so near me to deposit the burden that he almost touched me, and as he stooped to put it down, I gave the signal.

"Now," I cried in a loud voice and sprang upon my man. A scene of wild tumult followed as the series of tough struggles commenced. The men fought hard, and we stumbled and tumbled and wrestled in the darkness, blundering hither and thither, taking and giving fierce blows, often knocking up against one another, mingled at times in dire confusion, all straining with desperate effort, breathing hard and speaking scarce a word save when some sharp ejaculation of anger or pain, or a violent oath leapt from between tight-clenched teeth.

Ivan was the first to beat his man, and soon afterwards, as my hand chanced to knock against a heavy billet of wood, I seized it and dealt my antagonist a blow on the head which laid him out.

I was considering how to use the victory when some one came to the foot of the ladder, ran up a few rungs, and called—

"Start the fire."

At the same instant a tremendous crash was heard in the lower part of the house, followed by loud screams from the women and the gruff tones of men. Then Helga's voice came loud and piercing, calling to me for help.

CHAPTER XIV

CONCERNING THE VALUE OF HOSTAGES

THE noise in the house below ceased with ominous suddenness as I started to rush down in response to Helga's cry for help.

What to do with our prisoners embarrassed me for a moment. Every one of us might be needed below, and my first idea was to leave the men as they were. But happily I did not do that.

"Ivan, you must come with me. M. Boreski, will you and the servant watch the men here and try to find some means of securing them?"

"There is plenty of rope in one of the rooms above," said Ivan to the servant as we two hurried out.

The landing and stairs were dark, and we found the men we had left on the landing had clambered over to our side of the improvised barricade, where they were waiting, revolver in hand, in expectation of an attack from below.

"It is not safe to go down, my lord," said one of them. "They are waiting for us below there."

"Aren't the women in danger, you cowards?" I cried angrily, my thoughts on Helga. "Follow me," and I sprang over it and ran down.

"Mademoiselle, mademoiselle," I called as I ran, but no answer came. Ivan kept by my side, and as we reached the bottom some men sprang right at us. There were six or seven of them at least, and for a few moments we were in the thick of a pretty stiff fight. All four of us were struck several times, and finding it impossible to beat them, desperately as we fought, we had to retreat, losing one of the two servants who was made a prisoner.

Ivan fought like a fiend incarnate, kicking, lunging and using the butt end of his heavy revolver with tremendous effect, and but for him I should have been made a prisoner. I was surrounded and held by three of the men when he dashed in, and scattering them

91

with his tremendous strength, rescued me and dragged me up the stairway.

"To the landing, monsieur," he said; "our only chance;" and back we had to go, scrambling headlong up the stairs as best we could; while our assailants, exasperated at our escape, fired shot after shot after us.

That we were not hit seemed a miracle. The darkness alone can have saved us, aided no doubt by the excitement which prevented the men below firing steadily.

We had saved our skins but had failed in what to me was vastly of more importance—the rescue of Helga and the others; and the failure so maddened me that for the time I was incapable of consecutive thought. I was conscious chiefly of a fierce animal desire to wreak my vengeance upon the cowards who had captured her, and hugged the thought to my heart that I could certainly kill some of them. In other words I was for the moment almost out of my mind with baffled rage.

"We must save the mademoiselle, monsieur," said Ivan at length, perplexed by my silent inactivity.

"Or avenge her. My God, if anything has happened to her, they shall pay dearly," I returned.

"What shall we do next, monsieur?"

That question was soon settled for us, however; for suddenly lights appeared below and relieved the dead gloom of the landing.

"They are going to attack us," whispered Ivan.

"We shoot this time and shoot to kill, Ivan," I said, speaking out fierce wrath and with a sort of devilish pleasure at the prospect.

But the attack tarried, and while we waited Boreski came out.

"We have secured those three," he said.

"Bring them out and shoot them," I answered. "The others have taken mademoiselle and the Duchess."

"It will be no good to do that."

"Bring them out," I rejoined fiercely; and when he hesitated I added, "Then I will;" and I went into the room.

"For God's sake, don't do murder," he said, and Ivan followed in.

I paid no heed to the words, and seizing the first man I dragged him out, bound as he was, and dashed him down on the ground. The mere recourse to this brutality seemed to give relief to my rage, and I went in again and brought out another, treating him just as brutally. I was for the while both bully and coward in my frenzy.

When I got out I found Boreski speaking to some one below. I leaned forward and tried to see the speaker, and had I been able, I believe I should have shot him on the spot.

92

"You know whom we seek," the man said. "Give him up to us and we will go."

"Who are you?" asked Boreski.

"No matter. I speak for those who are with me."

"Not for all of them," said I, interposing with an unholy laugh. "We have three here who would like to speak for themselves. Come up and ask them why your scheme to fire the house has failed."

My reply seemed to produce far more effect than the sneer itself warranted, for we heard the men draw together and speak in low but excited tones. Suddenly the reason for this flashed upon me. I had spoken in Russian, and my accent had betrayed me for a foreigner.

At last I began to see the way out of it all, and my strange frenzy rapidly subsided.

"Are you coming, gentlemen?" I cried again. "We can promise you a merry welcome which will save some of you at least the trouble of returning. Or do you find it easier to gag women than to face men?" and I continued to pour in a broadside of sneers and taunts, speaking all the time in Russian.

"Who is that speaking, Boreski?" came at last in the same gruff deep voice that had spoken before.

"The man you have been fools enough to mistake for the Emperor," I answered with a laugh.

"Boreski, why do you not answer?"

"Tell him the truth, M. Boreski," said I in a tone loud enough to reach those below.

"If I tell them, it will turn their vengeance upon you for Vastic's death," he said in a low tone.

"Better upon me than upon mademoiselle," I replied quickly, in the same loud tone. "I am not afraid of the truth. Tell them I fooled you as well."

"It is not whom you think," he said.

"Holy Grace of God!" exclaimed the man below.

Realizing the effect which the discovery had produced, and believing firmly in the eloquence of acts, I obeyed my next impulse, and jumping over the barricade ran half-way down the stairs and stood where the light from below shone upon me.

"I will show you for yourselves," I said.

The suddenness of the action told, and perhaps the recklessness of it helped me. The men stared up at me as if astounded, and for a moment not one of them moved. Then two revolvers were raised and levelled.

"Stay," I cried in a loud voice of command. "If you fire at me it will be the sentence of death on your three comrades up there," and I pointed up the stairway. "You understand, Ivan?"

"By the living God, I do," he answered, and his voice, tremulous with earnestness, heightened the effect of the situation.

It was just one of those positions which a little impudence and bluff will carry when everything else may fail.

The leader of the men growled out a word, and the two revolvers were lowered. Then he turned to me.

"Who are you?"

"To the devil with your who are you? You can see who I am not, and that should be enough for you."

"It is Vastic's murderer," said one of the men then, and murmurs of rage followed. I recognized the speaker as Vastic's companion.

"You were with him, say what you saw," I said.

"I saw you shoot him like a dog," said the fellow.

"You lie, and you know it," I cried sternly. "I did not shoot him until he was in the act of shooting me. He mistook me, as you all have, for the Emperor; and it was his life or mine."

There was more angry murmuring at this, and I thought the men would break away from the leader's control. I have never been nearer death than at that moment.

"Come down that we may see you better," said the leader next.

"You can see me quite well enough here; but as you will. Ivan, remember, three lives for mine," I called, and I went down deliberately and stood face to face with them at very close range; and a very ugly-looking lot they were.

"He is not the Emperor, God curse him," cried one of the gang.

"I am not even a Russian," I said.

"Your name?" demanded the leader sternly.

"Is my own concern."

"I will know it," he insisted threateningly.

"While you threaten me, I'll see you damned before I'll tell you." This was only another bluff. It would be useless to deny my name. Helga had spoken it before Vastic's companion. But I dared not yield to the man's threats. A single symptom of weakness and the whole bluff would be exposed.

"You carry things daringly," he said.

"There are three reasons for it—up there," I retorted grimly. "You can take my life if you will and if you dare. You are all known well enough, and foreigners of my position are not murdered in cold blood without full penalties being exacted. Shoot, if you've a mind to face the public executioner. If you haven't, let's put an end to this."

"You killed our comrade."

94

"Yes, and three more will die if you kill me."

This was the trump card. I could see that. He had sneered when I had spoken of the executioner; but there was no sneer for this. He presented indeed the very type of concentrated furious perplexity. Like the rest, he was willing enough to kill me; but he believed my threat would be carried out; and fear for his comrades alone saved his hand.

"Do you still refuse your name?" he asked; and I believe he was utterly at a loss what to do or say.

"Not through fear of your knowing, but I allow no man to threaten me."

"Will you tell it me then?"

"Yes, when you speak in that tone. My name is Denver; I am an American."

"How came you to be here?"

"Under circumstances which led to my being regarded as the Emperor. Among those who fell into the mistake was the spy, Drexel, whose report to you has caused all the havoc."

"Where is he?"

"At present, alive. How long he lives depends on you." He liked this answer no better than my former threat.

"There has been a fearful mistake," he said.

"Which you have done your worst to add to."

"You admit you killed M. Vastic?"

"I haven't attempted to hide it."

"For that you and all concerned will have to answer."

"I am alone responsible. You know that. The man who was there knows it well."

"You are suspiciously anxious to shield others."

"I tell the truth, that's all. But come," and I resumed my former tone of authority; "we have talked enough. Are we to resume this fight, or will you leave the house and take your men away with you?"

"Are you dictating to me?" he asked, with a start of anger.

"Yes; for I hold the whip hand," I flung at him.

"You forget your life hangs by a thread."

"There are four threads and four lives," I retorted; and again he winced and bit his lip, and was silenced.

"If we go you must go with us," he said after a pause.

"Not alive, nor alone;" and I pointed this with a look he could read.

"You will release our comrades?"

I could have laughed aloud as I heard this. It was the proof that I had beaten him. But I answered as sternly as I could speak.

"It is not for you to dictate to me. Put mademoiselle and the rest back in the house here; then take your men away with you. When I am satisfied no treachery is intended, the three prisoners shall be released."

"By the living God of Heaven you shall answer for all this," he cried in a frenzy of rage. But impotent anger of this sort was nothing to me. I had him on the hip, and he knew it; and if he chose to vent some of his wrath in words, let him.

He stood many moments in desperate doubt, seeking for some other way out of the maze; but he found none, and he turned at length to consult his fellows. The conference was angry and excited, but no talk or excitement could alter the fact that to harm me meant the death of their three comrades.

Muttered oaths were as thick as corn on the cob; fierce threats were levelled at me, accompanied by glances of bitter hate. Once the counsel of violence seemed likely to prevail, and the looks and gestures grew so menacing that I intervened.

"You are listening, and ready, Ivan?" I called.

"Yes, monsieur, quite ready."

It was enough. The gesticulations ceased, and those who were against violence had once more the upper hand.

After that the end came soon.

Two of the men went out and returned with Helga, the Duchess Stephanie, and the women-servants.

Helga's face lighted when she caught sight of me as the knot of men fell back and made way for them all to pass.

"No one has been hurt?" I asked her.

"No, not hurt; badly scared, some of us," she replied. "But what has happened?"

"We have been arguing on the subject of hostages, and these gentlemen have taken my view of the subject. There will be no more fighting. Will you all go upstairs for a few minutes?"

As the men were leaving the house, I called one of the grooms down and told him to saddle a couple of horses.

"I shall ride a few miles with you," I told the leader.

"You do not trust me?" he said angrily.

"In my country we see to things for ourselves; that's all. Ivan," I called, "if I do not return in an hour, you will understand there is trouble. You will know what to do."

"Yes, monsieur."

"You try my temper," said the leader.

"Merely a business precaution," I replied lightly, and went out with him to the stables.

"I do not like your business precautions," he said. "You carry them too far."

96

"The fact is I wish to speak to you, and what I have to say cannot be said in the hearing of others. I can say it as we ride together."

I had some very pertinent questions to put to him, indeed, and when he had found his horse and the groom and I had mounted, I told the latter to fall back.

"Now," I said, as we all started, "I want to know what is to be the result of this night's work, so far as I am concerned."

CHAPTER XV

THE DANGERS THICKEN

MY companion was in no hurry to answer the question and we rode some distance before he spoke.

"Why couldn't you speak of this before the others—I mean those in the house at Brabinsk?"

"Why don't you all discuss your plans at public meetings? I suppose because you want to keep them secret. So do I now."

"Why do you lay such stress on secrecy?"

"Because my own safety is my own concern, and no one else's."

"Are you a secret police spy?"

"No; had I been, do you think I should have been in command of things at Brabinsk?"

"What are you then?"

"I have told you. I am an American; I have got mixed up in this thing and want to get out of it."

"You killed M. Vastic?"

"Do you think I was such a fool as to want to kill him? I had no feud with him, nor have I with you. It was a question whether he shot me—thinking I was the Emperor—or whether I got in first. And I had the drop on him."

"Our comrades do not die unavenged," he said with a grim significance anything but pleasant to notice. I chewed the reply a while in uneasy silence.

"I may take that as a declaration of war between us. You mean you will try to have my life for his. Not a pleasant lookout—for either of us." The pause and the last words touched him on the raw.

"What do you mean by that?"

"We Americans make ugly enemies when we're put to it. I know every man of you by sight, and have a rare memory for a face—when I want to remember it."

"God of the dead and living, have a care, monsieur," he cried.

"Ivan knows them too, and is a staunch friend of mine," I returned very quietly and meaningly; and when he made no reply, I added: "You've had a sample of American methods to-night, and if it comes to any of this vendetta business, I'll put up a good hand. You may gamble on that."

"How came you to be there as the Emperor?" he asked after a pause.

"For reasons that don't in the least concern you or your comrades; so you needn't ask for them."

Another pause followed.

"I happen to have a good deal of influence with very high authorities. It would be a mistake to drive me to use it."

Angered by this, he thrust his hand to the pocket where I had seen him stow his revolver.

"You'd better not," I said coolly. "The same authorities who will help me living would avenge me dead. You are all known. Besides, there are the three men at Brabinsk; and Ivan will keep his word."

He growled out something, an oath, I think, but he drew his hand back and rode on, presently asking abruptly—

"What is it you want?"

"A truce to the whole thing—for all concerned on both sides. Let it end right here. The thing, as you said, has been a terrible mistake. Let it stop at that."

"That is not in my power to say." He appeared to speak with some regret, and after thinking a while added: "No, it is impossible. If M. Vastic had not been shot, it might have been."

I had not expected to make much headway, so I was not very disappointed, and went on to try and get at what was the real object of my questions.

"I believe you yourself regret the thing," I said. "You mean, I suppose, that if it rested with you, your decision would be for a truce."

"Yes, I think it would. But the death of M. Vastic is too heavy a blow for the brotherhood. You will be all held to account for it."

"All. It was my act alone. You mean I shall be accountable."

Something in my voice must have betrayed me, for he started, and turning in his saddle looked at me.

"What are the others to you? The mademoiselle, for instance?"

"They are nothing to me," I answered as if indifferently; "except

98

that I have brought this thing on them and shall see them through it."

"You give yourself a troublesome commission, monsieur."

"You're a lot of damned cowards," I cried. It was a feeble thing to say, but it relieved my feelings, and soon afterwards I reined up my horse.

"I'm going back," I said curtly.

"Good-night, monsieur. As a man I am sorry for what has happened and for what may have to come. I hope we may not meet again."

"Wait till we do. Your sorrow may be wanted for your own side;" and without waiting for more, I wheeled my horse round and set off back at a gallop followed by the groom. And I took back with me a very anxious heart and a whole crowd of perplexing doubts and harassing fears.

Turn which way I would, dangers of some kind blocked the path—dangers for Helga or myself separately when they did not threaten us both in common.

I had had a fairly adventurous life, and in my time had run up against some ugly risks; but these had been of the nature of sudden emergencies to be met promptly and overcome. But never before had I been called upon to face such a danger as this threatened to be—enduring, shadowy, secret and all encompassing. And I am not ashamed to admit I was considerably shaken.

It is one thing to take your life in your hands, at a crisis, face the music and fight for all you are worth while the bother lasts; and quite another to pit yourself against a secret society, to find the music a perpetual dirge, threatening constantly to develop into your own funeral march, and to breakfast, dine and sup, walk, sit and sleep, talk, laugh and be merry with the cold circle of a revolver barrel pressed to your forehead.

But it had to be done, it seemed, so long as I remained in Russia, and how long that would be must depend upon an extremely explosive contingency—Helga's intentions.

My hope was to get her to give up her country and adopt mine; but it was impossible to be sanguine. They say a woman can bear pain far better than a man, and it seemed to me that, given the requisite courage and a sufficient motive, she could also bear the strain of ever-present danger with greater fortitude.

So far as I could judge, Helga had been for years risking the kind of danger which now loomed upon me as so formidable; and I saw very little reason to believe she would regard the new development as anything worse than just a fresh complication which had to be faced, and from which she would steadily refuse to run away.

When I got back to the house I very soon had reason to see that this was her frame of mind, and that there was more in this visit of the Duchess Stephanie than I had yet had time to learn.

The night's experiences, coupled with his wife's arguments and entreaties, had made an end of Boreski as a conspirator. He had persuaded himself, or she had persuaded him, which came to the same thing, that he had now nothing to hope for from the elaborate scheme by which he had designed to force the Imperial consent to his marriage and everything to gain by abandoning it. I found the two of them importuning Helga to take a similar view; and some high words seemed to have passed.

"We shall leave Russia for a time," the Duchess was saying as I entered.

"I think you are right to go under the circumstances," agreed Helga. "But what has occurred to-night has not weakened my position by a thread. The key of everything is the possession of these papers which the Government dare not allow to fall into other hands than their own. I still possess them."

"But even if you persist, you cannot use them, Helga," cried the Duchess Stephanie. "These wretches alone would not let you live to do that. I declare I tremble all over when I think of that fearful time when we were in their power."

"Why? They did us no harm. They just stopped us from crying out, took us over to the stable and locked us in with a guard until the mistake was discovered. As soon as that was plain, they released us and left the place. Surely it is no very awful thing to be locked up in a stable for an hour. It is not like a prison or a Siberian hell."

"You forget what I told you, mademoiselle," said Boreski; "that the men left us and released you only because we had caught three of their number and M. Denver threatened to have them shot. They would never leave you in peace—nor us, indeed, if we were to remain."

"If you think that, by all means leave the country."

There was a spice of contemptuousness in Helga's reply, although spoken with apparent earnestness.

"What do you think, M. Denver?" asked Boreski.

"I think as you do, that that is the only safe course."

"It will at any rate please M. Denver's friends among the authorities," said Helga, with a flash at me.

"We owe our liberty to M. Denver and probably our lives as well, and I don't think you should say such things."

This from the Duchess Stephanie surprised me vastly.

"We also owe it to him that the dangers ever arose at all," retorted Helga quickly. "But I congratulate him upon having won you over so completely to his side that you forget that. My memory is longer. But by all means take his advice."

"I shall help you best by taking no part in this discussion. There is still something to be done," I said, and left the room, in the middle of a protest by the Duchess Stephanie against what she termed Helga's rank ungenerosity.

It was the truth of Helga's bitter words that hurt me. I had caused the trouble and brought the danger upon them, and I knew only too well that the danger was but averted for a time.

I went in search of Ivan, and with him released our prisoners and Drexel and saw them well away on their return to the city. As we went back to the house Ivan said—

"You will not let the mademoiselle remain here, monsieur?"

"Why not, Ivan?"

"The brotherhood, monsieur. They will hunt her down, and you and M. Boreski."

"Do you think them really dangerous?"

"Great God of my fathers, can any one doubt it?"

"What of yourself, then?"

"What is to be will be," he answered with a shrug.

"You mean you don't care?"

"When the storm rages over the forest, monsieur, it is the big trees which feel it and fall, the little trees are passed over. I am only a little one."

"Would you like to have money to fly?"

"Lord of all Powers, if I had not seen you to-night, I should think you a coward to give such counsel. I am not a cur, monsieur, but a watchdog."

"I said it merely to test you, and I ask your pardon. I was certain of your answer, though. We shall work together to save the mademoiselle. But if we are to succeed, you must not do again what you did to-night."

"Your pardon, monsieur?" he asked, not understanding.

"You told her my plan and brought her to me."

"When you would have thrown away your life, and would not let me go with you, monsieur. What else could I do?" and he shrugged his great shoulders. "But I will follow you now anywhere and obey you implicitly."

"At present I do not know what to do. I see no way, Ivan."

"You will think of something—or Mademoiselle Helga will. But she should not stay here. There are places where she can hide safely, monsieur. We have done it before."

101

"Well, we shall see," I answered a little hopelessly as we entered the house.

Helga was waiting for us in the hall, and seemed angry and excited.

"Ivan, get M. Boreski's carriage, and, if he wishes it, go with him to the city. He starts as soon as possible. M. Denver will probably go with him."

Ivan looked the picture of perplexity.

"And yourself, mademoiselle?" he asked.

"Do as I say, Ivan, and at once."

He went away without a word but he glanced at me.

"To tell the truth, mademoiselle," I said, "I'm afraid I am rather too tired for so long a drive just at present."

Boreski and the Duchess came out as I finished and caught the last few words.

"It is not very long, M. Denver, only some three hours at most," he said, "and the Duchess will be very glad of your company. It will be an added protection."

"I hope you will come, monsieur. It is really the safest thing—in fact, the only safe thing."

"I think you had better go," declared Helga firmly.

"Of course you wish to get out of the country as soon as possible," said the Duchess.

"As soon as practicable, naturally," I agreed. "But I have one or two things to arrange first."

"If you are wise you will lose no time about it," said Boreski, who was manifestly eager for me to accompany him.

"You have completely forgiven me then for the deception I practised upon you in coming here?" I asked.

"Many things have happened since," he replied. "I have abandoned that part of my plan, and my wife has found a way of escape from the difficulties which troubled us. Our marriage need no longer be kept secret. Indeed, the Emperor already knows of it."

"The real Emperor," put in Helga quietly.

"Besides, we owe you much for to-night; I feel that," he continued, and went on to thank me in his courteous and dignified manner. I was so entirely surprised by this most queer and unexpected turn of things that I could find nothing to say.

Then the Duchess turned to Helga.

"Let me make a last appeal to you, Helga."

"It is useless, madame." The reply was curt, decisive and angry.

"You have no right to keep them. It was I who brought them to you, and they are mine. Why not do as I say, throw yourself upon the Emperor's mercy and seek his forgiveness?"

I stared from one to the other in amazement.

"The Duchess saw the Emperor this morning," said Boreski to me in an aside.

"You have had my decision, madame," said Helga coldly.

"I think you're a very wicked woman. You want to ruin me just when I have succeeded in everything."

"You make my position very invidious, mademoiselle," said Boreski, looking profoundly uneasy.

"M. Denver, you have some influence with Mademoiselle Helga," said the Duchess to me. "Use it now, I beg of you, to urge her to give back these papers to me."

"M. Denver has no influence with me," declared Helga. "The papers were obtained at my suggestion and for my own purpose, and no power in Russia shall drag them from me until that purpose is accomplished."

"But I have pledged my word," cried the Duchess with tears in her eyes.

"And have done your best to keep it. But the papers must remain with me. Nothing can change my resolve."

We heard the carriage at the door then.

"I think that in honour you should give them up," said Boreski.

Helga looked at him very angrily.

"I bid you good-night, M. Boreski," she said stiffly.

But the Duchess, having tried ineffectually entreaties and tears, had a last shaft in the quiver. She laughed angrily.

"They will do you no good. You have to account for how you obtained them, and I will swear, if necessary, that I forged them myself. You shall not ruin me. We have been your dupes too long."

"Your carriage is waiting, madame. Good-night, messieurs," and with a bow which included me as well as Boreski, she turned her back upon us and went into an adjoining room.

"We had better go," said Boreski.

"She is a dangerous, deceitful, treacherous woman," exclaimed the Duchess passionately. "Come, M. Denver."

"Excuse me, madame, I am remaining," I said.

"You will repent it, monsieur," she exclaimed angrily as she swept past me.

"Possibly, madame; but at present I see nothing but congratulation in being able to number myself among Mademoiselle Helga's friends."

"The Emperor will hear of it from me."

Boreski lingered a moment as if wishful to speak to me, but his wife called him sharply, and he contented himself with a glance which may have meant many things to him but nothing to me, and they drove off.

I looked after the carriage thoughtfully and went back into the house. Ivan was in the hall.

"You did not go with the carriage, then?" I said in some surprise.

"No, monsieur, mademoiselle said, if M. Boreski wished it, and he did not say so."

"I am glad, Ivan."

"Thank you, monsieur. I thought you would wish it. What are we to do next?"

"I don't know. I will see Mademoiselle Helga," and I went to the room where she was.

CHAPTER XVI

HELGA'S DEFEAT

WITH my hand on the door of the room where Helga was, I paused. The thought crossed my mind that I had not been alone with her since the critical moment in which the cloud between us had been swept away, and we had seemed to understand intuitively each the other's heart feelings.

The thought embarrassed me, and I turned back to try and think my way to some definite practical course of action.

The scene with the Duchess Stephanie had shown me one thing clearly. The failure of Helga's plans was no longer to be set down solely to me. The Duchess had herself seen the Emperor and patched up peace with him, the chief condition of which had been the restoration of the secret papers.

It appeared, therefore, that the Emperor and old Kalkov had been working for the same end at the same time by different methods. And if this were so, it was equally clear that the wily old Prince had misled me as to the Emperor's cognizance of my part in the affair. A course on his side which was quite in keeping with Helga's opinion and description of his methods.

For my part I cared little; he might throw me over if he pleased, and he had doubtless calculated upon that as a probable contingency. But it affected Helga very seriously now, because it had led the Emperor to take a line with the Duchess which he would never have taken, had Kalkov told him what I was doing; and it had thus closed the gates against Helga's chances of getting to the Emperor himself.

Up to the present Helga's position had been veiled, and if I could have secured her an interview, her story might have been listened to with an impartial ear. But now the Duchess was going in hot haste to prejudice Helga in the Emperor's eyes by pointing to her as the real source of danger in regard to the papers.

In other words Helga's scheme for the benefit of Boreski by securing the Imperial consent to the marriage had succeeded, while it had failed so far as it concerned Helga herself. And the very success of it made the failure for her all the more disastrous.

It seemed indeed that the further one went in the whole affair the more hopeless and complicated and dangerous it became.

The moment Helga's real part in the matter was told to the Emperor he would pass on the knowledge to Kalkov, and the whole machinery of the Government's secret police and spies would be set in motion for her detection and arrest.

And as if that were not enough, the ominous tangle with the brotherhood had arisen at the same moment.

Between us we had made just a horrible mess of everything; and as the more I pondered the thing alone the more hopeless it looked, I went in at length to Helga to see if I could get any ray of light from her.

The way of a woman is ever a paradox surely, and Helga was very much of a woman in that respect.

When I entered I found her stretched at full length on a sofa in what appeared to me to be an attitude of almost despairing dejection, and so preoccupied that she did not hear me until I closed the door behind me. Then she sat up quickly and looked at me. She had great mastery over her features, and she evinced neither pleasure nor surprise at sight of me.

"Have you forgotten something and returned for it?" she asked with a sort of conventional politeness.

"Returned?"

"I thought you were going with Boreski."

"Did you?" My glance said more than my words.

"The Duchess will have been disappointed."

"Her disappointment is nothing to me."

"No?" with a lift of the brows, as if in surprise.

"No," I repeated. "I have been thinking."

"You would have been better employed in getting back to the city. You would have covered a third of the distance by now."

"I am not going. I want to talk to you."

"Isn't it rather late?" She pointed this with a glance at the clock. I could not restrain a smile.

"Is this some new game we are playing?" I asked.

She sat drumming her fingers on the sofa arm.

"Is that what you want to talk about?"

"No. I wish to ask you what you propose to do."

"And I do not propose to tell you."

She said this very quietly and calmly, and then suddenly flashed out—

"What I do can be no possible concern of yours, M. Denver."

"On the contrary it is everything to me," I returned firmly. "You know that as well as I."

"I will not know it; I will not have it so."

"We shall see. What are you proposing to do?"

She looked as if about to make some sharp reply, but with one of her swift changes, she smiled.

"Do you really wish to render me a service, monsieur?"

"I hope to render you many."

"Then go back to the Palace—to those who sent you to me—and tell them you have failed in your honourable and secret mission. Tell them of me."

"Thank you, but that is not the kind of service I was expecting you to ask, and I shall not do it."

"There is no other that I care to ask, then."

"Why do you wish me to go?"

"Ought I not to be concerned for the safety of so welcome a guest?"

"What extraordinary creatures you women are—and you especially. Now if you were a man——"

"Would God that I were!" she interposed vehemently.

"You and I would just sit down and talk over the whole mess, as two friends should, and try to hit on the easiest and best way out of it."

"Friends!" she cried; but I took no notice of the interruption.

"And when we had hit on the solution we should try to work together to carry it out. But instead of that, here you are flying into a passion just because I ask you what you mean to do; and then you insult me for no reason that I can see or understand, except that I haven't run away like a coward, unless it is that there's nobody else around whom you can treat in the same way with impunity."

106

"Am I to throw myself on my knees in gratitude to every one who chooses to force the offer of his help upon me?"

"If it does you any good to say this kind of thing to me by all means go on. Only try to concentrate them into a few pithy and bitter sentences and get them over. I can only say they don't hurt me in the least except that I know you'll be horribly sorry for them after."

"I am serious when I say I wish you to leave here."

"I wish you'd try a cigarette," and I lit a cigar.

"You are intolerable," she cried.

"Let's have an agreement. This cigar will last about twenty minutes or half an hour; suppose you get through with all your nasticisms in that time, and then discuss things soberly."

"Will you leave the house, M. Denver?"

"Of course I will not—if it means leaving you here. Nothing will shake my resolution to see you through this."

"But if I tell you that your presence interferes with my plans."

"Good. Go on."

"I will not have your help, I say."

"Very well; go on."

"I may surely choose whom I will to help me."

"Of course you may."

"And I don't choose you, monsieur."

"All right, but you have a tendency to repeat yourself."

"Do you wish to provoke me?"

"A bit superfluous, surely. But if you would get into a towering rage and be done with it, it might help us."

"You dare to insult me only because you think I am defenceless."

"If you really think I wish to insult you, you are the most extraordinary woman in Russia. You know so much better than that."

"I wish you to leave the house, monsieur."

"Why?"

"And if you will not go I will call my servants."

"Ivan will have no hand in such madness."

"So you would even try to turn my servants against me."

"My cigar is half through," I said, very calmly.

"Ah, you have no answer to that."

"No, none. Ivan or you yourself can find one easily."

"You are insufferable," she cried, her eyes flashing, as she sprang to her feet. "I will not stay in the room with you," and she crossed to the door.

I went on smoking and would not even turn my head to watch her. At the door she paused.

"Will you leave my house, M. Denver?"

"I have given you my answer already, Mademoiselle Helga."

"I did not think you could be so grossly discourteous."

"There's a good deal about me you seem to persist in misunderstanding. But one thing you shall know clearly—that my will power is every whit as strong as yours."

"Then I shall leave."

"That's precisely what I wish you to do, and Ivan and I will go with you."

She opened the door and I rose and flung my cigar away.

"I've thrown the rest of it away. Now let us be sensible and face things, and stop this wrangling. Come and sit down again."

"I will not. I will not be insulted."

I looked her very steadily in the eyes as I crossed the room to her, and she may have divined something of my thoughts, for it seemed to cost her an effort to meet my gaze. And when I was close to her, she shrank slightly and her fingers left the door handle. I closed the door then, and she bit her lip and frowned in the struggle to appear firm. After an intentionally long pause, I said, slowly and deliberately—

"You have been horribly unjust to me. In your anger you have said things that I would suffer from no one else. You know that, and—" I paused and lowered my tone—"and you know why. We both know why, Helga. We learnt it to-night."

She shook her head quickly.

"I don't see why you should shake your head. It has changed all my life for me——"

"Don't," she interposed.

"Why not? It is true—do or say what you please. You are first in the world to me."

"I will not hear you. I will not."

"Then I won't say it again. But it will always be so. I just want you to feel that and to know it's in that spirit I wish to talk over things with you. That's all."

That she was deeply moved she could not hide from me. She stood with lowered head, her bosom heaving, her lips trembling as she bit them, and her fingers interlocked, until with a deep sigh she appeared to come to a decision, when she lifted her face and answered steadily—

"I do not pretend not to understand you; but I cannot and will not accept your help. You must go away."

"I will not take that answer, and I will not leave you."

I spoke as I felt, quite resolved on that point.

The answer pleased her, and the hardness of her face relaxed.

"You are very obstinate," she said, and her eyes were almost smiling; certainly the light in them was soft.

"It doesn't matter what we call it. It is the thing that matters. Tell me frankly why you try to refuse my help."

She did not answer directly, and her eyes were troubled.

"Yes, I will tell you. You have a right to know," and she recrossed the room to her former place. I followed to mine.

"How far would you go with your help?" she asked, leaning her chin on her hand and gazing at me earnestly.

"I should like to know what that look has behind it, but I can answer the question only in one way. I wish you to be my wife, Helga, and let me help you at every turn in life. I love you."

"And know nothing of me."

"I know that you are the one woman the world holds for me. That is enough for me to know."

"You saw me yesterday for the first time."

"It will be the same when yesterday is ten or twenty years old. It is no question of mere time."

"Yet I am not as other women."

"I don't love the other women."

"I do not mean that. You know. I mean I am not a good woman—as women are counted good."

"I am accustomed to form my own judgments and to trust them."

"I should only ruin you. It is impossible."

"Wait until I am ruined and then see. But you would not ruin me, on the contrary I should save you from ruin."

"You are very self-confident."

"Because I love you."

The directness of the reply seemed to please her, for she smiled.

"You are very concise, monsieur."

"This is no time to waste words. We have a crisis to face."

She paused, and her face hardened a little as if in defiance.

"I have been wooed before—do you realize that?"

"You have not been won."

"I mean I have led men on to woo me and have jilted them."

"You did not love them."

"You mean——" she began with a flash of her eyes which changed to a smile as she stopped abruptly. It died away when I said nothing, and the air of defiance returned. "It is that you will not understand me. I did it to use them for the purpose of my life—and when they were of use no longer I flung them away."

109

"Then why not use me?"

"I meant to—at first," and she threw up her head.

"Why not at last then?"

"Ah, you drive me to speak so plainly. I tell you I am bad—bad to the core, heartless, heedless, sexless if you will, where my revenge is concerned. Now will you go?"

"No."

"Well, then, if you will have the full truth, you shall. So long as I thought you were the Emperor I set myself with all my woman's wit and cunning to make you love me. I planned it, schemed for it, and knowing all that it might mean, I yearned for it. I told you I would have made any sacrifice to have won your power to my side. Now, perhaps, you see how base a thing I am."

"Well, you have succeeded, and have made me love you—though Heaven knows I needed no making. What then?"

"My God, will nothing open your eyes and drive you from me?"

"One thing; but you have not said it yet."

She looked at me, and emotion seemed to master her till she said passionately—

"You are no use to me. Had you been in truth the Emperor, as God is my judge, I would have been your mistress. But being what you are, I will not be your wife."

"You are very anxious to blacken yourself in my eyes," I said after a pause.

"You at any rate shall know the truth—see me for what I am."

"Why?"

"I wish you to know it."

"I will tell you why, Helga. There are limits even to the recklessness of your self-slander. I have done you more wrong than I deemed. You had caught yourself in your own toils and come to—to love the Emperor."

I spoke slowly and deliberately, and as the words left my lips she started as if to make some indignant retort; but checked herself and leant back in her seat, pale and set, her brows wrinkled in intensely earnest thought. I watched her closely, and presently a flush began to spread over her cheeks, and she said slowly, without looking at me—

"Why should I deny it? You wish the truth and shall have it."

Then she sat up again and bent forward toward me.

"Yes, I love you—if it be love to long to do what you ask, and yet be strong enough to put all thought of doing it out of my heart. I do love you, I believe, and yet I am resolved never to look on your face again. I hate you for the deceit you practised, which has ruined everything for me at the very moment when all seemed to be won.

110

And yet"—her voice and eyes softened and she sighed—"and yet I—I am glad you came."

"I ask no more than that—at present. Except leave to ask for more when I have undone the mischief I have caused. You will grant that?"

"No—no, a hundred times no."

"You may make it a million. It will not alter my resolve."

She laughed with delicious softness.

"Now, you know why I will not have your help."

"Now, I do not care. I mean to force it on you; I will make it necessary to you. You have shown me the road in what you've said. You will marry me when I have helped you to revenge upon old Kalkov. Very well."

"No, no, I said I would never marry you."

"I know you did, but that was because you declared I was no use to you. I will make myself of use. I accept your own terms, and from now on I take hold of the thing and handle it in my way."

"You are very masterful," she cried.

"No, only American. I've a large interest in it now, and on our side we believe in good management. You've bungled things awfully, you see, made a holy mess of them all round and wasted no end of opportunities. For all I know you may have spoilt every chance. But there's still one way, and I shall try that."

"I can manage my own affairs," she protested.

"You can mismanage them, you mean; I'm too deep in now to trust your methods any longer. We go my way from now."

"Indeed, and what is your way?"

I believe all women at heart like to be forced to submit, and Helga's manner now was a curious mixture of the resentment which her pride dictated and pleasure at meeting a will just a bit stronger than her own.

"I am going to get you to the Emperor before the Duchess can prejudice him."

"How?"

"Never mind how, I'm going to do it. What you have to do is to go and get some sleep. You can have three hours, and then you must be ready to start, and Madame Korvata must be ready too."

"But I——"

"I'm not going to let you talk any more," and I got up and opened the door.

She rose and laughed with a shrug of the shoulders.

"It's a new sensation to be ordered in this way."

"In three hours we shall start," was my reply.

"My nerves are tingling with desire to rebel," she said, as she

111

came across the room slowly, and when she reached the door she stood and looked at me, smiling. "Do all you Americans make—make love in this way?"

"I'm the business man at present; the lover will come afterwards. You won't mistake him when his turn comes."

"Good-night, Monsieur—l'Empereur," she cried, her look a challenge and her whole expression radiant.

"You will make the lover rush things, Helga, if you look at the business man like that. You ought to be asleep already. Good-night."

"Asleep? After to-night!" and with a toss of the head she was gone.

CHAPTER XVII

AT THE GATES OF THE PALACE

AS soon as Helga was gone I sent for Ivan, and told him to have everything in readiness for the start in three hours' time; and that of course he would go with us.

"Where are we going, monsieur?" he asked.

"I don't know. You spoke of some places where mademoiselle could safely lie hid for a while. Which is the safest and nearest to Petersburg?"

"There is a house in the city itself, in the Square of San Sophia, monsieur; quite safe, if the mademoiselle will adopt her old disguise."

"What disguise is that?"

"A Sister of Charity, monsieur."

"Is it safe from both the police and the brotherhood?"

"Quite, monsieur."

"Then we could go there. Is it ready for her?"

"I can send on a carriage with a couple of the women."

"Good; then see to it at once."

"But if we leave here, there is one thing, monsieur. Have you forgotten—the body of Vastic?"

"Yes, indeed, I had forgotten. Go and see to the other things, and I'll think what to do."

It was a prickly problem in truth. To leave it at Brabinsk

appeared out of the question; to bury it and try to hush the thing up equally impossible; and to take it with us to the city more hazardous than either. He threatened to be as much trouble to us dead as alive, and I smoked a cigar and tried to think the thing out.

My intention was to make a clean breast of the matter to Kalkov, leaving him and his police to do what they liked; and I did not doubt they would find little difficulty in arranging matters.

But where should I tell them to look for the body? To bring them after it to Brabinsk would only put them on the scent after Helga, a result full of dangerous possibilities.

Yet how to get it away? It occurred to me that Ivan and I might carry it off some miles from the house and hide it in a wood or pond or somewhere; but the personal risks attending such a venture were too considerable, and in a way unnecessary.

Thus in the end I was driven back upon the decision to leave it at Brabinsk; and Ivan and I had to undertake the exceedingly gruesome and revolting task of burying it under the floor of a distant out-house.

I shall not readily forget that experience. Ivan was cool enough; but for my part I felt nearly as bad as any murderer could have felt when seeking to hide the body of his victim; and when I got back to the house, a stiff glass of brandy was necessary to enable me to shake off the feeling of chilly horror.

Then I had to plan my further movements. Roughly, my intention was to get back to the Palace and obtain an audience of the Emperor at the earliest possible moment, and beg him to see Helga.

Prince Kalkov I did not wish to see until after that. I took Helga's view of matters, and believed that if she could get the story of her father's ruin straight to the Emperor, before the Duchess Stephanie could influence him, she would succeed in working upon his old friendship for her father sufficiently at least to cause some kind of investigation into the affair.

But in that we should have to reckon with Prince Kalkov, of course; and he would be an ugly enemy. Fight he would, naturally, to the last gasp; and his influence, position, and parts would ensure that such a struggle would be a desperate one. It was like challenging the whole force of the Government; and however good our case might be, there were a hundred things likely to arise to defeat us.

When I am trying to think out a course coolly, I have an unfortunate knack of seeing all the dangers and obstacles through a kind of mental magnifying glass; and I saw so many now, and they all appeared so great that I could only regard our chances as little short of hopeless.

Then added to everything was this infernal Nihilist complication. Not only would it afford Kalkov a lever of tremendous power against Helga, but it threatened to dog our every movement with perilous personal risk.

It was in this respect that Vastic's death was so threatening. The instant I told Kalkov of it he would be in possession of the fact that Helga was implicated with the brotherhood. He would recognize in a moment the importance to him of denouncing his accuser as a Nihilist of the Nihilists, and would find or invent a thousand proofs in support of the charge; and her whole case would be instantly tainted and ruined.

The one thin slender chance of averting this catastrophe was to hide the fact that Helga Boreski the Nihilist and Helga the daughter of Prince Lavalski, the Emperor's former friend, were identical; but even this forlorn hope would be cut off when the Duchess Stephanie got to the Emperor and told her story. Boreski himself knew all about it, and in all probability had told his wife.

Still, whatever we might attempt, there were big risks, and we must be content to take them and deal with them as they threatened us. The first consideration was to get at the Emperor before the Duchess and strike the first blow.

A glance at Helga's face when she came down told me she had not slept. She was very pale. I told her where we were going, and added—

"You have not taken my advice and got some sleep."

"I wish to speak to you earnestly a moment. I have been thinking. You must not do this thing for me."

"I will give it up on one condition—only one."

"What is that?"

"That you give it up also, and, instead of going back to Petersburg, you cross the frontier with me!"

"That you know is impossible;" and her face clouded.

"Come, then; and don't keep the carriage waiting."

"But if you are to run this risk, it will be so much harder for me. I cannot bear it."

"So long as you remain on this side of the frontier I remain too; so that you'll have to bear it, I'm afraid;" and I took her out to the carriage in which Madame Korvata was already shivering in the nipping morning air. That good lady was not in a pleasant temper, moreover, at having been dragged from her bed at such an early hour; and as she did not know all that had occurred, and was not fully in our confidence, Helga and I could not speak much during the long drive.

Helga lay back in her seat most of the time wrapped in thought, and I on my side was equally absorbed; but once, when Madame Korvata had fallen asleep, we exchanged a few words.

"I am going straight to the Palace," I told her; "and shall do my utmost to get to the Emperor at once. If I am successful I shall send immediately for you."

"You will not succeed. Prince Kalkov will not let you," she replied.

"I hope to evade him altogether."

"He is a vigilant watchdog, and all those about the Palace are at his beck and in his service."

"Then I shall try to hoodwink him. I know I can get to His Majesty. What you have to do is to be prepared with all the proof of Kalkov's infamy—all particulars, so as to hit right home at once, and as hard as possible."

"Do not be afraid that I shall fail at such a moment—if it ever comes."

"It will come. It shall," I said firmly. "But there is another thing. If we get our chance and yet fail—what then?"

She looked at me and paused before replying.

"If I could answer your question as you wish, I would. But I shall never give in. Nothing will ever satisfy me but victory."

"All the greater reason, then, for me to do my utmost now," I answered; but she saw I was disappointed at her reply.

"No. It is the greater reason for you to abandon the attempt and leave me to fight on in my own way."

"That is not how we Americans fight."

"But in America you know nothing of the conditions of such a trouble as this. You do not yet know the risks you run. If we attack Prince Kalkov and fail, do you think he will not know how to wreak his revenge upon us—upon all concerned? Ah, monsieur, what can a Republican know of the ways of Russia?"

"I'm beginning to get an insight, at least," I said lightly.

"You fight with your votes over there, and risk perhaps some of your money; but here the stakes are human life and liberty. God help us."

She spoke so vehemently that Madame Korvata awoke, and our conversation ended.

When we neared the city I told Helga I should not drive with her to her destination, and asked her to tell me exactly the location of the house.

"Every one knows the Square of San Sophia—close to the

cathedral. The house is called the Retreat, and was formerly a mission house. A small red-brick building in the north-east corner."

I took out a scrap of paper and scribbled the words "Retreat, Square of San Sophia, N.E. corner."

"You are not writing it down. It is dangerous to write addresses, my friend," said Helga cautiously as I put it in my pocket.

It was a very small thing, but it startled me. I seemed to feel, as it were, the first chill of the atmosphere of intrigue which the simple caution suggested.

"It is in English, and no eyes but my own will ever see it," I said.

"Yet it is dangerous," she repeated. "You are not in America."

"Perhaps you are right. I'll tear it up;" and I took out what I thought was the paper, tore it up, and was flinging the pieces out of the carriage when Helga again stopped me, and smiled.

"Not all in one place. You have not been reared in this school, my friend. It is safer to burn papers which tell tales."

"The pieces with the writing on are gone already," I said, glancing at those still in my fingers. "See, these are blanks."

"It may not matter, but caution can never be exaggerated."

I tossed the remaining fragments away, and tried to regard the incident as neither important in itself nor significant of anything serious. But Helga's evidently sincere earnestness affected me; and the bothersome trifle was in my thoughts when I left the carriage soon afterwards, and she renewed her injunctions to me to be cautious.

"Do not deceive yourself," she said very earnestly as we parted. "I know you will do your best for me; I believe it with all my heart. But you do not understand these things—and we may never meet again."

"If I get into a mess I will contrive to let you hear of it."

"Not in Russia, M. Denver. I shall wait, how anxiously I cannot tell you, for news of you. And if I get none, I shall not misunderstand. I repeat—we may never meet again."

"If you do not hear from me to-day, or at latest to-morrow, you will know there is a check somewhere, and you must fly."

"I shall be quite safe in the Retreat."

"You can safely communicate with me at the American Embassy. Remember that."

"I shall not forget, and need not write it down," she answered with one of her smiles. "And do you yourself remember—caution, such as you have never had to use. Good-bye. May God prosper us and our cause."

"And our love, Helga," I added in the lowest of whispers. A pressure of her fingers and a glance from her eyes answered me.

The carriage drove off rapidly, and left me to set about a task, which in its way was perhaps as difficult as any that ever plagued the wits of a sorely perplexed man.

It was still early in the morning, and I had to walk some distance before I could secure a drosky. The driver, when I told him to take me to the Palace, appeared to think I was either some overnight reveller who had not shaken off the effects of the drink, or else a lunatic; for he laughed and swore good-humouredly, and then flatly refused to do as I bade him.

While we were wrangling, I saw some police approaching, and, having no mind to be interviewed by them, I ended the dispute by giving him a double fare and telling him to drive to a point near the Palace.

As we rumbled along innumerable difficulties suggested themselves as obstacles to my gaining admission to the Palace at all at such an hour; and the all but hopelessness of doing so without Prince Kalkov getting to hear of it was too patent to be denied.

The attempt had to be made, however; and as impudence and a show of authority go for much in Russia as elsewhere, I put as bold a face on things as possible. When I left the carriage I wrapped my military cloak about me, and strutting with as much of an officer's swagger as I could assume, I marched past the first sentry without a question.

I returned his salute in an off-hand way and walked on to the great building. Just as I thought my bluff would succeed, however, I was stopped by an official.

"Your pardon, monsieur," he said, "but no one is permitted to enter."

"I suppose I may go to my own rooms," I replied in French, with a smile.

"Of course, but this is the Palace, monsieur."

"And my rooms are in it. I am a guest of His Majesty."

"A thousand pardons for this interruption, but we have very strict orders, and have had no notification of your visit. Will you be so good as to come to my bureau?"

"I'd rather go to my rooms; but if this is the way that His Majesty's guests are usually treated, by all means lead the way."

He bowed very ceremoniously and took me to his office. Here he repeated his apologies and asked me my name.

"There will doubtless be some directions here," he added, taking a book from his desk.

I didn't want to give my name if it could be helped; and I hesitated.

He noticed the hesitation and frowned.

"My name is Harper C. Denver. I am an American. I arrived here three days ago. You will probably recognize this ring of His Majesty's as a guarantee of my position."

But there are always two views as to the possession of a Royal jewel; and this blockhead took the wrong one. I might have known he would; and I could almost read in his eyes that he suspected me of having obtained it by some wrongful means.

He pretended to search in his book for some mention of my name, while all the time he was asking himself how I could have got hold of one of His Imperial Master's rings.

"I regret exceedingly that I find no reference here to you," he said, his manner still excessively polite. "It is very awkward and very unfortunate. But I am afraid I cannot permit you to enter the Palace—without further instructions, that is. No doubt, however, you can suggest some one to whom I can send?"

He said this with the air of a man who feels he has got you.

"You can send to His Majesty," said I quietly. "That will be the simplest way."

He looked at me steadily, and his manner changed.

"You wish to see His Majesty, then, at once?" he asked.

"What I wish is to go to my rooms first, and see His Majesty afterwards. Nothing unreasonable in that, is there?"

"Unreasonable, no, monsieur, and yet, perhaps, unusual. But I will see what I can do. I will send and make inquiries."

He had returned to his former polite deferential air.

"So long as you are quick, I don't care what you do," said I.

"This is very trying to me. I am deeply sorry. But perhaps you are used to these needs for caution in other countries;" and he went on in this style until a servant entered.

"Send Gravok to me," he said, and accompanied the order with a significant nod.

I wondered what was coming; but was not long left in doubt, for half a minute later a sergeant and three soldiers entered, two of whom placed themselves instantly one on each side of me.

"This is a mere formality, of course; but you will understand."

I laughed then.

"You mean I am under arrest, I suppose."

"Yes, of course; what else?" he answered in curt quick tones. "Are you armed?"

"I have a revolver; here it is," and I put my hand to take it out.

"Stop him," said the official sharply; and a soldier caught my arm, while the sergeant plunged his hand into the pocket I had indicated and drew out the pistol.

The official smiled with dry significance as he examined it and said—

"Ah, and loaded, I see. I expected it. Take him to the guard-house."

CHAPTER XVIII

PRINCE KALKOV'S WELCOME

MY first inclination was to burst out laughing at the egregious absurdity of the blunder, but I restrained myself. Had I had no one but myself to think for, I would have had my laugh, if the next minute had seen me in the deepest dungeon in Petersburg. But I was carrying too many responsibilities.

There are certain classes of officials at whom it is extremely dangerous to laugh. You meet them in all countries; but on the continent of Europe, they are able to resent your merriment practically by clapping you into gaol and perhaps keeping you there. It is safer consequently to laugh at unofficial people.

There was one quick way for me out of the bother, to refer the thing to Prince Kalkov—and although I was loth to take it, I saw immediately that I must adopt that course or be marched off by the soldiers who were only too ready to obey the command.

"You must not permit yourself to commit this mistake, monsieur," I said, quietly, "or you will incur the serious displeasure of Prince Kalkov, as well as of His Majesty. I do not wish to bring trouble upon so courteous an official, and consequently urge you in your own interest to communicate with the Prince without delay."

Nowhere in the world does a big name properly used carry more terror than in Russia's capital; and I put all the authority I could into my tone and manner.

"What have you to do with His Highness?" asked the man, hesitating and yet suspicious, and motioning to the soldiers to wait.

"It happens to be the case that I have told you the truth about myself and you have disbelieved me. You have sent for these gentlemen and ordered my arrest. I will overlook that insult if you send a letter which I will write to the Prince. And if you will not, I warn you in all seriousness that I can and will obtain from His Majesty your dismissal and disgrace."

"I have done no more than my duty," he returned sullenly. He was obviously unwilling to give way before his inferiors, and yet secretly afraid to persist.

"On the contrary, monsieur, you are exceeding your powers now. I have shown you how to obtain instant confirmation of what I have told you from the highest authority, and in the simplest manner. Refuse, and take the consequences. I am like yourself in one respect—my patience has its limits."

"You had this upon you," he said in the same tone, as he fingered my revolver. "And, as I said, it is loaded."

I turned to the soldiers.

"Gentlemen, I am at your disposal. Take me to the guard-house and send to me the officer of the watch;" and I moved toward the door.

The sergeant himself had no liking for the job now, however, and hesitated; and the official in a surly tone gave in.

"You can write," he said, and laid paper and pen on the desk.

"I will not write now," I said curtly, for I began to see another ending to the affair. "I gave you the opportunity and you declined it. I will go to the guard-house. His Majesty and Prince Kalkov shall find me there, and you can explain. Come, gentlemen, if you please; or shall I go alone?"

That any one should exhibit a preference to be arrested was so novel an experience for Russian officialism that they were all staggered. The official took refuge in anger.

"Are you attempting a joke with me?" he cried.

"I do not joke with persons in your position," I retorted sternly.

"I have my duty," he replied, shrugging his shoulders.

"If you deem it your duty to degrade Prince Kalkov's friend by imprisoning him, do it, monsieur—if you dare."

"It is an impossible position."

"You have created it, and must find the way out. But every minute I am detained here will count against you with the Emperor;" and I pulled out my watch as if to mark them off. He was sorely perplexed.

"I will consider the matter. Withdraw your men, sergeant;" and they filed out again, the sergeant manifestly relieved. "I will send to His Highness."

"You will do nothing of the sort, monsieur, now," I said. I saw that he was now practically convinced of my good faith, and I meant to gain my end in my own way.

"You can enter the Palace, monsieur, but I must retain this," and he held up my revolver.

"We Americans do not consent to be robbed even in an Emperor's Palace," I retorted, bent on winning with the honours of war.

"It will be returned to you, monsieur; but I cannot consent to allow you to pass with a weapon in your possession. I dare not take the responsibility."

"There's reason in that, perhaps," I agreed after a pause. "You can keep it until I come to reclaim it."

He opened the door for me then, and murmured an apology.

"I am sorry for what has occurred, but you will understand the difficulty in which I found myself."

"If you do not mention it, monsieur, I shall not; but if you do I shall make the worst of it. In your private ear I may tell you I have been away on urgent business of the Prince's, and he wishes neither my departure nor my return to attract notice. I need say no more to so zealous a servant of His Highness;" and I gave him a look which I hoped would secure his silence.

I was passing out when a thought occurred to me.

"It will perhaps complete your satisfaction if you accompany me to my suite of rooms."

He was more than pleased; and so was I, for by this means I secured myself from all further interruption at the hands of the numerous members of the household whom we met on the way.

I had some difficulty in finding my rooms, but succeeded at length, and taking my companion in with me, was soon able to convince him thoroughly of his mistake. He overwhelmed me with profuse apologies, returned my revolver, begged me to overlook his action, and what was much more important, assured me I could depend upon his silence as to my return.

It is always an intense satisfaction to turn a check into an advantage, and I was disposed to plume myself upon my adroitness and to regard the incident as of good omen for the start of things.

I dressed myself in my own clothes once more, and then had to consider how best to reach the Emperor. I was, moreover, desperately hungry, and how to get a breakfast puzzled me.

It is so often the little fiddling trivialities which cause so much embarrassment. The servant who had waited upon me before had been Kalkov's confidential man, Pierre, and I was naturally unwilling that he should know of my return, as he would instantly inform his master.

Some breakfast I must have, however, and to get it I must of course ring the bell and take my chance. The luck was with me this time. The man who came was a stranger.

"I will have my breakfast served in my room this morning," I said in an off-hand tone, as if I had lived in the Palace half my life. He was too well trained to express any surprise even if he felt any; and in a few minutes he returned with a breakfast and stayed to wait upon me.

I ate the meal in silence, and then lighting a cigar I said in a casual way—

"You have not waited upon me before, I think. I don't recall your face."

"I have been absent from the Palace, monsieur."

"Ah, that explains it."

"I returned the day before yesterday, monsieur," he said with a quick glance and in a significant tone which showed his thoughts.

"I see, that was while I was away. Is His Majesty recovered from his indisposition?"

"By the blessing of Providence, completely, monsieur," he replied earnestly. "But it was not serious, happily."

"That is good news," I said; but it struck me as singular that his recovery should be complete before my return. It seemed to lend some kind of confirmation to my former suspicion that Kalkov had played me false in regard to the Emperor.

"By the way, you will be waiting upon me for the future, I suppose?" I said after a pause.

"Yes, monsieur."

"I am glad of that," and I gave him a couple of gold pieces as a material proof of my pleasure. "I wish to have an audience of His Majesty this morning. Can you get my request to him? I will write it. It is important."

"There will be no difficulty, monsieur."

I wrote a note urging His Majesty to grant me an immediate interview and handed it to the man.

"You know who I am, of course," I said, with a smile.

"His Highness Prince Kalkov's man, Pierre, told me that the suite was reserved for M. Denver, an American gentleman. But he described you differently, monsieur."

"Oh, you mean my beard. Yes, I had to shave it off. Well, get my letter to His Majesty as soon as you can."

All was going so easily that when he had taken away the letter I indulged in a little pardonable jubilation, as I ran hastily over the heads of what I had to say to the Emperor.

It had not been so difficult, after all, to break through the

122

cordon with which the Prince surrounded the Emperor; and my direct American methods had done well.

If I could only succeed half as well with His Majesty, Helga and I—and then my thoughts branched off to her, and all other considerations slipped out of my mind.

She was worth winning indeed, let the fight be as stiff as it might. Victory now meant a life full of radiant happiness with her—a veritable queen among women. Let the price be what it might, it was worth paying to see the light of loving gratitude which would spring to her lovely face when I should claim her for my own and take her in my arms and tell her that my ways had conquered when hers had failed, and——

I had reached somewhere about that point when my rhapsodical reverie was interrupted by a knock and the servant entered. I sprang to my feet eagerly.

"His Highness Prince Kalkov to see you, monsieur," he said, and in came the Prince, hands extended and face beaming, as if in genuine hearty welcome.

"My dear M. Denver, I cannot say how glad I am to see you back again," and he seized my hands and shook them warmly. "I have been really anxious, painfully anxious, about you."

For the life of me I could not for the moment shake myself free from the chagrin and disappointment caused by his arrival and play up to the part of appearing glad to see him.

"I am very glad to get back, Prince, I can assure you," I said, with a sort of tongue-tying hesitation, as his sharp eyes were playing about my face like the blade of a skilful fencer round a novice.

"I thank my God you are alive and well, and have suffered no more hurt than the loss of your beard. How it has changed you!" and as he looked at me his grim wily old features relaxed into a smile.

"Yes, I had to shave," I said.

"You are the Emperor no longer, monsieur. No one will make that mistake again."

"Thank God for that. I don't care for the part at all."

"That means you have had an exciting time," he answered. "There are two emotions which I make a rule to deny myself rigidly, monsieur, and you have made me break the rule. They are enthusiasm and impatience. Now I am enthusiastic when I think of your act; and impatient to hear your account of it."

But I was very far from impatient to give it him, and was indeed cudgelling my wits how to colour it.

"In the first place I have a pretty heavy item against you, Prince," I said.

123

"For having let you embark in the thing, you mean. My dear M. Denver, I give you my solemn assurance I had no idea there would be anything like this result."

"I don't mean that. I mean the breach of the agreement between us that Boreski's carriage should not be followed."

"Ah, that!" and he threw up his hands. "Yes, that was bad. It failed; but those responsible for the failure have paid the penalty. They should have known that Boreski might bring one of those cursed motor-cars and thus be able to distance pursuit. I was served by short-sighted fools—and fools of that kind I do not keep in my employment. When I heard of it I was maddened."

I let him run on in this way in the effort to draw me on to a side issue, for my object now was to gain time in the hope that the summons to the Emperor would come to interrupt the interview.

"I don't refer to the failure, I mean the attempt. You promised that no attempt should be made."

"My dear M. Denver, I give you my word that the thing was necessary. I should have done precisely the same had you been in truth the Emperor himself. Of course, you know, monsieur, that there are times when the commands even of kings have to be secretly disregarded."

He gave the last sentence with a kind of semi-confidential air.

"I don't know anything of the etiquette which surrounds kings, but I do know, Prince, had I not trusted your word I should not have gone," I replied with the severe manner of a man with a genuine grievance.

"I am deeply sorry, monsieur, profoundly sorry; but, as I say, I only treated you as I should my august master. And what effect, then, had it? It must have been serious, of course. I can tell that by the stress you lay upon it."

"It was a breach of faith with Boreski."

He waved his hand carelessly and smiled to show his indifference to that.

"He was clever enough to elude the pursuit, and had evidently come prepared for the trial of wits."

"It made him suspicious, of course; and jaundiced his view of the documents I had to lay before him."

"I am afraid you have failed with him, then. You did not get the papers?"

"No, I did not." I spoke reluctantly, angry at the adroit manner in which he had got at the pith of the thing so quickly.

"That is very disappointing," he said. "Yes, very disappointing. But I am sure it is no fault of yours."

He appeared to be quite earnest in expressing his

disappointment at the failure; but his manner of referring to the papers was in such contrast to his former reference to them that I could not fail to be struck by it. I jumped to the conclusion consequently that he knew of the interview between the Emperor and the Duchess Stephanie and thought they were still to be recovered through her.

"No; it was no fault of mine," I replied.

"I am under a deep obligation to you, M. Denver, for having made the attempt—an obligation which will find expression in a way that I think you will appreciate. I mean in regard to your projected journey. Everything that the Government can do to help that shall be done. I give you my word."

"That is very good of you."

He looked at me very shrewdly as I spoke.

"You have not abandoned the idea, have you? I know that many of your countrymen act on impulse," he said with a smile.

"Abandoned it? Oh no. Why should I?"

"Well, I did not know whether anything in your present experiences might incline you to think our country not as—as safe for travellers as some others."

That there was something underneath his words and his calm smiling suavity was as clear as an ant in amber.

"One has to take risks, of course," I replied indifferently.

"What I mean is that if you would rather turn back, you would of course have our protection to the frontier. If, for instance, you thought you would rather approach our Asiatic dependencies from the other end?"

"I have seen nothing of the capital itself yet, Prince."

"True, comparatively nothing; but this is a bad season of the year for Petersburg."

"You have some meaning behind that," I said pointedly.

"How could I, M. Denver? You have told me nothing yet of your experiences."

He was blandness itself, with just the necessary shred of reproachful reminder of my omission.

"I am waiting to see the Emperor. I have asked him for an audience this morning; and as my story to you will take rather long in the telling, it would be better to postpone it."

"His Majesty will be charmed, I am sure. Did you hear of the ruse de guerre about his indisposition?" and he smiled again.

I was getting to be rather afraid of these smiles of his.

"Yes, a paper was shown me."

"I hoped it would be. I hoped it would be. It was a rather ingenious bit of colour. But His Majesty had to recover yesterday."

"Before I returned," I put in drily.

"He had to go to Moscow to meet the Crown Prince, you see."

"Do you mean His Majesty is in Moscow?" I cried.

"Did you not know it? The servant should have told you this morning. These men are really addlepated fools," he cried with an excellent indignation, as his sharp glittering eyes fixed on me. He was enjoying my momentary confusion, I am sure.

"No, I did not know it," I answered, with difficulty smothering an oath.

"He was overwhelmed with regret that you had not returned before he went—the more so as he knew you would have left Petersburg before his return." He continued to enjoy my discomfiture, for a moment, and then added lightly: "But at any rate there is one compensation for me. It will give ample time for me to hear your story, for which, as I told you, I am really impatient. Will you tell it here, or would you like to come to my apartments?"

"It doesn't matter, one place is as good as another," I answered, in any but an amiable tone.

I was no match for him at this game of fence. Already he had contrived to fill me with a kind of fearsome speculation as to how much he had managed to hear of my doings and concerning Helga. There was suggestiveness in every word he uttered, and every look and gesture he made.

"Why did the Emperor think I should not be in Petersburg on his return?" I asked after a pause. "You are perplexing me, Prince."

"I told him so, my dear M. Denver," he replied, as if frankly.

"Why?"

He spread out his hands and smiled.

"May we not find a reason in your interesting narration? I have really never known myself to feel so much impatience for anything of the kind before. I entreat of you not to keep me in suspense."

And he threw himself back in his chair and folded his hands in the attitude of an interested listener and looked to me to begin.

CHAPTER XIX

TURNING THE SCREW

BEFORE I complied with Prince Kalkov's request I took out a fresh cigar and spent some time over lighting it.

"You have quite a stage instinct, monsieur, in pausing thus at the critical moment. If I did not know you, I might be tempted to think you were arranging the duly dramatic unfolding of the tale, or perhaps," he added lightly, "considering what part of it you need not tell."

"It is after all only the story of a failure, Prince, and naturally one does not care to dwell too long upon it. I went to Boreski, as you know, led him to believe that I was the Emperor, laid before him the papers as we arranged, and he took the objection I had anticipated—that he must have the money in cash instead of a draft."

"You told him the reason—that the money was a dowry?"

"Of course, and he immediately checkmated me by saying he was already married to the Duchess and that the consent to the marriage must be dated back."

"He is a daring fellow. It was a tight corner. What did you say?"

"I couldn't alter the date, of course, for the reason that I could not write in the same hand, so I put up what we Americans term a bluff," and I described to him what had passed, withholding, of course, all mention of Helga and her part in it.

"It was very clever, M. Denver. And why did you not come away?"

"If I had come the papers would have been placed in the hands of the Powers' representatives at once. I stayed, therefore, in the hope of finding the means to avert such a catastrophe."

"That was almost reckless, but under the circumstances no more than I should have expected." He was a fiend at the game of implied suggestion, and again I was convinced he had secret information of some kind. "But in the end you found you could do nothing?" he continued. "They made you a prisoner."

Why did he use that plural? What "they" had he in his mind?

"A prisoner in effect, because, if I left, Boreski meant to use the papers at once. But I could have left at any moment."

He smiled and nodded.

"Ingenious, highly ingenious. And then?"

"Then there was nearly the devil to pay. By some means or

other the Nihilist brotherhood got wind of the fact that I was at Boreski's——"

"At Boreski's?" he shot in, as if in surprise.

"Presumably it was Boreski's house, and a hurried flight followed with the object of saving me from them, but it was ineffectual. They found me, and an attempt was made upon my life by a man named Vastic, and I only averted it by shooting him."

"What infernal villainy! It shows, of course, that Boreski is in league with this brotherhood. And where was this?"

"I can find my way to the place, I think."

"It would be at Brabinsk, of course."

How the devil did he know that?

"It was a very close shave, I assure you," I said, trying to conceal my surprise. "It was Brabinsk; I remember to have heard the name. How did you know it?"

"Through my agents. As a matter of fact, an anonymous communication has been laid in the matter to the effect that murder was done there last night—the murder of this man, Vastic."

I felt my nerves chill at this, with sudden dread for Helga. He noticed the change instantly. Nothing seemed to escape those piercing eyes of his.

"The facts are as I have told you. His revolver was at my head when I got the drop on him and fired. It was his life or mine."

"Exactly. I don't think you need bother your head about the matter. My men are out there by this time, and we know how to deal with such cases. Vastic was one of the few really dangerous men in this brotherhood, and by killing him you have added to our obligation. We shall try to avoid any fuss. By the way, were there any witnesses?"

He was the devil with these quietly-put, probing, torturing questions.

"What was the account they gave of it? A second man was joined in the attempt and witnessed it."

He saw the obvious parry.

"Naturally nothing was said of that," he answered with a laugh. "I mean, was Boreski present? You see, it would be most valuable to be able to connect him with it, and his presence would be enough."

"No, Boreski was not in the house," I answered, cursing him in my thoughts for torture he inflicted.

"Then why did you stay there?"

"I have told you—because of the threat to use the papers."

"Oh, yes, of course. It is a pity. I should like to have had that link in the chain against him." He frowned as if genuinely concerned, and added after a pause, "Of course, you will see the desirability—the necessity, in fact—of telling everything, everything in the fullest sense, I mean, in such a case?"

"Do you think I have not?" I retorted sharply.

"Where are the papers now?" he asked, putting my implied repudiation on one side.

"I should think we had better ask M. Boreski," I answered, attempting a light tone and forcing a smile. But it was an effort. I recognized that, and recognized too that I was afraid of him. Not for myself, he could not harm me; but terribly afraid for Helga.

"I should have thought that, too," he answered, copying my light tone. "But it's just there I am puzzled. You see, Boreski says he doesn't know either." He spoke for all the world as though we were just talking over the thing in full mutual confidence.

"It's scarcely likely, is it, that he would tell everything?"

"No, no, of course not. But he declares, or at least the Duchess Stephanie does, and it's the same thing, that he hasn't them." Then he started as if an idea had occurred to him. "By the way, you haven't said anything about this mysterious lady, Mademoiselle Helga Boreski? Didn't you think it worth while, or didn't you see her?"

His eyes were on my face, and he saw the wince I gave at the sudden thrust. He had known about her all the time.

"I didn't wish to bring her name into the affair."

"Ah, monsieur, that was a mistake. May I ask the motive?"

"Certainly. She is the lady whom I hope to make my wife." It was my turn to surprise him now, and a long pause followed, while he sat smoking and thinking over the new turn.

"Well, M. Denver, I am genuinely sorry for you; sorry that I ever sent you on this business. You cannot save this lady, and it would of course be idle for me to pretend that I do not see how your feeling for her has actuated you. She is a Nihilist; she has had chief part in this plot; she holds these papers; she was present when the attempt was made on your life—and probably instigated it——"

"No, she did not," I interposed angrily. "At that time she knew quite well I was not the Emperor."

"So you told them that?" he returned in his quiet suggestive manner.

"I did my utmost to obtain the papers," I protested.

"We are getting at cross purposes, monsieur," he answered with dryness. "I will not question you about her. Probably you know who she is and what her motive is in the strange course she is taking. I do not yet; I am speaking frankly—more frankly than you dealt with me—but I have now certain information, and shall soon have more. But already I know enough to warrant me in ordering her arrest."

129

"You have seen the Duchess Stephanie this morning?"

"Yes, and shall see her again—and others. You must face the facts, monsieur; and the facts are that this Mademoiselle Helga will not be long at liberty, and that any thought of marriage between you is absolutely out of the question. She will go to the mines."

"On the contrary, your Highness, she will be my wife," I said firmly. Now that the mischief was out, and I was no longer clogged by the need to hide things, my embarrassment was at an end, and I recovered my self-possession. There was a prospect of a fight too, and my spirits rose to it.

"We shall see, monsieur. I am, as I say, deeply sorry for you; but, believe me, you will not improve your case if you attempt to espouse this reckless young woman's cause and fight our Government for her sake."

"Fight you, you mean, Prince?"

"As a member of that Government, yes: in a way it is fighting me."

"You forget the Emperor is my friend."

"But not the friend of desperate young women Nihilists, monsieur," he answered with calculated deliberateness. "You must give her up."

"That I will never do."

"Then the consequences will be disastrous. But now," and he waved his hand as if putting that matter aside, "there is another matter. Your killing of this man, Vastic, has made you many enemies. Your name is known to them as well as your appearance, and your life may be in danger at their hands. You were mentioned by name in the charge which reached us. We shall of course protect you."

"I can protect myself, thank you," I interposed.

"We can run no risks of any trouble with the American Embassy on your account, and we must therefore charge ourselves with the task of protecting you. What I propose to you, therefore, is, as I said at first, that you either return to the frontier, or that you start on your journey to Khiva under strong escort, and that you adopt one of those courses forthwith."

"I thank your Highness, but I shall not go. I shall not leave Petersburg, at any rate until I have seen the Emperor."

He rose then and tossed away his cigar.

"I hold you for a man of decision, monsieur, but in this case I will give you an opportunity of reconsidering this one. I will see you again in an hour."

"You will not find me here. I shall go to an hotel."

"For that hour at least it will not be convenient to us for you to take such a step."

"Does your Highness make me a prisoner?" I demanded indignantly.

"I will see you again in an hour, monsieur," he replied, and with that left the room, without heeding my angry retort.

As soon as he had gone the servant entered and asked my permission to attend to the rooms. I gave it to him, and throwing such things as lay to hand into a grip I went to the door.

"I shall not be back," I said to him, and he turned and looked at me curiously.

"Very well, monsieur," he answered. "But I believe His Highness wishes to see you here."

I flung the door open, for my temper was up, and then found I was indeed a prisoner. Three men were posted there on guard.

Affecting to believe their presence had nothing to do with me, I made as if to brush by them.

"Your pardon, monsieur," said the man in command, "but my orders are to desire you to be so good as to await His Highness's return."

"I have told the Prince I will see him another time," I returned.

"Deepest regrets, monsieur; but my orders were very precise;" and as it was quite evident that he was prepared to prevent my departure by force if necessary, I gave in, went back into the room and slammed the door. Just one of those childish acts a man commits in a rage.

But the situation was far too grave for my vexation over the mere personal indignity to last long. The thing had to be considered as an indication of the length to which the Prince was ready to go in the absence of the Emperor. He would stick at nothing; and the treachery which had destroyed Helga's father years ago was still a practical policy with him.

The question was what he could do to me and whether he would attempt to keep me from seeing the Emperor. It was clear that his suspicions had fastened upon Helga. He had had his own reasons for asking so pointedly about her real motives.

"You probably know who she is; I do not—yet," he had said; but he had a connecting link almost in his hands in the person of Boreski. Moreover he had accepted my news as meaning that I should associate myself with her. If then he guessed that she was so dangerous to him as the daughter of the dead Lavalski would be, I could not doubt he would strain every nerve, not only to secure her and put her away as a Nihilist, but also to keep me as her champion from getting to the Emperor's ear.

131

But what should I do? That was the question. Drive me out of Russia he should not; that I was resolved; but shut up in my room in the Palace I was as powerless as if I had been in New York. He could set his dogs to hunt down Helga and have her half-way to Siberia before I might get a chance to escape; and the thought was almost maddening in my then state of mind.

Presently it occurred to me to try and meet craft with craft, to pretend to accept his offer of a safe conduct to the frontier and then return. To get out of the Palace by way of the frontier was a long route, but it was better than remaining where I was, and things being as they were it appeared the only course for me to adopt.

It was nearly three hours, instead of only one, before he returned, and when he came I saw that he had fresh news. I could read him sufficiently well by this time to see that.

"I regret the delay, M. Denver, but it has been unavoidable," he said in suave apology. "Have you considered your decision?"

"I protest in the strongest manner, Prince Kalkov, against my forcible detention here. I demand, as a citizen of the United States, to have an opportunity of communicating with our Embassy here."

"That course is open to you naturally, and if you press it I cannot and shall not oppose it. You may indeed find it necessary—in your own defence."

"Then I am free to go to them?"

"Not exactly that, but you will have the usual opportunities," he answered with one of his infernal implied threats.

"What do you mean by usual opportunities?"

"Our legal procedure in regard to foreigners is not perhaps very swift, but it is very just; and if you prefer an open investigation into this man Vastic's death to the course I indicated before, I cannot of course object. And as an American accused of murder you would be fully entitled to all the help of the American embassy."

"But you know the truth as to that," I cried.

"And personally have not a doubt that your act was committed in self-defence. Still it was committed, and——" He finished with a shrug of the shoulders and a lifting of the hands.

"Do you mean that you accuse me of murder?"

"I? God forbid I should do you such an injustice," he said, as if in indignant repudiation of the idea. "It is others who do it."

"You are the devil, Prince Kalkov," I cried furiously. "This is just another of your infernal schemes."

"Is that quite just to me, when I have offered you a safe conduct across the frontier, or to anywhere you please? It is you who place me in this awkward situation."

"To hell with your hypocrisy," I exclaimed, losing my head in

132

my rage. "Speak out bluntly, and say what you do mean—that if I won't consent to leave the country you will take this devil's way of getting me into one of your cursed prisons while you carry out your other plans."

"Really, M. Denver, this language to me is beyond bounds—even for a free-speaking citizen of the United States. It is true we might not be able to get the proceedings finished for some weeks; I have known it take months, indeed. There was the case of——"

"The devil take your cases. Do your worst, and we'll fight it out on those lines;" and I turned away and flung myself into a chair.

But he was my match at that tactic also. He sat down, drew a small table to his side, took out some papers and studied them with slow methodical deliberation. He calculated that my temper would not last, and that I should then see the utter futility of resisting him. And of course it proved so.

"I'll accept your terms and leave Russia," I said, when the silence had lasted many minutes.

"Pardon me," he said, as if he was buried in some other matters. "Just one minute," and he went on with his papers, and then folded them up neatly. "Now I am at your service again. Let us talk it over. Why do you treat me as an enemy?"

"I would rather not discuss anything except my departure."

"As you please, but the matter is not quite where it was when we last spoke of it. I know a great deal more than I did, and I am compelled to regard you as more dangerous than before. You are at liberty to leave, but I shall have to ask you for a written declaration on your word of honour as an American gentleman that you will go straight to America, and that you will make no effort to communicate, directly or indirectly, with my August Master. Further, I shall place at your disposal a courier, who will accompany you to the port you select—I would suggest Hamburg—and attend on you until you reach New York. This I do partly for your personal safety."

"And chiefly as a spy to see that I do go, you mean."

"He will of course report to me."

"And if I refuse?" I asked, when I could force myself to speak without anger.

"I hope you will not refuse, because if you are still in Russia when the man Vastic's death is investigated—and time in that matter presses, of course—it will be very difficult, I fear, to avoid your being implicated." The perfect command he had over his expression and tone aggravated me almost as much as what he said.

"I will make a condition on my side—that Mademoiselle Helga Boreski be allowed to leave the country at the same time."

133

"Mademoiselle Helga Lavalski, you mean?"

I nearly broke my teeth as I clenched them at this.

"I have said whom I mean."

"Well, there are two objections. You know her story of course, and so do I—now. She is, as you are aware, unwilling to leave until she has ruined me for some fancied wrong; and she is a dangerous Nihilist, with whom the authorities can have no dealings except in the usual legal way. She will go to the mines, as I told you, if we deal with her."

"And if you have found her, perhaps," I cried with a sneer.

"True; and true also that we may not have to deal with her at all. She has, as you know, incurred the vengeance of this brotherhood, and it may be less troublesome to leave her to them."

"Thank God, she is as safe from them as from you."

"Yes, but not more so. You left a paper in your coat which the servant found and handed to me. You had scribbled on it two or three words which I thought might have reference to her—about a small red-brick house in the north-east corner of the Square of San Sophia. I followed up that clue, and by this time the information we gained is in the hands of the brotherhood. They will know how——"

"Stop, for God's sake, stop," I said hoarsely, jumping to my feet in horror. "I can bear no more. If you say another word, I swear to God I shall find it in me to kill you where you sit."

CHAPTER XX

A DEATH TRAP

THE Prince had nerves of steel, and met my threatening look with a calm and steady gaze, absolutely unmoved by my passionate outbreak.

"You had better calm yourself, M. Denver. It will not help the case of an accused murderer to attempt my life, and such an attempt must fail, as a single cry from me will bring in the men at the door."

"Get out of the room then," I cried bluntly, "lest the passion to choke the life out of you passes control." I flung myself back in my chair.

"I wish you could realize that I am indeed grieved for you. Your violence now shows——"

"To hell with your sympathy," I said brutally. "It is all a lie, like the rest of you. Do what you please with me."

He took the insult, as he did everything from me, unmoved, save for a shrug of the shoulders, and for a minute was silent.

"You cannot save this woman. Will you leave Russia?"

"Will you spare her if I do?"

He pretended to think for a space.

"No, I will not," he said implacably. "She has sown the seed and must reap the crop. That is the law of intrigue such as hers. Moreover," he added as he glanced at his watch, "it is probably already too late for me or you either to save her."

"Have you no jot of humanity in you? Are you utterly cold, calculating and brutal? You could send her warning."

"It is possible nothing may be done until to-night. But it is no part of my duty to warn a Nihilist who betrays her comrades."

"Russian chivalry is a noble thing," I sneered. "But, by God, remember this," I added fiercely, leaning forward, "if harm comes to her, you shall pay for it with your life, if I come from the other side of the earth to take it."

"I have been threatened many times, M. Denver, by men as desperate as yourself—and still live. But now," he asked as he rose, "will you leave Russia, or do you compel me to order your arrest on this murder charge? You are young, with a bright future."

"Never mind my future," I put in. "Do what you will."

"Your violence to me will be added to the charge now, and our influence with our judges is great."

"Go, before there's another death to be added also."

He went to the door and turned.

"I am still very reluctant, for you tried to serve us. Take another day to think, and give me your word of honour to make no attempt to escape. You can then stay here."

"Go," I cried, turning my back on him, and I did not look round until he had left the room.

Desperate as my own plight was, my thoughts were not for myself, but for Helga. I cursed myself a thousand times for my insensate blundering stupidity which had brought all this danger upon her, the very blunder against which she herself had warned me.

I remembered scribbling the words in the carriage, and saw now that instead of tearing up the paper on which I had written I must have torn up the blank sheet. I recalled that when she had warned me not to throw even the fragments in one place, I had found none but blanks in my fingers, and I could have torn my hair out to think I had been such a reckless idiot as not to search my pocket again to make sure.

I had destroyed her. I who would have given my life to save her; and that bitter hour of miserable unavailing remorse held horrors for me no description can convey. It will never pass from memory, and I marvel that in my agony I did not go insane.

I was far past caring what happened to me, and when the door opened and I looked up expecting to see the police with the warrant for me, I was ready to welcome this arrest as a distraction from my thoughts. Anything, anything to get away from the maddening oppressiveness of my gloom.

It was not the police, however, but the servant who brought me food.

"Don't bring that here," I cried, when the man set it down.

He looked at me in surprise.

"You are in great trouble, monsieur," he said, not unkindly. "But one must eat, even in trouble."

"I wish to God I was dead," I exclaimed desperately; "and you talk of eating. Take it away, man, take it away, or I shall do you a mischief," and I turned to the window and leaned my fevered head against the sash.

Helga was being pursued by these sleuth hounds and would be killed—killed for having tried to save my life—and it was I—I who had laid them upon her trail and brought destruction upon her. Already they might have struck the blow. And I could barely keep myself from moaning aloud in my impotent anguish.

Then suddenly I started. I had made a discovery.

A man came into sight in the ground below. It was one of the gardeners, and he crossed from the right until an abutment of the Palace hid him from my view on the left.

I was only two storeys from the ground, and the roof of the out-building behind which the man had been lost to sight could probably be reached from my bedroom window. Then by a curious memory freak an old joke dashed into my thoughts, and I smiled. It was the story of the man who languished in gaol for twenty years racking his brains with elaborate plans for escape, and then—opened the door and walked out.

My God, the way of escape lay right here. I might still get to Helga. I had to steady myself against the window frame now in the rush of this new excitement.

I turned back to the servant. He was still there.

"Why don't you take those things away when I tell you," I said, trying to speak in my former tone.

"I hope you will try to eat, monsieur. You have fasted long."

I was conscious suddenly of hunger. I might have work to do for Helga, and must keep up my strength. My new thoughts had changed me.

"How long is it since I breakfasted?"

"Many hours, monsieur. It is now nearly five o'clock."

Five o'clock. How the time had flown! My interviews with Kalkov, and the intervals, had eaten up the day. Five o'clock! I groaned. The dusk would soon fall, and if Helga were not already in the hands of her enemies, the time in which a warning could reach her might almost be counted by minutes.

I must get rid of the servant, and perhaps if I ate the food he had brought it would save time.

"I will take your advice." I sat down to the table and ate with the speed which only Americans have cultivated as a fine art. In a few minutes I had swallowed almost everything he had brought.

"I am glad, monsieur. You were then hungry after all," he said with a deferential air of satisfaction.

"I have finished. You can take it away," I replied.

I lit a cigar and watched him as he piled the things on the trays. He was very slow and methodical, and I fretted and fumed over the time he took, until I felt I could have kicked him out of the room and thrown the trays after him. Then he showed an inclination to talk.

"You are an American, I think, monsieur," he said, playing at rearranging the things.

"Yes."

"It is a fine country, I believe, monsieur."

"Yes."

"I have a brother there. He is doing well. He is in Chicago."

"Oh."

"They seem to earn very large sums of money there, monsieur. He is married and has a business of his own. He sells birds and animals."

"Ah." Would he never stop his gabbling and get away?

"Yes. He wishes me to go to him. I think I shall some day. But there is the sea to cross, and I have never seen it. You have crossed the sea, monsieur?"

"Yes."

"But I should not like his trade, monsieur. I am fond of birds and animals—but not in cages; oh no, not in cages. It is like imprisonment, is it not, monsieur? And here in Russia one does not speak lightly of prisons."

"No." I gave him nothing but monosyllables, but his chatter seemed to thrive on it.

"No, I should not like his trade," and he shook his head dolefully. "I have a heart, monsieur, and if I went there I think I should ruin him. I should want to let the birds out of their cages, monsieur."

A new interest in him and his chatter sprang to life in my thoughts. I looked up sharply, and caught his eyes fixed on me with an inscrutable expression in them. Did he mean anything by the words?

"A kind heart is a good thing," I said.

"Yes, monsieur, but"—he sighed—"it is sometimes liable to get one into trouble." He had finished now with even his pretence of packing the things together, and he paused and said, "You are a prisoner, monsieur?"

"It looks like it."

"It is very sad, monsieur. Well, I will have these things taken away."

"You can take them away yourself," I said.

"I am very sorry, monsieur, but my orders are not to leave the room again. I am to stay with you."

And my heart sank as he touched the bell, and we waited, in silence until the trays had been fetched. Then he stood close to the doorway between the two rooms.

It began to look as if there would be a tussle of strength before I got away, and I measured him in my eye with this thought present to me. He was a slightly built wiry little man, no sort of a match for me if it came to a trial of strength; but I preferred another way if it could be managed.

"Where shall I remain, monsieur?" he asked after a time.

"Was it you who ransacked my pockets this morning?" I asked, recalling Kalkov's words.

"By the Prince's orders, monsieur. We all fear him—but we all hate him. We dare not disobey him."

Whether he meant me to understand anything by this or not I could not tell, but the time was pressing so fast that my anxiety drove me to bring matters to a crisis, and soon I had a plan. Any moment might now find me in the hands of the police.

I got up and passed into the bedroom, my purpose being to catch him suddenly at a disadvantage, fling him on to the bed, and smother his cries with the pillows while I tied him up and gagged him.

He seemed suspicious of my intentions, for he hung back, but one is always tempted to suppose that others may divine such thoughts. So I fooled around with some of my clothes, and then called him to help me move a bag. I got him near enough to the bedstead, and then with a significant look I said—

"You have a good heart, I can see that. Now, assuming I am like one of your brother's caged birds, will you help me out?"

"Monsieur, I dare not, I dare not."

But he neither called out nor attempted to get away. Instead, he fixed his eyes on mine, and there was no fear in them.

"I will make it worth your while," I said firmly. "Come."

"Oh, monsieur, if it were found out. I am sorry for you; but if it were found out."

"It won't be. We'll fix that all right," I answered. "Listen. I intend to escape by the window there, drop on the roof below, and from there to the ground."

"Oh, monsieur, monsieur, I dare not," he cried.

"I shall give you five hundred roubles to help me."

His eyes gleamed avariciously.

"I will help you," he said; "but you must make it seem that you have forced me. You must bind me and stop my mouth, so that when they come and find me they shall see you have forced me."

It was a very thin device, but if it satisfied him I had no reason to care, especially as I had contemplated doing it in earnest.

"Very well."

"And you must not go yet, monsieur, not until dark. You would be seen; the grounds are alive with guards and soldiers. You must wait till seven o'clock."

"Why till seven o'clock?"

"It will not be dark enough before; and besides, a number of men go away at that hour—the gardeners—and I can tell you how to get out so that no one will see you if you wait till then."

"That's all very well, but I may be arrested first," I said suspiciously.

"No no, monsieur. You are to stay here all night. I heard his highness say so, and I was told to remain here until ten o'clock, when I am to be relieved."

There was Helga to think of, however, and to remain there an hour and a half longer while she was in momentary peril seemed intolerable. At the same time, there was wisdom in what the man said. To get out of the grounds in daylight, while the gardeners and others were about, was just a forlorn hope, and bitterly as I chafed at the delay, I resolved to wait until dusk came.

That hour and a half was the longest in my life. The man did his best to occupy my thoughts, telling me over and over again exactly the way I had to go so as to avoid meeting any one, pointing out part of it from the window, and giving me a hundred hints and suggestions.

As the time approached I gave him the sum I had promised, stowed the rest of the money about me, and then fastened him up. He himself suggested an ingenious method. I wrapped a sheet round him, and then wound certain cords about him, until he looked like a mummy in clean clothes, and could move neither hand nor foot; and then I fastened a pillow over his head.

Bearing all he had said in mind, I opened the window, got down on to the roof below, crept along it, and finding the coast clear, dropped to the ground. I fell on to a flower bed, and darted at full speed across the lawn to the point he had told me.

He had earned his money well, for I was able to follow his instructions to the letter with the greatest ease. He had told me to make for that part of the gardens where the greenhouses stood, and past them to take a path to the left until I came to a spot where an out-house with a low sloping roof stood against the high outside wall. By means of this I was to climb to the top of the wall, and then drop into a dark unfrequented road. I was to go along this to the right for about half a mile, when I should find myself at a point from which I could easily reach any part of the city.

I remember being struck by the fact that a part of the Palace grounds so near to the building should be so deserted, but I had not a thought or suspicion of treachery of any kind.

I reached the road within a very short time of leaving the room, and turning, as he had told me, to the right, I ran along it at a sharp speed. It was overhung with heavy trees and very dark, but on this fact I congratulated myself as I ran.

I had covered half the distance when the path narrowed between the high wall of the Palace grounds on one side and an equally high hedge on the other, and it was so dark that I could not see the ground beneath me. I was so keen to get to Helga that I pressed on at headlong speed, until my foot slipped on something wet and greasy and down I went all a-sprawl in the dirt.

My hat flew off and my head struck the ground, and my face slid along in the mud, but beyond grazing my skin and griming myself considerably, I suffered no hurt. I fell on the soft mud and thus made scarcely any noise, a fact to which I believe I owed my life.

I sat up, and was groping about for my hat when I heard a sound some way ahead of me. Thinking some one was coming I rolled under the shadow of the great hedge and waited.

I have said before that my sense of hearing is very acute, but though I strained it now to the utmost I heard nothing for some

140

time. In the meanwhile I found that in the dark I had blundered into a kind of broad ditch which crossed the path, the bottom being of soft wet mire.

I pulled myself cautiously up on to the dry ground, and putting my ear to the earth lay as still as death and listened.

Presently I heard the sound of the shuffling of feet, and as it was repeated after a few moments' interval, I could tell some one was waiting at a distance ahead of me.

I must find out what it meant, and that at once, for minutes were precious. I sat up, therefore, and took off my boots, and as I was rising my hand struck against my hat.

I crept forward now as cautiously as before I had ran heedlessly, stopping every few yards to listen.

That any one could be waiting for me did not even then cross my mind; but I was carrying too great a responsibility to run risks and although the slow progress I made chafed and worried me, I dared not quicken it. And well it was indeed that I exercised this restraint.

There was very little wind moving, but what there was came from the direction I was going, and in one of the pauses I made to listen, I caught the sound of a voice, and then heard the tread of heavy feet. In a moment I rolled myself under the hedge.

The steps came nearer, and I could tell there were two men. They were speaking in low guttural tones, but I could not at first catch the words, until one of them said in a louder voice, with a touch of impatience—

"Yes, seven o'clock, of course."

In a flash my eyes were open. It was the hour the servant had insisted upon for my escape. The whole thing had been planned by Kalkov himself. And these men were—who?

I was not long in doubt on that point either.

The two came on, drew level, and passed; and as I held my breath I heard a muttered reference to the brotherhood and Vastic's murder, which told me all I needed to know.

The Prince had adopted the same policy toward me as toward Helga, and having planned the means of my escape through that treacherous scoundrel of a servant, had managed to convey to the brotherhood an intimation of where and when I could be found.

But for that fall of mine into the mud the plan would have succeeded, and there would have been an end of any interference from me in his plans.

I had no time to waste in cursing him, however; and as soon as the men were well past I rolled out from the hedge and crept on as quickly as I could.

141

I was afraid there would be a third man to be dealt with at the mouth of the place, but to my infinite relief the coast was clear, and putting on my boots again I turned into the road and walked briskly in the direction of the city.

I was in a deplorable mess from my tumble, and tried with very little effect to get rid of some of the mud from my clothes and face.

It was while I was doing this, and puzzling how I should get admission to Helga's house that the need for some disguise occurred to me. I should probably have to pass some of the brotherhood spies near the house, and if I were recognized the consequences might be vitally serious.

The means for the disguise were in fact supplied by the mud into which I had fallen. I knocked in the crown of my hat, took off my coat, tore my shirt-sleeves half-way to the elbows, daubed them and my arms and hands with mud, and in a minute was changed into a dirty disreputable loafer, whom any one would have the greatest difficulty in recognizing as Harper C. Denver, the smartly groomed New Yorker.

And in this guise I hurried as fast as I dared without exciting suspicion from the police in the direction of the square of San Sophia.

CHAPTER XXI

AT THE SQUARE OF SAN SOPHIA

FROM Czar to street smouch was a big change of parts, and had I had time to think and opportunity to choose, I would have selected a different character.

But I had little conscious thought beyond a burning impatience to get to Helga in the shortest possible time. I was jostled and pushed as I hurried on; now hustled off the side walk, now grazing the house fronts, and at times dodging through the traffic: but all the while pressing on with feverish haste through the people, followed constantly by curses and angry threats from those who shrank from my dirty presence or shouldered me roughly to one side.

There is no lack of disreputable-looking beggars in the streets of Russia's capital at any time, and at night one drunken man more or less attracts little attention, provided he keeps quiet. I was taken for a drunkard; and my dirt-begrimed face and clothes, my coat slung over my shoulder, my half-bared arms and muddied shirt-sleeves lent colour to the part, as I scrambled and scurried along with a wary eye for the police, whom I avoided with scrupulous care.

I had not much difficulty in finding the square of San Sophia, which had once been a fashionable quarter. It was a dismal-looking cul de sac, with a winding entrance at the southern end, in shape like nothing so much as a tennis racket with a bent handle.

At the entrance stood a woman, who came toward me, half paused, stared sharply at me, and passed on. I guessed she was a spy of some kind, posted there to mark all who entered and left the square.

I lurched past her, keeping up my part of a drunken man, and reeled on into the square—a small open space, unrailed and unprotected, with two or three forlorn-looking stunted trees in a clump in the centre.

From the shelter of these I was able to make out Helga's house—standing well back in the shadow—a wider, shorter building than the rest, with a deep porch. Not a light showed in any of the windows, a fact that gave me a momentary qualm.

Having assured myself that no one was watching me, I stole out from the trees and made for the porch, knocked gently at the door, and waited. No one came, and fearing to give any noisy summons, I was feeling and peering about for a bell—for inside the porch was very dark—when I heard footsteps in the square. By the flickering lamplight at the entrance I saw the woman who had met me returning in company with a man, and, to my dismay, they came with rapid steps toward the spot where I stood.

I lay down and squeezed myself as close to the side of the porch as possible, trusting that the gloom of the place would prevent them seeing me.

The footsteps came right to the house and then stopped.

In a fever of impatience I dragged myself cautiously to the entrance and peering out, watched them.

They stood a moment talking together in whispers at the other end of the house. The woman seemed to be giving the man some information and instructions, for I saw her point several times toward that end of the building.

After perhaps a couple of minutes she left, and the man shrank back into the deep shadows, until the sound of her footsteps had ceased. Then I heard the scrape of his feet against brickwork, and

143

could just make out that he had climbed on to a low wall which ran by the side of the house.

At the risk of discovery I felt that I must know where he had gone, so I drew off my boots and stole after him. By the side of the house ran a very narrow passage guarded by a heavy iron gate, and crawling on to the wall I followed the man with as much haste as the need for extreme caution permitted.

The house was as still as a charnel vault; but I was no longer dismayed by this. It was evident that such a visitor must have very strong motives for this kind of secrecy; and as I judged that the woman had pointed out the means by which an entrance to the house could be gained, it was easy to understand that this was all connected with the threatened attack upon Helga. This meant therefore that she was still safe, and that I had arrived in time to take a hand in matters.

When I had gone far enough along the wall to get a view of the rear of the house, I lay down and looked about for the man, and soon discovered his plan. There were no underground rooms to the house, but there were cellars, and the way to these was protected by a heavy grating. He had removed this, and when I caught sight of him he was standing below in the act of replacing this grating above his head.

As soon as it was in its place, I slipped off the wall and listened. He entered the cellar, and when once inside struck a match, the feeble flickering light from which enabled me to watch him.

He looked round for a moment as if in doubt, and then went to a door in the far right-hand corner and knocked: three double knocks, repeated at short intervals. After a while I heard the door open; the sound of muffled gruff voices came to me; the door was closed, and then all was silent as the grave once more.

For a moment I hesitated whether to follow him or to go back to the front and try again to get into the house that way. But my former failure to attract attention there decided me against that course.

It was just possible that Helga had arranged these precautions in the critical need to conceal her presence in the house, and in that case, if I once gained admittance, I could easily explain my presence. But it seemed far more probable that a very ugly purpose lay under it all, and this I resolved to ascertain, even at the risk of finding myself face to face with one or two members of the brotherhood.

I slipped on my boots and coat, therefore, and following the man's example, I got through the grating, and finding the inner door, gave the signal I had heard. It was an anxious moment as I huddled up against the door awaiting the result. It was a long wait, until I heard a stealthy movement; the door was opened slowly and cautiously, and a man, holding a light, looked out.

Not caring for any scrutiny of my face, I put my foot in the crack and my shoulder to the door, and shoved my way in.

"Why keep me waiting?" I asked in a whisper. "I am followed."

"Who are you?" asked the voice.

"One who should be here," I answered at random, as I closed the door and shot home the bolt. "Lead the way," I said, in a tone of authority.

He was for thrusting the light in my face, but I brushed his hand away and growled out an oath.

"Who is here?" I asked then, under my breath.

He made no reply, and seemed quite undecided what to do; so I decided for him, and pushed him very unceremoniously before me into the darkness beyond.

He led me into an inner cellar, unlighted, save for the candle he carried. I followed, prepared for almost anything except that which I saw; and seeing it, I could scarce restrain from laughter, so complete was the relief from the tension of the previous few minutes.

There was only one man there—obviously the same I had followed—and he was staring hard at us with an expression of mingled fear and expectation. It was Paul Drexel. He was shaved, and disguised in the shabby clothes of a beggar; but I knew his flabby coward's face in a moment, although he did not recognize me. And I took care that he should see my face as little as possible. For an instant the question flashed upon me: What Drexel was doing in the affair? But I had to act, not think, because if my supposition was correct, we should soon have more of the men upon us.

There was no longer any reason for fear. With no one but a fat coward like Drexel and the man with the light to oppose me, I should soon find a way out of things.

"Who are you?" asked Drexel, as I entered.

"I am here to take command," I replied, muffling my voice. I turned to the other man and asked: "What part of the house are we in? How do we get where we have to go?"

"These are the cellars. They didn't think of them," he replied, with a grin of cunning.

"Show me," and I made him light the way for me.

My examination of the place revealed nothing but bare cellars.

My guide pointed out a flight of stairs, and explained that there was only a door at the top, which would not be difficult to force.

My first step was to get rid of him; and as he was now quite unsuspicious of me, this was easy.

I found that one of the cellars had a door with bolts on the outside, and as we stood in it, I made an excuse to take the light from him, and catching him unawares, I gave him a blow on the side of the head which sent him staggering over the floor, and before he could recover himself I had shut the door and bolted it upon him.

He began a clatter at the door, and I called to Drexel sharply—

"Come and help here, quickly."

He came hurrying out, but before he could ask a question I caught him by the throat and shook out of him all his little courage and most of his breath.

"Up these steps, quick," I said, dragging him up, and reaching the top I hammered and kicked at the door until some one came.

"In the devil's name what's this?" cried a voice threateningly, as the door was opened.

"Thank God it's you, Ivan," I said, more glad than I can tell to see him. "The mademoiselle; is she safe?"

"M. Denver!" he exclaimed, in profound astonishment.

"Mademoiselle Helga, man, tell me, is all well?"

"Yes, monsieur, but what——"

"Thank God for that," I interrupted, the sense of relief filling me with indescribable delight.

"How do you come here, monsieur?" he asked. "And who——" he paused to peer into Drexel's white face. "M. Drexel, Great Lord of the Skies, what has happened?"

Helga was safe, and for me at that moment the whole world held no other matter of concern. But there was much to do, for which even the ecstasy of that knowledge could not wait.

"Take this treacherous snake, and have him kept safe somewhere until we can question him. And now——"

"What has happened, Ivan?" It was Helga's voice from above stairs, and hearing it, I smiled and caught my breath.

"M. Denver is here, mademoiselle," said Ivan.

"M. Denver?" in a tone of intense surprise. "Where?" The voice was nearer. She was coming to me.

"Yes, I am here, mademoiselle;" and I went to meet her.

On catching sight of me she stopped as if aghast.

"I don't look pretty, I'm afraid," I said, with a laugh. "But it's about the best show I can make for the moment."

Her eyes were now full of sweet concern.

"You have been in great trouble?" she said.

"Nothing's the matter that a bath and a clothes brush won't cure. But it's been a near thing."

146

"Tell me."

"I will, everything; but not now. Let me see you presently; there is some work to be done first. You will have to leave here; go and get ready."

"Leave here? I cannot. I must not."

"The place is known to Kalkov's police and to Vastic's friends. There has been hell's work; but you will be safe now."

I drew Ivan aside then and told him what I knew and surmised, and how I proposed to act. My idea was that he should take some of the servants down into the cellars with him; let the men who were expected enter one by one, seize them and make them prisoners.

Ivan was the man of all men I would have chosen for such a task. He possessed enormous strength and a courage equal to any demands that could be made upon it; I knew I could leave the affair safely in his hands.

When I had explained my wishes and seen him start, I went to question Drexel. He was in a condition of abject terror, and was to me such a repulsive creature that I hurried my examination of him.

"If you know how to speak the truth, I advise you to do it now. I know much about you and your doings, and if I find you lying to me I shall denounce you as a traitor to the men you were to have met here. And you know what to expect at their hands." I gave him a second to chew this, and then asked: "Now, whose spy are you, police or these men?"

"Neither. I have not come to help in this thing; I have not on my soul: I know nothing of them."

"Why are you here?"

"I came to get the papers from Mademoiselle Helga for Prince Kalkov."

"Oh, you are his agent, eh? How did you get in?"

"I was told to meet a woman in the square who would tell me what to do to get in." This might be true, for I had seen the two together. "I expected to find the house deserted."

"Who gave you your instructions?"

"Prince Kalkov himself. If I refused, he threatened me with the mines, monsieur."

"For what?"

"As a Nihilist."

"How did you get to the Prince?"

No answer.

I repeated the question.

"I went to clear myself," he said slowly and with hesitation.

"To offer yourself as a spy, you mean?" I replied sternly.

"I was a suspect, and I wanted to clear myself."

"And he told you you could clear yourself by getting these papers. I think I understand you. He told you also that mademoiselle would be assassinated, and that you could do your present work safely."

"On my soul, no. I had no thought of that. I had not. I was told she would be arrested."

"Who gave the information to these men?"

"I don't know, monsieur; indeed, I don't. I don't know who they are. I was told only police would be here. You can kill me if you will, but that is true."

I was disposed to believe him, and to regard him as a mere tool of Kalkov, sent to the house as being likely to know where to look for the papers; and in this case he knew too little to be of much help to me.

It was quite consistent with Kalkov's methods that he should use Drexel for the purpose he had described; and although there were discrepancies in the statement, I did not think it worth while to waste valuable time in interrogating him any further.

What we had now to think about was the vital question of Helga's escape, and I left the miserable wretch, glad to be out of his presence, and went to urge upon Helga the necessity of immediate flight.

CHAPTER XXII

FLIGHT

AS I hurried out from Drexel, intending to try and find means to render myself more presentable by getting rid of some of my grime, I found Helga waiting for me.

"I am all mud," I said apologetically.

"I am all impatience, and that is worse," she returned.

"Let me get rid of some of this;" and I spread out my hands and glanced down at my clothes, and looked up to find her smiling. "You can't tell how glad I am to see that," I added.

"You will see no smiles if you keep me waiting. I will forgive the dirt if you will only tell me."

"I could tell you more comfortably if we were en route for the frontier."

"Perhaps we shall be soon. Come," and she led me into a room, all dirty as I was.

"Disaster is easy to tell. Prince Kalkov knows everything about your plans, your name, your real part in Boreski's business, your fight against him—everything;" and as shortly as I could I told her all I knew and had learnt from the Prince.

She listened with scarcely an interruption, and when I finished sat thinking with pursed lips and gathered brows.

"It was very clever and very devilish," she said. "And for the time it means failure. You are right. I must fly, and that to-night."

"I am glad you see that."

"I have had to do it before—for a time. But I shall, of course, come back. I am not beaten. Flight is only one of the tactics in the fight I am waging. I shall never cease to fight until I win or they kill me. But he has beaten me for the time, and now that he knows my motive, he will be harder to fight than ever."

"It is I who have ruined you by betraying this place through my stupid blundering."

"Ah, I had not thought of that," she said, turning and smiling to me. "You will have suffered. It was a mistake, but it would have made no difference in the end. With the new clues which the Duchess Stephanie and this Drexel could give him, the Prince would have found me here. I should not have waited for him indeed, so that by warning me now you have more than made good the mistake."

"Do you think Boreski has told him anything?"

"No, not Boreski; I am sure of him. It is Drexel. A man when he is afraid for his life is a contemptible creature. But it is his nature," she said scornfully. "I knew it and knew him. I used him as a tool, and when a tool breaks in your hand, you are fortunate if you are not hurt."

"The sooner we start the better." But she was thinking and appeared not to hear me.

"I shall have to begin again," she said, with quiet resolution. "It is no new experience. I have had to do it two or three times before. My next attempt shall be better planned. Each time I do better—learning from my failures. Next time I shall win."

"When shall we start?" I asked, as she paused.

"We? If you are wise and take my advice, you will go to your Ambassador, tell him frankly all that has occurred, and get his help."

"And if I am not wise?" I sought her eyes and we both smiled, and she sighed.

"No, no, you must not."

"You know that I shall, Helga. Let us be frank."

"You wish me to be frank?" and she looked up calmly.

"Why not?"

"Then I would rather you did not attempt to accompany me."

"Do you mean to leave me in the lurch?"

"Don't," she cried, with a little wince of pain.

"I didn't mean that—but you know what I do mean."

"You know nothing can come of it."

"Call it nothing or something, it is just all in all to me."

"Please!" she said, almost pleadingly.

"I will have no mercy when you speak of parting."

"But I mean it. You must not come with me. I am stronger alone."

"Why?"

"You can be very stupid—when you wish," she cried, with another smile.

"Why?" I repeated. "Why stronger alone?"

"Because—ah, you know."

"May I not wish to hear you say it?"

She looked up steadily, and said in a quiet, firm tone—

"Because when you are with me I weaken in my purpose."

"That is just my object. I hope to win you from it altogether."

"It is impossible. You must not go with me."

"You wish never to see me again?"

"How cruel you can be!" Then defiantly, "Yes, I do wish it."

"Very well," I cried decidedly, as I rose. "Then I will go." I paused, and she started and gave me a glance in which surprise and pain were blended. I went to the door, and turning, saw she had paled slightly. I waited for her to speak.

"I—I am glad." The tone was very low, and her lips faltered.

"Yes, I have put up with it long enough. I can bear it no longer."

A quick questioning, half-indignant light was in her eyes as she rose.

"You can bear it no longer. I am sorry——"

A laugh from me checked the words on her lips.

"I have never been so dirty in my life. I must wash."

She turned away with a toss of the head.

"You treat it as a jest—at such a time."

"When I am earnest you won't take me seriously—you won't take me at all! indeed, it seems. But in any case you can't travel with

150

a man who looks like a tramp. I am going, as I was saying, to try and get clean again."

She turned then, and there was neither pain nor surprise on her face, only relief and intense gladness.

"I thought you were in earnest." It was only a smiling reproach.

"I am always in earnest where you are concerned." I took a step or two towards her. "And you are glad?"

"I am ashamed of my weakness."

"A weakness of which such a smile as that is a fitting confession."

"I hate myself for being weak at all," she cried in protest.

"It would be worse if you hated the cause of it. But now it is my turn to be weak, and to lean on you. I have no clothes to travel in."

"We can help you there. We have many disguises here."

"A travelling coat is all I need, and an idea of how we are to leave."

"I have always found the simplest is the best. If you are right about the Prince, he will have given no orders for either you or myself to be watched, and the railway will be open. The mail leaves at ten o'clock; open to tourists of all nations."

"And the frontier difficulties?"

She laughed.

"The Russian officials are the stupidest on earth. We shall, of course, have passports, and our papers being in order, all will be simple. A passport can be a very valuable friend, and those who need them always take care they are in order."

"I brought mine with me."

"Then you reckoned on my going?" she asked, smiling. "You count upon your influence with me, it seems."

"But Kalkov may communicate with the frontier folk?"

"How should he know and why? He has, no doubt, spies who are able to convey information to the brotherhood; but do you think they would return the favour? He will think they may be trusted to do as he wished to us, and when he hears of the failure we shall be beyond his reach."

It was an ingenious thought and probably correct.

"Good," I said. "You see how you help me. We are stronger together. We will get ready."

I went first in search of Ivan, and heard from him that our plan had succeeded entirely, and that the men who had come in quest of Helga had all been secured.

With his assistance I soon got rid of the traces of the evening's work, and when I saw Helga again she was ready for the start.

"About Madame Korvata?" I asked, suddenly remembering her.

151

"She has gone to the station for our tickets. She went long ago, before you spoke to me and while you were with Drexel."

I looked at her and smiled.

"Then you had made up your mind before—before what you said to me?"

She flushed slightly and her eyes brightened.

"I—I foresaw what I should probably have to do," she answered, and laughed softly. "You see, I knew I must go."

"And that I should not let you go alone. I did not see, but I do now."

"It is time to start, I think;" and she turned away.

Helga had indeed concluded all the arrangements, thinking of every detail with all a woman's eye for small things. Madame Korvata was not to travel with us, but to follow later. Ivan was to remain and see to the difficulties in regard to the presence of the men in the house, and then go into hiding until he heard from Helga.

The whole affair was just cut and dried, as though a flight from the police were an ordinary incident of life.

I felt abominably nervous, I admit; disposed to look for spies and police at every turn. But Helga was as cool as if we had been in the States, and were running up from New York to Saratoga for a few days' change of air.

"There is only one point of possible danger yet—the police may have a spy somewhere near at hand. I doubt it, because the Prince will rely upon Drexel, and knows that if his spy were seen, the plot against us would fail. But I have taken care. There is a house in the square here where the people are constant travellers. Our carriage is there, and we shall leave here unobserved, and pretend to come out of that house."

"Is such a thing likely to trick them?"

"You smile; but it is just these little simple acted lies which make all the difference. Spies are trained to believe what they see; no more."

We did as Helga had said, and whether or not we were seen I cannot say; but I saw no one, and we found not the least difficulty with the railway officials, who were indeed exceedingly courteous to the young handsome French widow, Madame de Courvaix, the name conspicuously written upon Helga's luggage.

The cars were well filled, and we were not alone in our compartment, so that I thought we had better speak very little. But that was not Helga's intention. She gave me a very meaning look, with a glance toward our fellow-passengers, and began to chatter at once, with all the vivacity of a Parisian.

152

"I am glad they did not come to see us off," she said, as soon as the train started. "Train good-byes are so inane."

"Sometimes they are."

"Yet I think the General should have come, and young Lablache from the Embassy. He promised me. A ball-room promise, of course;" and she laughed merrily and threw her hands up.

"Lablache? Do I know him?"

"Know him? Not by name. He is that dark handsome man who was so nice about the flowers, and at whom somebody I know, a stupid, jealous somebody, looked daggers;" and she made a pretty grimace at me.

"Oh, that fellow!" I growled.

"He is coming to Paris next month, and has promised to call;" and then we plunged into a conversation about a wholly imaginary set of people, in the course of which Helga managed most adroitly to include a purely fictional history of herself, with side-lights upon our relationship as an engaged couple.

Having done that, she settled herself in her corner, said she was going to sleep, and advised me to do the same; and as I was putting the rugs about her, she managed to whisper a sentence which gave me food for thought all through the night.

"The woman's a spy. Be careful."

As she said it she laughed gaily, and in a few minutes closed her eyes and appeared to sleep soundly.

But there was no sleep for me. I forced myself to keep my eyes closed, a continuous effort that was infinitely taxing; and during the long, weary hours, I think I must have pretty well exhausted in thought all the possible dangers that might result from the presence of so dangerous a fellow-traveller.

Helga was more than equal to the emergency, however. In the early hours of dawn she woke, or pretended to awake, cross and fretful, and roused me.

"How soundly you sleep," she said crossly. "How can you in this abominable stuffy atmosphere? Let the window down, please."

"I think it's very chilly," I said, not understanding her.

"Am I nobody?" she cried, with a stamp of the foot and a shrug of the shoulders. "Shall I do it myself?"

I put it down a little way.

"Wide open, I mean," she said angrily.

"It's very cold," I protested; and indeed the cold, keen air came rushing in and made me put my collar up.

"Nonsense, I'm stifled. Wide open, I said. That's better," as I put it right down.

Our fellow-travellers stirred, as well they might indeed, for the temperature ran down swiftly several degrees. The man having heard Helga's request was too polite to interfere, and suffered in silence, drawing his wraps closer round him.

But the woman had no such scruples, and after a while asked me pretty sharply to close the window.

"It is open by my request, madame," declared Helga in a very angry tone. The woman grumbled to the man, and at her instigation he appealed to me.

This was Helga's opportunity, and she and the woman began an altercation, which lasted for several miles, and was waged with such bitterness that had they been men they would have come to blows. Helga's fluency was too much for her opponent; besides, we were masters of the situation; so that the window remained open, and we shivered in victory.

At the first place where we stopped the quarrel began again, and the woman appealed to the officials.

They were sorry, but could do nothing.

The conductor offered a solution, however. There was an empty coupé on the train; would Helga remove to it? Certainly she would not. In her beloved France people could have a window up or down as they pleased, and she was not going to yield her privileges for all the cantankerous old women in Russia put together.

This settled it, and with many a parting shot at France and Frenchwomen in general, and Helga in particular, the two got out and followed the conductor to the other carriage.

As soon as we were out of the station Helga, who had kept up her show of vociferous and gesticulating anger, laughed.

"Do put the window up, please. I'm nearly frozen to death. I hope I haven't given you a cold."

I closed the window and laughed.

"I thought you were in earnest at first," I said.

"Thank you; but I am not quite such a crochetty, ill-tempered individual, even after a sleepless night of doubt in a railway carriage."

"Sleepless?"

"I was planning that little coup all the time, of course. She suspects nothing, or she would have frozen to death before she had left the carriage. She is new to her work, so I could take a risk."

"You are a wonderful actress."

"I have had a long training, and life and liberty are bigger incentives than any salary," she answered thoughtfully. "Now we can sleep safely for two hours, and then we stop for breakfast."

When we reached the station she said she would not leave the

154

carriage, so I fetched her some, and after I had had mine, I strolled up and down, smoking.

Presently she called me.

"Something has happened, and whatever it is, the officials are uneasy and excited. Go and hear what those two are talking about;" and she pointed to a couple of men, one of whom held a despatch in his hand, which both were discussing eagerly.

I strolled over to them and caught my breath quickly as I heard one of them say something about Nihilists and supposed flight.

I went up to them and put a casual question about our train being late, intending to follow it up with others, when some one exclaimed in English:

"Just like my infernal luck!" Recognizing the voice, I turned, and the speaker clapped me on the shoulder and then seized my hand.

"What, Harper, old fellow! What on earth brings you here?" It was an old Harvard chum, Frank Siegel.

The two officials glanced at us, and moved off as we shook hands.

"Rather; what are you doing?"

"I? Oh, I'm out for the Frisco Eagle—the Screecher. I've been round the world for them. Trotting home, and, like my infernal luck, I've just missed a scoop in Petersburg."

"What is it?"

"What is it? By gee, it's just what I'd have given my ears to get. A big Nihilist raid. No end of arrests; but the biggest birds are flown. May be on this very train."

"I heard nothing of it, and I came from Petersburg."

"Are we on the same train? My, that's bully. Say, I'll get my traps and join you."

"I'm not alone, Frank."

"Don't you worry about that; I shan't mind your friends. I'm used to all sorts of mixed company;" and with a grin at this gibe he ran off.

I went back to Helga and told her what I had heard.

"Can you trust your friend?" she asked, after a short pause.

"Oh yes, as myself."

"Then let him come."

"And you?"

"I have already had to explain our relationship once!" she answered, with a glance.

"But if I tell him we're engaged——" I paused.

"Well?" with a challenging smile.

"It will have to be in earnest."

155

"Well?"

"Then the sooner he comes the better," I said.

"We must know the news, even if we make concessions to learn it."

"I guess my news will surprise him as much as his will us."

And we were both laughing happily, despite the ominous turn in things, when Siegel came running up and bundled his wraps into the carriage, as I introduced him to Helga.

CHAPTER XXIII

AT THE FRONTIER

FRANK SIEGEL was one of those enthusiastic journalists to whose zeal the press of America owes its distinctive position. Enterprise, unhampered by too much discretion, was the gospel which had been hammered into him. Be first, down the other fellow, make the scoop, get the facts, discreetly if possible, but get them, serve hot for the public taste, and let all else go hang. The editor and the public will forgive anything except a beat for the opposition show.

Siegel lived up to this. All the world and everything in it was to him so much copy; and he looked at everything with an eye, and that a very sharp one, for its newspaper possibilities.

When off duty his eye could also appreciate a beautiful face, and he was charmed by Helga, who did her utmost to win her way into his favour.

In particular, she was sympathetic in regard to his present disappointment at having left Petersburg at the moment of a Nihilist trouble.

"I'd give a sackful of dollars to get at the bottom of a Nihilist show," he exclaimed. "Either side, Government or the other. What a country this would be for a pressman, if they weren't so tight lipped! I've sent some stuff across, but of course I've had to pad it a lot."

"What have you heard about this, M. Siegel?" asked Helga.

"The conductor gave it away to me. There was a telegram telling him to look out for a woman on the train—and a man, too, he thought; but he wasn't clear. It seems a swoop was made on a haunt

156

last night, and a lot of arrests there and elsewhere followed. But they wanted the woman most, and she'd gone."

"Oh!" I murmured, and Helga and I exchanged glances.

"Lord, what asses those Russian police must be. Imagine what a mess we should have if we muddled our press inquiries as they do their business. They should apprentice a few of their fellows to the Screecher, and let 'em learn the art of making beats."

"Beats, M. Siegel?" asked Helga, puzzled.

He explained the enormous virtues of exclusive news, and gave her a telling illustration.

"If this were the States, which thank God it isn't—I can say that safely as none of us are Russians—what would happen? Probably we should have known all about this raid before it was ordered; but assume we hadn't, and it caught us by surprise. Well, we should have had some one on the spot right there, and the moment we heard the birds had flown we should have wired our men to watch every train—this one for instance, most likely with a recognizable description of the fugitives. Say, Harper, wouldn't it be bully to do the trick with no machinery and spot them on the train. What a scoop!" and he laughed pleasantly.

"The fugitives might not relish such a press," said I, with more meaning than he divined.

"I'm going to have a try," he replied. "Do you remember Marvyn, Harold Marvyn, at Harvard; that thin dark chap we used to call the spectre? He's at the Embassy here, and I've wired him to wire me a description of them if he can get it. I'm going to look for 'em at the frontier, and if I don't find 'em there, I'm off back to the capital to look up things. I wish I'd never come away; worse luck."

"You would like to hand them over to the police, M. Siegel?" asked Helga.

"Gee wiss, no, madame. If we were in the States, yes; but here, what are the police to me? I'm thinking of the Screecher and the interview I could get." Helga laughed and said:

"And being in Russia, monsieur, if you interfered you would probably be clapped into one of their gaols as an accomplice."

"Say, Harper," he cried, turning to me, "wouldn't that be just lovely! Gee, think of the headlines. Russia's prisons from the inside. I could make half a column of them. Ah, I wish it could be worked," and he sighed.

"You have some queer ambitions, Siegel," I said. "You might find it easier to get in than to get out again. There's Siberia, you know—not exactly a pleasure resort, either."

"I came through there. Looks all right from the outside; what

157

they let you see of it, you know; but I'd like to scratch the surface off."

"You might not have far to look for the fugitive Nihilists, M. Siegel," said Helga steadily.

"Don't excite his zeal," I put in hastily.

"Can you help me, really?" he cried.

"I am one and M. Denver is the other," she replied calmly.

He stared at her and then at me in amazement, and laughed.

"You're pulling my leg," he said.

"I don't know what that means, but what I say is true," replied Helga.

He turned serious then, being convinced.

"Just light the gas for me, Harper," he said.

"It is true. We are both Nihilist suspects and are making a bolt for the frontier;" and I went on to tell him something of what had got us into the mess.

"Can I use it?" he asked, his first thought naturally, for the Screecher.

"No, not our part; but if you care to take a hand you can use your own experience."

"It's the chance of a lifetime. Of course I will," he declared at once, adding characteristically: "I may do you a turn at the same time."

Then Helga told her plan and we discussed it together. Siegel's enthusiasm rose and fell as the risk of his being arrested in mistake appeared greater or less. Indeed he was just as anxious to be caught as I was to escape; and in the end we came to an arrangement.

Siegel was to take my place as Harper C. Denver and to carry my passport, and I was to take his. Helga was to remain Madame de Courvaix and to act independently of us both; and we were all to travel in separate carriages and endeavour to pass the barriers at the frontier alone.

"I am candid with you, M. Siegel," said Helga; "I think you will be stopped. M. Denver's name is known and we ought to have had another passport. I think I shall get through, and I'm sure he will. And that is my principal concern."

"I'll try and act up to the part," said Siegel gleefuly.

"If you are stopped, I shall not attempt to get through," I said to Helga.

"But that is just what you must do. You must go first. Think, if we are both stopped, how disastrous it may be. You will take these with you;" and she handed me the papers which had played so great a part in the past few days. "With these, and your freedom and your Embassy at your back, you will gain the Emperor's presence, and then his friendship for you should do the rest. It is our one sound chance."

"But it looks like deserting you," I protested. "You ask too much. It's cowardly."

"What could you do if we were both detained? You must do this. You must. And you must be the first to pass the barrier."

"Say, Harper, you can give the thing the necessary colour by asking for that wire from Marvyn for me."

I gave in, reluctantly; and at Dunaberg, the next stop, feeling something like a coward I left the carriage to find a seat elsewhere.

"Courage, my friend," said Helga, giving me her hand with a smile. "Courage, and we shall make the rest of the journey to Berlin safely and together."

"Pray God it will be so," I answered.

"This is just bully," cried Siegel in the highest spirits. "See me do the conspirator when you two are through. I hope to glory they won't let me pass."

During the remaining run to the frontier I was profoundly anxious and miserable. I knew Helga would not have taken such a step as to bring Siegel into the matter if she had not felt there was real danger for us both; and that she gave into my care the papers which were of such vital import, showed that she regarded her own chances as very doubtful.

I had unbounded confidence in her wit and ready resource. She would get through if any one could; but the gate was a very narrow one. If the new development came from Kalkov, as I could not doubt, she was so well known that a personal description of her would be sent in full.

And then I perceived the shrewdness of her present manoeuvre. Siegel and I were sufficiently alike for a written description of one to pass for that of the other. We were both clean shaven, somewhere about the same build and height and colour; and when I read his description in his identity paper—drawn up for the purpose of his long journey through Russian territory—I saw it was quite possible to apply it to me.

When we reached Vilna the official preparations began. A number of men were at the depot and made a careful scrutiny of the passengers, and eventually all of them boarded the train. One got into the compartment where I sat with Siegel's writing case open on my knee.

He watched me write for a time and then asked me for a light.

I handed him Siegel's matchbox—a curio he had picked up in China—and made a commonplace remark in execrable Russian. I had heard Siegel's Russian.

159

"Monsieur speaks French?" he asked me politely, returning the box.

"Un poo, pas bocoo." He recognized the accent immediately and smiled. "Je suis Americain; San Francisco, voo savvy."

"German, perhaps?" he ventured.

"Ya wohl, etwas; aber Englisch am besten;" and I laughed.

"I speak English," he answered, "and have been in England."

"Been in America?"

"No, sir."

"Ah!" and I smiled indulgently as if he had missed Heaven.

"You are a writer?" he asked next with pleasant inquisitiveness.

"Yes. I'm Siegel of the Screecher; which means that," I added in reply to his look of bewilderment, and gave him one of Siegel's cards. "Screecher is American for Eagle," I explained. "And what are you?"

But he was not communicative. He smiled and gestured deprecatingly, as if he were of no importance.

"Just a private individual."

"Travelled much?"

"No, not far. To England and in France and in Germany."

"Ah, I've just been round the world;" and I rattled away with a general description of many things I did not know and many places I had not seen; but I took care to say nothing about any part of European Russia.

What did I think of Petersburg? I had only stayed there long enough to see my friend Harold Marvyn at the Embassy. If I'd known I'd have stayed longer; and I skated on to the thin ice of the Nihilist raid, playing Siegel's part as he had performed for us. I ended by saying I was expecting a telegram from the Embassy at Kovna—could he tell me how to get it quickly?

He could and did and offered to help me. On this I became professionally confidential. I told him my wish to know more of the Nihilist business, and asked him whether it would probably be worth my while to return to Petersburg; and so managed that he was led to ask all about me and my newspaper. Then I showed him enough to convince him of my good faith.

I watched him gradually lose interest in me and my concerns; and I knew from this that any suspicions or hopes about me, with which he had entered the carriage were dissipated. I was not a Nihilist; no credit was to be gained from detecting and arresting me; and he wished to bother himself no more about me.

We were in this stage of the proceedings, and I was wondering whether Siegel had also been interviewed and if so with what results, when my companion said we were close to Kovna and that I

160

had better put my things together. He was kind enough to assist me and I noticed that he was at great pains to see as many of my papers as he could and to read them. I gave him ample opportunity; and an easy-going fool he no doubt thought me in consequence.

At Kovna his confidence in my good faith communicated itself to the other officials and my path was made easy in consequence. He walked with me to the barrier; a significant glance or two passed between him and the officials; a very cursory look was taken at my passport and I was through.

I had not risked looking for either Helga or Siegel; but when I had passed through I hung about and soon made a discovery which filled me with concern.

A great distinction was made between the men and the women. Scarcely any difficulty was made in regard to the men; some sharp glances and a few questions at the most. But all the women between twenty and fifty years of age were taken away for separate examination.

I saw Helga come up, hand over her passport, and submit to the close and searching scrutiny with a kind of impatient frankness that was admirable acting. But she was led away like the rest for further examination of her papers.

I was waiting with an anxiety which can be imagined for her to appear again, when I was witness of the little comedy in which Siegel played the chief part.

He had put up his coat collar and drawn down his cap so that as little of his face as possible was to be seen, and he came striding along casting quick suspicious glances on all sides, much after the manner of the conventional conspirator of burlesque.

In this way he tried to thrust his way past the officials. Any one with the faintest sense of humour would have seen he was fooling; but humour is not the strong point of Russian officialism. The men by the barrier whispered together as he approached and then clustered close like wasps round an over ripe peach.

"Your passport, monsieur, if you please," said one, stopping him.

"Passport, what do you mean?" he asked in a truly cosmopolitan language.

"Your passport; you know what that is," said the man trying French.

"Haven't one," he answered. He told me afterwards he had intentionally torn up mine, thinking he had better leave the officials to connect him with me. "Americans don't want passports."

"Your name, monsieur."

"Shan't tell you. I'm an American, that's enough. Don't you interfere with me," he said threateningly; and made as if to go on.

Half a dozen hands were thrust out instantly to stop him. One man tried to see more of his face and was glancing at a paper. He whispered something to his colleague, who asked—

"Will you raise your hat, monsieur?"

"No, I won't."

"You cannot pass, monsieur."

"We'll see about that;" and he drew his hands from his pockets and clenched his fists. I really feared he was going to show fight.

"Will you step this way, if you please, monsieur?" said an elderly man coming forward. Apparently a man in higher authority.

"What for?" asked Siegel brusquely.

"There has probably been some mistake which I can put right for you," was the suavely spoken reply. "You can then resume your journey."

"All right," said Siegel, after a moment's pause; and the two went off followed by several of the other men.

"Do you think it is?" asked one of the officials at the barrier of his colleague.

"I'm sure it is," was the reply. "He'll resume his journey all right, but—" he jerked his thumb backwards and winked. And the incident was closed so far as the public were concerned.

The women passengers were now beginning to come out from a separate door; but I saw nothing of Helga and my hopes for her safety ebbed as the number of the women increased.

Some of them were speaking of their examination, and I heard to my dismay that in more than one case there had been a most rigorous personal search. They were loud in protest at the indignity.

"She actually made me take down my hair to see if I had anything concealed in it," said a German woman to a friend, as the two passed me. "You never saw such a disgraceful scene."

Still there was no sign of Helga; and keen though I was for news of her, when we were told the train would soon start, I dared not linger lest I should draw attention and suspicion upon myself.

I was in a fever of anxiety during the last few minutes as I stood by the door of the car straining my hungry eyes in vain for a sight of her.

Then the detective who had been on the train with me came along, his face wearing a satisfied expression. He caught sight of me, smiled and nodded as he passed, then stopped, turned and came up and spoke.

"Bon voyage, monsieur. Then you are not going back?"

"I'm still in two minds. But I suppose it's nothing serious."

162

I spoke as indifferently as I could.

"Oh no—not for your country. I don't know, though. I could give you some news."

"I'm always ready for that," I replied with an eager smile.

"I'm a police agent," he said, as if the admission would astound me. I was therefore promptly astounded.

"You!" I cried. "Impossible. Why, I thought——" and left the thought to his imagination.

"What did you think?" He chuckled.

"I put you down for a merchant or a landowner. But a police agent!" and I waved my hand in amazement. "I've always heard you are the smartest men in Europe. Now I know it. A police agent!" I was lost in wonderment.

"Do you know what I thought you were?"

"You didn't take me for another, I suppose?" It was a joke and he enjoyed it and laughed.

"No, I thought you were a Nihilist!"

"A Nihilist! Well, that's worse than ever. An American a Nihilist?"

The thing was incredulous as my tone showed.

"They come from all countries, monsieur. I was looking for a countryman of yours, a Mr. Damper—no, Denver."

"Great Scott. You don't mean it!"

"We caught him, too. He was in the train; and a woman too—one of the most dangerous Nihilists in the Empire."

"A woman! Oh, you police agents are wonderful! But do you mean that women are in this?"

"They are often the worst. She is a pretty woman, too, this one. You'd better get in, monsieur, there's the signal—unless you think of going back to Petersburg."

"When is the next train?"

"Starts in an hour from now. But you can catch the return mail at Insterburg."

"Perhaps that'll be better. I can get my baggage. If I do come back I shall look out for you," I said, as I got into the carriage.

"I am going back at once to Vilna. Bon voyage, monsieur."

"Good-bye. A pretty woman you say? Will it go hard with her, do you suppose?" I asked in a compassionate tone as the train moved.

He shook his head and smiled significantly.

"She'll go to the mines, if what they say is true."

That was what that infernal old Kalkov had said; and he was making his words good.

And it was from that I had to save her.

163

Thank God she had been shrewder than I; and that I was free to make my effort.

If I had been in Siegel's place—and then despite the tragedy I thought of the comedy and smiled.

But the smile was very fleeting.

CHAPTER XXIV

THE FRESH CAMPAIGN

IT was fortunate for my peace of mind in the hours which followed Helga's arrest that I did not know a number of grim facts that afterwards came to my knowledge about Russian methods in dealing with certain classes of offenders.

Her case was bad enough at the best. Prince Kalkov was one of the most dangerous men in the Empire to have for an enemy; and that he was Helga's bitter enemy he had shown already. Her secret attack had threatened his influence and position and had thus roused him to vigorous measures of self-defence.

As I recalled my last interview with him, I saw now that he had deliberately goaded me to passion and then let drop the hint of possible escape in order to drive me to make the attempt which he had planned to end fatally for me. And in thus goading me he had shown his hand against her so openly, because he believed I should not live to speak of it.

I thought I could see something more, too. He had not scrupled first to use the brotherhood for his own purposes against Helga, and then had swooped down upon them at the moment they were serving his end and had made the raid upon them. In this way he had probably calculated not only to demonstrate the vigilance of his agents but also to secure the silence of the men he had used, should anything compromising to him transpire.

As the result of that raid he had found that Helga had slipped through his net and had taken the papers with her; and had learnt from Drexel no doubt, that I had been with her at the house.

The hue and cry had followed which had led to the arrest of Helga and, as he had no doubt been informed, of myself as well.

The net had been cast wide and, as both the birds had

seemingly been caught in its meshes, he would probably feel easy enough in mind.

There was only one point in which he had failed. He had not secured the precious papers; and I had to consider what he was likely to do in consequence.

I came to the conclusion that under the circumstances although he might possibly see Helga to question her, he was not likely to see Siegel. In my last interview he had threatened to have me charged with Vastic's murder, and I had left him to do it; and this was no doubt the charge which Siegel would find himself called upon to face. He would have no difficulty whatever in meeting it, of course, the moment he chose to open his lips; but as he wished to learn at first hand the secrets of the Russian prison, he would not speak for a while.

I should thus have time to operate, and my course was fairly clear. I had to get to the Emperor himself with my story before Kalkov had any suspicion that I was not safely under lock and key. If he knew I was still at liberty he would put insuperable difficulties in my way, as he had before.

I left the cars at Insterburg accordingly and caught the limited back to the capital. The journey was without incident. I was recognized at Kovna; but no questions save those prompted by curiosity were asked me.

My friend the police agent had spoken about me to one or two of the officials, and what he had said had apparently been very much in my favour. The elderly man whom I had seen lead Siegel away at the moment when he seemed about to show fight, was particularly gracious to me; and after a general query or so, he asked—

"Was the American whom we arrested here a friend of yours, monsieur?"

"Of course, in a sense all Americans are friends," I replied evasively.

"Do you know his name?"

"There are some sixty millions of us Americans;" and I laughed. "Are you sure he was an American?" I preferred to do the questioning.

"He would say nothing, not even his name."

"Could I see him? I might by chance know him. A newspaper man gets to know a lot of faces."

"He has been sent back to the capital. If I can venture to warn you——" he paused and looked at me.

"I shall be only too glad of a hint."

165

"I should not seek him out then, if I were you. We know little about him, but in our instructions the charge is an ugly one."

I laughed.

"Well, when we Americans take a thing up we generally do it in earnest, whatever it is. But I don't believe any American would ever turn Nihilist."

"Yet you have had Anarchists in your country. Some of your Presidents have been assassinated, monsieur; is it not so?"

"By madmen or wild European scum; not by honest Americans."

He raised his eyebrows, smiled, and shook his head.

"The disease is the same in all countries. This man is a murderer, monsieur," he answered slowly and emphatically. "He was escaping."

Poor Siegel! I could have laughed again; but did not. I was appropriately shocked, almost horror-struck, at the news.

"It is terrible," I said, gravely. "One cannot wish to help such a criminal as a murderer, even if he be one's own countryman;" and with that we parted.

The one item of fact I had gathered was that the prisoners had been sent back to Petersburg; and in the hours of my journey I had ample time to consider my plans, and had them pretty well cut and dried when I reached the capital.

I chose a quiet hotel for the night, registered myself as Frank Siegel of San Francisco, and after a supper served in my own rooms, I went straight to bed.

I took all the precautions I could to avoid observation, of course, as I had to face the double risk of recognition by the Nihilists and by any of Prince Kalkov's agents.

In the morning I commenced my work. I drove to the American Embassy and sent up Siegel's card to Harold Marvyn.

I was shown up to his room and as I entered he jumped up from his table and came toward me, with hand extended. Then he stopped suddenly and with a very sharp look said—

"They brought me Mr. Siegel's card."

"Do you recognize me?" I asked.

"Good heavens, you are Harper C. Denver."

"Yes." And we shook hands. He was obviously perplexed and stood fingering Siegel's card.

"I'm afraid I've puzzled you; but for the moment Siegel and I have changed personalities. It's a queer show. But he's in prison and I'm here to tell you all about it."

Marvyn was never a very demonstrative man and his diplomatic training had increased his capacity for self-restraint. But my quiet statement was too much for him. He went back to his seat, and as I drew a chair close to his table, he stared at me, his thin sallow face all lines of surprise, and letting out a long breath in a sort of mixed sigh and whistle he exclaimed—

"Well, I'm gormed."

I remembered his expression at Harvard.

"I haven't heard that since you left Harvard," I said, with a smile.

"But what does it all mean? What are you doing here? How is that—here, show me."

"It means a most infernal mess, which can all soon be put right, however, if I can keep my head and you can keep my secret."

"My dear Denver, I'll do anything in the world for you. It was your father got me into this, you know. But is it official?"

"It's a bit of everything, I think. But you give me your word not to repeat anything I tell you?"

"Of course I will."

"For one thing I want your people here to get me a personal audience with the Czar."

"The Czar! Well, that's a pretty tall proposition as a start. But I daresay it can be done. We're on excellent terms with Prince Kalkov who arranges such things."

I laughed.

"But old Kalkov's just the man who must know nothing about it. He's the man I'm fighting; so I'll drop that part of the business."

"Fighting? How's that? Give me some facts."

"I think I'll begin backwards," and I told him about Siegel's arrest; and then little by little most of the story.

"Don't tell me anything about the contents of those papers," he said. "It might be very inconvenient knowledge."

"I can't; I don't know them myself; but it's in regard to them I want your assistance. Of course I don't mean to compromise you in any way officially."

"I'm afraid you're trying to weave cloth of spider's webs with a hornet's sting for the shuttle, Denver. My advice to you in regard to those papers is—burn 'em."

"And if I were in your place here, I daresay I should; but you understand that officially you know nothing about them. All that I wish you to do is to receive for safe custody the property of an American citizen to be dealt with as that citizen desires."

"That's all very well, but if any fuss came and enquiries were made about them, think what a stink there might be," he objected nervously.

"I tell you for all I know to the contrary they may be mere

sheets of blank paper. I hand you two packets of valuable securities, that's all; and I ask you to accept instructions as to their disposition. You can surely do that? If an American can't get a trifle like that done for him in his own country's Embassy, it's a pretty pass."

"And what are your instructions?" he asked suspiciously.

"I shall either call here every day before twelve o'clock or send you a letter before that time, requesting you to hold them for a further twenty-four hours. If you do not see or hear from me, you are to hand them over to the person who produces a letter from me dated to-day, requesting you to deliver them to the bearer, and signed by me in this fashion: 'Harper Clarence Denver, sophomore, citizen of the United States.'"

"Who will present that letter?"

"What has that to do with the Embassy? It will be signed in that way to prevent any forgery."

"I think I can do that," he agreed after a pause.

"I know you can; and there is only one thing further. The day you part with them ask your friend, Prince Kalkov, in what prison he has ventured to lock me up, and use all the powers of the Embassy to find me. You may gamble on it that I shall need all the help you can afford."

"I don't like it, Denver, and that's the truth. I wish you'd let us take the thing up in the usual way."

"My dear fellow, that's just a sheer impossibility. I know where I'm walking in this thing. I mean to win right along. This is no mere bluff I'm putting up: I hold a straight flush."

I pressed the matter very insistently and in the end gained my point, although I should not have done so, had not Marvyn felt under a considerable obligation to me as the son of the man who had helped him, and whose influence could be depended upon to see him through any bother. He yielded with great reluctance. Still, he yielded, and that was all I needed.

"And what about Siegel?" he asked, when my point was settled and I had written the necessary letters and given into his charge the papers.

"You may safely wait until you hear from him or me. When the mistake is discovered they will be as anxious to get rid of him as he was that they should make it."

"He's a queer fellow."

"He's getting the 'copy' he wants."

"There may be a row about it," said Marvyn, who appeared to have a far scent for trouble.

"Only for newspaper purposes," I answered as I left.

I was in high spirits at my first success. I had planted the compromising papers where even Kalkov's iron hand would be powerless to reach them, and I had now only to complete the machinery by which they were to fall into the right hands if trouble came my way.

I drove to the Embassy of the Power chiefly concerned and asked for the man there whom Helga had mentioned to me. I sent up no name at first and consequently met with a courteous refusal and a request to put my business in writing.

Give my own name I could not just yet, so I sent up one of Siegel's cards, marking it on urgent private business. After some little farther trouble this had the requisite effect, and I was shown into the presence of a man some fifty years of age, thin and tall, with a military carriage, clean shaven, with one of those straight almost lipless mouths you see in men of secretive mind.

"Mr. Siegel?" he asked in English.

"Are we quite alone?"

His eyes asked me what I meant.

"You can see, sir," was what his lips said.

"Will you answer my question, please?" I persisted. I had my reasons; for there was a big screen in the room and I had heard things.

"You can rely upon everything being confidential."

I pointed to the screen and looked at him. He started.

"A screen always suggests draughts to me. Permit me to——"

"There is no need," he interposed quickly, as I was moving toward it. "It is usual to have a memorandum of matters that pass here."

"I am much obliged for the thoughtfulness, but I can trust my memory," I answered drily; and then he sent some one out of the room and himself folded the screen together.

"Now, Mr.—er—Siegel," he said referring to the card.

"I am not Mr. Siegel and have no connection with the press of any country. I wished to see you on something of extreme importance and of a vitally confidential nature. I used that name to gain this interview."

"And your own name?"

"Is for the moment of no concern. You would not know it, but will of course learn it if this interview ends as I wish."

"Will you be seated?" and he motioned to a chair.

I drew my chair close to his and waited.

"Yes?"

"I can speak more easily to you here;" and I pointed to the seat at his desk.

"You are mysterious, sir."

"No; only cautious. I don't intend to be overheard," I replied quietly. He took his seat then and turned to me a listening but impassive face.

"You had some negotiations recently in regard to certain papers?"

"Ah!" Recognition and interest now took the place of impassiveness.

"They have come into my possession."

"How?"

"That is of no consequence. I have them. And—" I paused and met his intent gaze—"they may find their way to you."

He thought rapidly.

"The price, sir?"

"You mean money? I am not for sale. I say they may find their way to you."

"I do not understand you."

"Yet my words speak my meaning."

"From whom do you come?"

"On my own initiative."

"Where are the papers?" and his eyes shot at me as if to pierce to my pockets.

"They are in perfectly safe keeping."

"What is it you wish?"

"I am in some personal danger—possibly great danger—and if anything should befall me, I intend those papers to come to you."

He saw my meaning in a flash.

"You intend to use that as a means to restrain those who threaten you?"

"Exactly." There was no change in his expression but I read his silence, and added: "You can get them in no other way."

He made up his mind then promptly.

"Your terms?"

"I ask little except absolute secrecy about myself. If you consent, I shall leave with you a letter to those who will upon receipt of it hand you documents which will tell you precisely where and how to get the papers you wish, and will be a full authority to secure their being handed to you. There are two sets of documents. One is for your use: the other you must give me a pledge to have placed in the hands of the Czar himself."

I did not tell him he would get the papers themselves from Marvyn, nor that they were actually at the American Embassy.

"If that is all why not give them me at once?"

"You will only present the letter I shall give you under certain conditions."

170

"Those are?"

"That on any day you fail either to see me or hear from me by noon."

"You ask nothing from us?"

"Nothing more than I have said."

"No assistance, should you get into this danger you anticipate."

"You could render none."

"It is very extraordinary."

"Your answer?"

"I accept your conditions, of course. But I wish you would give them me at once. We would find means to protect you."

"Thank you. That is impossible."

I wrote the letter in the terms I had agreed with Marvyn and handed it to him.

"My name you will see is Denver," I said.

"Mr. Marvyn, of your Embassy. I know him."

"Your pledge of secrecy must be kept, or the whole thing falls through. I have arranged that. The slightest breath, and the papers are lost to you."

"Does Mr. Marvyn know?"

"Mr. Marvyn knows no more about them than the secretary you sent out of the room. I have left with him the particulars which will enable you to get the papers."

"On your side, Mr. Denver, you will observe confidence?"

I smiled as I answered.

"If they are to fall into your hands, I shall be in a place where my silence will be very effectively secured."

"I do not ask about that," he said as I rose. "But you will render us a service we should never forget, Mr. Denver."

I smiled.

"You mean, I may do so. There's an 'if' in the matter, and I hope it will be the strongest word in the whole conversation."

I left him then to set about the still more difficult task of getting my audience with his Majesty.

CHAPTER XXV

THE LUCK WAVERS

I WAS very preoccupied with my plans as I left the Foreign Embassy, and, crossing the side path quickly, ran against a man, who turned, stared, started, and muttering some words I did not catch, passed on.

Something about him struck me as familiar, and I glanced after him with half a mind to follow and speak to him. But time was pressing. It was already mid-day, and I had yet to devise a means of getting at the Emperor; so I entered my carriage and drove back to the hotel.

The incident had served to revive my caution, however, and when I alighted I had a good look about me. There were but few people about, and none to take any notice of me; but while I still stood in the lobby, a drosky drove rapidly past, and in it was the man whom I had jostled some minutes before.

Obviously I had been followed; and having ordered my lunch to be sent to my rooms, I went up feeling vaguely uneasy and worried.

The man's face would obtrude itself into my thoughts, and my vain efforts to place him in my memory troubled me. In the last few crowded days I had seen such a number of different faces that my recollection of this one was lost in the crowd.

That any one should have recognized me at such a moment was annoying; and whoever the man might be, and whatever his object in following me, I foresaw the possibility of embarrassing complications, and even of dangerous ones.

Without interference from any one, the difficulties in the path of getting to the Czar's presence were of themselves likely to tax my ingenuity to the utmost. Even when I had been his guest in the Palace they had proved insuperable, and now they threatened to be no less troublesome. A hundred different suggestions occurred to me, only to be put on one side.

You cannot walk up to an Emperor's door, send in your card, and see him without any fuss; and if I was to succeed now, it would only be as a result of some ruse.

For this there was only one thing which might tell in my favour. I knew my way about the Palace, and on the night of my arrival I had been seen by, and my name was known to, one or two of the gentlemen-in-waiting. If I could get inside the building, therefore, I might by the use of a little impudence and ingenuity gain my end.

172

In this connection I had a stroke of luck. I learned from the papers that the Czar had returned late on the previous evening with his guest, the Crown Prince of Denmark; and I saw how to make use of this visit for my purpose.

The Crown Prince and his staff were staying in the Palace, and the fact of there being so many new faces to puzzle the officials would help me. I resolved to go to the Palace quite openly, ask for one of the Prince's staff, and while he was being sought, I proposed to lose myself somewhere in the building, and trust to my wits for the rest.

To ask openly for an audience of the Emperor would, of course, be useless, because, as Marvyn himself had admitted, all such requests were referred straight to Prince Kalkov.

I found a list of the members of the staff in a morning paper and picked out a name at random: that of a Colonel von Kramen: and over my lunch arranged the details of my venture. If I came actually face to face with him, I could easily use Siegel's connection with the Screecher to carry me through.

I fixed the time for my visit for about five in the afternoon. I knew the Czar's habit was to devote himself to matters of business for an hour or two from five o'clock; and if I could get my name before him then with a pressing request for an audience, I reckoned all the rest would be plain sailing.

I ordered a carriage to be ready by half-past four, and sat down to wait for the time to pass with such patience as I could command; and I was just finishing my cigar when the waiter interrupted me with an announcement that brought me to my feet in a moment.

"Your brother to see you, monsieur."

"My brother!" I exclaimed, and got no farther before the man who had followed me to the hotel rushed in with both hands extended and face beaming with smiles.

"Ah, Frank, my brother, my brother," he cried in broken English, and with a very effusive foreign manner.

I drew back and stared at him.

"I don't know you," I said.

The waiter stood staring at us in amused astonishment. The ways of these Americans were always droll, of course, to him.

"Oh, Frank, brother, why receive me thus coldly? Why this cruel estrangement? This freezing stare?" exclaimed my visitor as the waiter, after lounging a moment, went out and closed the door. Then the newcomer's manner changed. "Or am I mistaken, and is it—the Emperor?" the last sentence in a low, sly tone with a look of intense cunning.

"I don't know who the devil you are, but you've no business here anyway, so get out, right now," I said angrily.

He took no notice and stood staring at me with the same smile of cunning. Then shaking his head as if in reproach, he sat down.

"This is my room. Get out of it," I cried.

He did not move, so I crossed to the bell.

"Shall I call some one to pitch you out?"

He spread his hands and wagged his head.

"They will not do that."

"We'll see;" and I touched it.

"They will not do that," he declared, unmoved. "You will not tell them to. I should only say I am looking for an American gentleman I had the good fortune to meet at—Brabinsk, and think I have found him."

He smiled with the same serene cunning.

"What do you want?" I asked angrily.

The waiter opened the door then.

"Ah, that is more like my brother. I will have cognac and cigars and coffee. The sight of your dear face, brother, is a delight."

"Bring cigars, coffee, and brandy," I told the waiter.

"Was I not right? You no longer order me out. On the contrary, we drink together, and smoke and—and talk."

I waited until the drinks came.

"Help yourself," I told him; and he did, generously. Russians can all drink like fish, and this one took half a tumbler of brandy and very nearly forgot all about the water. Then leisurely he lit a cigar, and having got rid of the waiter's curious eyes, rose and locked the door, and tossed the key on the table.

"You may have another brother, monsieur, and he would not be so welcome;" and with a fresh smile he sat down again and puffed away in silence.

"A good cigar," he said appreciatively.

His coolness was amazing.

"You said you were going to talk—well, talk, and say what you want."

"I want to do you a good service, monsieur; I am your friend."

"Never mind that, what do you want?"

He took up his glass and looked at the liquor in it deliberately.

"A toast, monsieur. To the memory of—M. Vastic," and he tossed off half the liquor at a gulp. "You do not drink?"

"No; I'm waiting for you to speak."

"He was a great man—Vastic. But you were too quick for him."

"Were you—?" I began.

He nodded his head quickly.

"I missed you. It is not often I miss. I am counted a dead shot;" and with a glance the mingled threat and cunning of which no words of mine can convey, he took out a revolver and laid it on the table in his hand.

The interest of the situation heightened considerably.

"Have you come for a second shot?"

"I hope not; I hope it will not come to that. I should not miss a second time. Perhaps you have arms here?"

"Perhaps I have," I answered coolly, meeting his eyes.

"It would help to give them me."

We stared steadily at one another, and then I noticed that the door key was within my reach. I leaned forward slightly, as if to be nearer him, and then picked up the key with my left hand, and thrust back my chair so that my right hand rested on the bell push. As I moved, he watched me like a cat, and partly raised the revolver.

"This will do for me," I answered, slipping the key into an inner pocket and putting my finger on the bell. "You can shoot me if you wish, but at the slightest movement from you I shall ring this bell, and you will find it difficult to get out of the room before the people come—and equally difficult to explain your presence. Now we can talk."

A dead tense silence followed my words. I sat staring at him, with my finger on the push. His fingers left the revolver and he smiled.

"You are clever, monsieur. But it would not have saved you. You are right, however. We will talk."

"Say what you have to say," I answered, keeping my hand on the bell.

"If I spare you, you can save me. And we shall be quits."

"Go on."

He took his hand from his revolver and used it to lift the glass which he drained and immediately replenished.

"You remember me then, monsieur?" he asked.

"Yes, perfectly, now. You were with M. Vastic at Brabinsk."

"When you shot him," he added significantly.

"At the moment he was attempting to shoot me. Yes, go on."

"For that you were condemned by the brotherhood, and I was one of those chosen to—to find you."

"And murder me, you mean—after having been a witness that I acted only in self-defence. Go on."

"We know what occurred," he answered with a wave of the hand, as if putting my words aside. Then his look sharpened. "I am now the only one at large of all who were at Brabinsk that night."

"Which means—what?"

175

"That I am your only source of danger—from us, monsieur. It is fortunate that I chanced to see you to-day."

"There may be two opinions about that," I said drily. "I have mine."

"It is fortunate—for both."

"That gun of yours is scarcely a promising circumstance, is it?"

"You can make me your friend, if you will."

"How?"

"I am in danger, almost at my last turn. I am being hunted down—and you can save me. Every refuge is closed by these dogs of police."

"Do you think I can call them off? I'm no longer even playing at being Emperor."

"I have no money, monsieur—and dare not go where I could get it."

So the cat was belled at last. To my profound relief, the desperate Nihilist and picked assassin was just a common beggar, and his six shooter and threats mere picturesque bits of stage colour, and no more. An almost ludicrous bathos, but yet unutterably welcome to me.

A moment's reflection convinced me that he was in earnest. I knew of the raid on the Nihilists and that there had been a great number of arrests. Panic had no doubt seized the bulk of them, as it will do at such moments, and this man had caught the infection: oaths, pledges, revenge, the brotherhood, friends, everything had been blown to the winds by the passion of the panic and fear for his skin.

I took my hand from the bell and rose.

"Come," I said quietly, in a tone of reassurance. "Put that gun away and don't monkey with it any longer. I'll help you if only to show I've no cause of enmity with you. You shall get out of the country if you wish. How much do you want?" and without more ado I pulled out a roll of notes.

This readiness completed his conquest. He tried to maintain some show of stolid indifference, but the sight of the money and the knowledge of all it meant was too much for him; and for the moment he could not speak.

"How much?" I asked again. "Five hundred roubles?" and I laid notes for that amount on the table.

"I don't need so much as that," he said.

"If you'll comply with one condition, I'll double the amount."

His quick glance asked my meaning.

"You are the one man whose evidence can prove what took place when Vastic was killed. Leave Russia and go to any place you

176

please, but let me know where to find you; you can write to Mr. Harold Marvyn, of the American Embassy here. And if I need your evidence, be ready to swear to what occurred at Brabinsk. Do this, and I'll see that you have a fair start in a new country. You're not of the stuff that makes good conspirators. Come; your gun, right now, as a pledge you trust me and will do what I say." And I held out my hand for it.

He hesitated, looking at me nervously.

"I'm a prisoner, monsieur," he murmured.

"Rubbish! Here," and I tossed the key of the room over to him.

"By God, you're a man!" he cried. "You make me feel like a vile wretch of a coward;" and he pushed the revolver toward me. "I was drawn into this thing, like so many others, and the net was too strong to break. But I could get away now, and if you'll give me a chance——"

"All right. Here's the money. I'll have your story when we meet outside your infernal country. Now go, I'm busy. By the way, what's your name?"

He picked up the notes almost like a man in a dream and as if he could not believe in his good fortune, and put them away.

"I am Anton Presvitch. What can I say to you, monsieur? I——"

"Say au revoir or any other old tag you please, and keep clear of this sort of business for the future. I wish you good luck in getting away;" and I opened the door, gave him back his revolver and bundled him out.

The time was now close at hand for me to start, and I hurried my final preparations.

My chief concern as I drove to the Palace was lest any of the men who had stopped me on the previous morning should be on duty and recognize me; but the luck continued to be on my side.

No difficulty was raised about taking Siegel's card to Colonel von Kramen, and I was shown into an ante-room to wait. But I was not left alone, and could not therefore find means to get further into the Palace. But I was in luck again. Instead of the colonel, a young officer came to me, who said he was his secretary, and politely asked my business.

I invented a reply to the effect that the paper I represented wished me to get the career of so distinguished an officer as the colonel, and that I was very anxious to have a personal interview. I would not detain him more than a few minutes.

"I'm afraid it's out of the question just now. The colonel is with his Royal Highness, and can scarcely be interrupted," he said, as if with regret. "Cannot I tell you what you wish to know?"

"I'm also going to ask the colonel to endeavour to get me a word with his Royal Highness," I answered glibly.

"Really!" He smiled. "I have heard of the enterprise of American newspapers, but I scarcely expected this."

"It's a usual thing," I replied, as if it were. "In fact I am known to the Czar himself, and have had the honour of a long conversation with him."

This impressed him, as I intended it should.

"I'll go and see what I can do," he answered.

He was a very pleasant young fellow, so I ventured a step further.

"Is there not some place where we could be more private than here? In a confidential matter of this sort——"

I left the rest to his imagination.

"Will you come to my apartments? I shall be delighted."

Of course I agreed, but felt rather like a shame-faced impostor at having to trick so frank and good-natured a fellow. There was too much at stake, however, for me to hesitate, and we went away together, talking gaily, up the stairs and along the corridors to his room.

I was going to win after all, in spite of old Kalkov and his Argus eyes, and my spirits rose as success came nearer and nearer within my grasp.

We sat chatting for a few minutes, the young officer exhibiting a strong curiosity on the subject of American newspapers, what information I wished to obtain, the use I should make of it, and so on; and I did my best to satisfy him.

He was satisfied at length apparently, for he went off on his search for the colonel and left me alone.

I gave him just time to get well away, and then hurried off in the direction of the rooms where I knew the Czar would be at that hour.

What happened when the young secretary returned to find I had hoaxed him, I do not know, and never had an opportunity of ascertaining. He went out of my thoughts there and then, and the occurrences of the next few hours were too vital for me to think of him again.

I had to get to the Czar, and assuming an air of as much importance as I could, and feeling, it must be confessed, not a little nervous, I strode into the ante-room, my pulse beating with the fear that Prince Kalkov might be there, and said to one of the aides-de-camp, as I handed him my card—my own card this time—

"Kindly let his Majesty know that I have obeyed his summons and am here."

The aide looked up and frowned.

"I have no note of your name, monsieur. What is your business, if you please?"

"I am here by his Majesty's request. I was staying in the Palace as his Majesty's guest until the last two days. I am going to Khiva, and his Majesty wished to see me first."

"Oh yes, I heard of that. Pray pardon me; you are the American, M. Denver, yes. His Majesty is engaged at present, but the audience will be over directly, and if he sent for you, of course he will see you."

"I was to see him before I left. But my name will be enough."

"Will you wait, monsieur?" And he waved me to an adjoining room.

Good old bluff! The finest of all tactics, I thought as I sat, very anxious and impatient I admit, but very confident now. Once get the Czar's ear, and then—

The door was pushed partly open, and there came a dramatic pause. I got up, eager and expectant; and the luck turned with a rush.

It was Prince Kalkov, pale, urbane, cool and dangerous.

"I am afraid, M. Denver, his Majesty is too much engaged to grant you an audience to-day."

This in the suavest of tones, for those outside to hear. Then he closed the door and smiled.

CHAPTER XXVI

I WIN

MY feelings as Prince Kalkov and I stood thus face to face for some half minute or so without speaking were not wholly those of disappointment and chagrin. Disappointed I was, of course, and chagrined; but I had throughout had the secret expectation that he would succeed in blocking my way to the Czar; and it was in view of this that I had taken the elaborate precautions in regard to the compromising papers.

My surprise passed very quickly therefore, and I was conscious of a feeling of amusement mingled with conjecture as to the course which the interview would take. I had no fear of him whatever, for I was absolutely confident.

He might do what he pleased, but I had the stock of the whip in my hand, and there were two long biting thongs on it.

I sat down on the edge of an office table, and swinging my leg carelessly, smiled and opened the business.

"I am not so entirely surprised to see you as you may think—nor so sorry. I would rather see his Majesty, but that will come presently."

"You play very adroitly and very confidently, M. Denver. Who is in your place yonder—your cell?"

I affected not to understand him.

"My cell?"

"Need we pretend? What American has personated you?"

"No one, Prince; I am not an Emperor." Then in an indifferent tone I added: "Have you got an American? I heard as I came back through Kovna that your people had blundered and had made an arrest. I think something was said about a murder, but, of course, we know that's all mere wishwash and wind baggery."

"You will find it serious enough, monsieur. Who is he?" he asked sharply.

I pretended to think a moment, then slapped my knee and laughed.

"By Jove, I believe I can guess it. Splendid. There was an American, a newspaper man, on the train, represents the most sensational papers in the States; he was dying to get the secrets of your prisons at first hand, and it's just like him to have played for this arrest. You'll have a flaring description of the one he's in sent across the Atlantic. Lovely!" and I laughed with unnecessary heartiness. "You'd better get him out as soon as you can."

His eye kindled with anger.

"If there has been a conspiracy, monsieur, it will not help you now, and he will pay the penalty. We are not to be fooled with."

"That's just the point. The worse you treat him, the better he'll like it, and the more his papers will make of it," I replied, taking out my cigar case.

"Where are his papers, monsieur?" he retorted pointedly.

I grew serious and looked up at him out of the corner of my eyes.

"Are we to talk about—papers yet, Prince?"

His momentary discomfiture was a thing of joy to me.

"You do not realize the fix you have got him into."

"No indeed, for I don't believe he's in any fix at all. By the way, shall I have time to smoke a cigar before I see his Majesty?"

"Yes, many," he rapped out drily.

"Well, here goes for one, then," and I lit mine deliberately. "Now I suppose we are going to have a little chat together. I think you'll be interested in an account of my adventures since—yes, since the night before last at—seven o'clock. You know them up to then."

"It is unusual for me to grant an interview to a man charged with murder."

"Then I'd better go straight to his Majesty."

"You will not see his Majesty."

"I think I can persuade you that I shall, Prince. As you said just now, I am very confident."

"If you desire to lay any mitigating facts before me, I will listen to you in my apartments. I am wishful to deal with you leniently."

"Mitigating facts, that's a pretty phrase. I like it. I am also ready to go anywhere you please—gaol if you like; and I can understand that you would prefer me to be a little farther removed from the Czar than we are at the present moment."

"I shall send you there under guard, monsieur."

"No, decidedly no," I said firmly. "If you send me anywhere under guard, it will be to a prison, and then—well, things will happen, and you'll be sorry. I am enjoying this interview, and am quite willing to continue it where and when you please; but you are vastly mistaken if you think that I am only bluffing you now. I am really dangerous, Prince. You know the jargon of poker—well, it's up to you to see me—if you think it safe."

Apparently he did not, for after a second's pause he said—

"We'll go together, monsieur."

And together we went accordingly.

I was well satisfied with the progress of things so far. I had told him nothing yet; had merely hinted at the power I held; and the hint had forced him to yield. Nothing more was said until we reached his apartment, and once there, he sat down to his desk, while I threw myself into an easy lounge chair. It was my cue to appear absolutely unconcerned, and I played up to it.

"Now, monsieur, for the reasons why I am not to hand you over to the police at once."

He spoke sternly and curtly.

"The main reason is the blunder of your men at Kovna. They first let me through with things that were of great importance, and then let me back again to take ample measures for the safety of myself—and others. I owe them an infinite obligation."

"You will find it better to drop this jesting tone and speak plainly."

181

"Why should I adapt my tone to suit your convenience? You are presuming to address me as if I were a prisoner."

"You are a prisoner."

"Why persist in this ridiculous delusion? I am not anything like so near a gaol as—well, say as you are."

"This is insolence, monsieur," he cried angrily.

"Yes, calculated insolence, your Highness. I resent your attitude. You have behaved infamously to me—infamously. And you would carry your infamy to the last extreme now, and send me to rot in one of your gaols, were you not restrained by your fear of the consequences."

"You shall not speak thus to me," he cried passionately, striking the desk with his fist.

"I shall speak as I please to the man who laid a treacherous trap to lure me to my death."

"This is not the way to obtain my leniency."

"Damn your leniency! Do what you dare—right now. I am as safe from your threats as I am indifferent to your anger. I am a free-speaking American citizen, monsieur, not a Russian serf; and I can prove my innocence as clearly as I can prove your guilt."

"You tempt me to end the interview by your arrest. Had you not been a friend of his Majesty——"

A laugh from me cut him short.

"Exactly. I understand. You mean it's safer to hear me out, no matter what tone I adopt. And so it is."

He knew well enough I was dangerous to him; and filling up a pause by drawing some large sheets of official paper before him and selecting a pen, he said—

"Your statement, monsieur."

"You won't find it advisable to put it all down there; but you can please yourself. First, we'll clear up the mystery of your prisoner. His name is—but wait, here are some of his papers, including his passport. I used that with his consent to pass your men at Kovna;" and I handed over such of Siegel's cards and papers as I had with me.

"You admit this?" he asked.

My action surprised him.

"Oh yes. Fortunately I met him on the train, and we arranged that I should use his passport."

"You conspired together?"

"Put it how you like. It doesn't matter five cents. If I didn't know that, I shouldn't have told you. Shall I wait while you write that down?" I asked, for his paper was as blank as my hand.

182

"I can trust my memory for his crime," he replied when I waited for an answer.

"Then you can have my first condition. M. Siegel must be liberated the moment he expresses the wish to leave. I don't want him to lose material for his article. He was so useful to me, you see."

The Prince bit his lips savagely and sneered.

"It is good of you to name your conditions."

"If I didn't, how could you comply with them?"

"Perhaps you have some others?"

"Certainly I have. The next is the immediate release of Mademoiselle Helga Boreski—or Lavalski, whichever name you prefer. When that trap of yours for me failed—and only an accident caused the failure, for it took me in completely; you may like to know that—I went to the Mademoiselle and told her your intentions in regard to her, warned her and assisted her in attempting to fly. Your quick swoop on the place afterwards—a fact we had not counted on—broke up our plans, and she was arrested. I tell you of the mistakes we made in regard to you, so that you may feel perfectly sure I have not made any miscalculations now."

"By your own admission, you aided the escape of this Nihilist leader. You are frank, monsieur."

"Except that she is not a Nihilist leader, but your personal enemy, you are quite right. I admit I helped her to get away. I went with her, of course, as you now know."

My frankness was having precisely the effect upon him which I calculated. He felt I should not make a number of hazardous admissions if I had not some strong cause.

"You must, of course, be held answerable for this; even my desire to save you would be useless in the face of this," he said, for all the world as though he were my best friend and protector.

"I am ready right here and now. But about Mademoiselle's release?" I asked when he paused.

"It is preposterous—monstrous—out of the question."

"Still, it's got to be done; how, I leave to you;" and I leant back and smoked placidly.

He sat thinking, and then shot the question at me for which I had been waiting, and with it a sharp lightning glance.

"Why?"

"I have those papers."

I enjoyed the start and frown which the words fetched, and his evident discomfiture and perplexity.

"Your men were very good to me; I should like to recommend one of them in particular for promotion." I couldn't resist the chance for this little gird at him. "I had them on me when I passed

183

the barrier and again when I came back. And now they're in good safe keeping."

He bore the gibe without retort, without a sign of any kind, although I knew how deep I had thrust the blade in.

"A queer turn of the wheels, isn't it? The very papers you sent me out to recover, when I do recover them, become my weapon against you. And, by the way, they are not the only ones I have."

"Well?"

"There's the full case—with dates, details, names of witnesses, proofs, everything—in the charge against you in that Lavalski matter."

I saw his hand tighten on the arm of his chair, and a muttered oath slipped out from the pressed lips in a whisper. Save for that one truant whisper, his face was as pale and immobile as death itself.

The sight of his tense emotion satisfied even my bitterness against him, and I held my tongue, speculating what he would do.

He found the problem beyond even his ingenuity for a time at least, and sat thinking, trying to see a course that was not fraught with real danger. He had guarded this secret jealously; fought for it with desperate vigilance; flourished on it prosperously for years until he had reached so high; and now exposure menaced him with all its consequences of overthrow, ruin and disgrace.

I knew he would fight on doggedly, if only he could find the means of fighting. But where he would look for them I could not see.

The silence lasted for minutes, and then he moved. He had apparently thought the thing out and made his choice. At length he spoke.

"This Lavalski charge is false, monsieur," he said.

"Intentionally false, no," I answered. "Mademoiselle Helga is incapable of deliberate falsehood. Mistaken, possibly. The inquiry which his Majesty will order on hearing the charge will no doubt settle its truth or mistake. That is all that is needed."

"His Majesty will order no inquiry, monsieur."

"We shall see."

"The Duchess Stephanie has seen his Majesty."

"When?"

"This morning, in a long and painful interview. I was present. What passed has convinced his Majesty of the character of this mademoiselle."

This was the one thing I had feared.

"I do not believe that of the Emperor," I said firmly. Our eyes met and I tried in vain to read the expression in his.

"From that quarter the mademoiselle can look for no countenance—now," he returned, with slow incisive significance.

I began to understand.

"I have yet to see him and tell my story," I answered.

"I repeat, there can be no inquiry, monsieur."

"It will arise out of any trial of the mademoiselle," I said significantly.

"There need be no trial." He accompanied the ambiguous sentence with a look which further enlightened me. Helga must look to him and not to the Czar for help.

"What does that mean?" I asked.

"It rests with you," he answered, slowly, as if the words were wrung from him by torture. As indeed they had been.

I drew a long breath of relief. I had won, and the intense significance of my victory rushed upon me, filling me with a gladness that deprived me for the moment of the power to speak.

I got up and walked two or three times across the room. Helga was free, and I had freed her. The luck was indeed with us. Looking at the Prince I found his eyes riveted upon me.

"You are satisfied, M. Denver?"

"Yes. What remains to be done can be arranged easily. When can Mademoiselle Helga be set at liberty?"

"As soon as she agrees to abandon this ridiculous charge against me, and arranges for the surrender of the papers."

My face clouded. I had not thought of that. Helga had to abandon everything—the very purpose of her life. Would she?

"They cannot be surrendered until she is beyond your reach."

"You do not credit me with much good faith," he said bitterly.

"If you held my life in your hands would you put the weapon into mine and expect me to kill myself?"

"Yet you expect me to credit you."

"You cannot help yourself. Besides, I have gone straight. I am not a Russian diplomatist."

"Will you tell me where those papers are?"

"Will I put my head in a noose and hand you the loose end?"

"How do I know that you have them?"

"I tell you so. My word is enough; but you know pretty well I shouldn't have ventured here if I had not had them?"

"You came expecting to see the Emperor?"

"And should have forced my way to him just now—if I hadn't known that, having them, it was safe to trust myself with you."

"Who else knows where they are?"

I started and looked at him. I began to see his drift, and led him on.

185

"No one," I answered, and I saw by the way his eyes fell that my new suspicions were correct.

"Will you give me a pledge on your honour that if I do what you ask you will hand them to me?"

Again he would not trust me to see his eyes.

"Yes. Any pledge you like, written or verbal," I answered, helping him out. "But write me first that you grant my conditions."

"Yes. I agree to that. It is fair." And he began to use for the first time the paper with which at the start he had made so much show. "Will that suffice?" he asked, handing me the writing.

I appeared to read it carefully, but I was watching, and noticed that iron-nerved as he was, his hands were trembling.

"Yes, that will do," I said, and put it away in my pocket.

"Now write, then," and we exchanged places, he standing up by me, I sitting at his desk.

"Let me see, how shall I word it?"

"I will tell you," he said, his voice trembling. "Write where those papers are, or by God it will be your last moment alive."

I was turning to look at him when I felt the cold circle or pistol barrel pressed to my head.

Move, I dared not, for I knew that at the least sign of resistance from me he would fire. I saw how he had reasoned. He believed that I alone knew where the papers were, and that if he shot me the secret would die with me. If I refused to write what he demanded, he would kill me and take the risk of their never being found; while if I did tell him, he would kill me just the same and get the papers afterwards.

But my precautions spelt checkmate to his ingenious scheme. Bitterly as he hated me, I knew he would not indulge his hatred at the expense of his own inevitable ruin.

"I will write something you had better read," I said steadily, and wrote: "I have placed the papers where, if anything happens to me, the one set will pass at once into the hands of the Embassy"—I named the Power concerned—"and the other set straight to the Czar."

I ceased writing and felt the pressure of the barrel increase as he bent forward to read the words. He gave such a start that I wondered his fingers did not pull the trigger.

"I was only testing you," he said, then, and he tossed the revolver back in the drawer from which he had secretly taken it.

"Testing my folly, you mean, Prince Kalkov," I said as I rose. "Seeing whether I was fool enough to put my finger in the cobra's mouth without making sure that the fangs were drawn."

"I am sorry. I was not myself," he said, his voice strangely weak;

186

and he fell into the lounge chair where I had been sitting, and lay there ashen white and trembling, so that I thought he would faint.

I could guess from that what he had undergone.

He was so long in this condition that I began to think he was seriously ill, and would collapse altogether.

"Shall I summon assistance for you, monsieur?" I asked.

"No," he murmured faintly, with a feeble wave of his white hand.

It was several minutes before he could rally sufficiently to resume.

Then he got up and changed to his own chair by the desk. He was like a man more than half dead, and when he tried to write, his hand shook so violently that he could not form the letters.

I waited in silence and watched him. Unscrupulous, treacherous, subtle, and vile as I believed him, he was so broken and beaten that I could almost have found it in me to pity him.

He succeeded after a strenuous effort in mastering his feebleness sufficiently to be able to write.

"I shall trust your honour, M. Denver. Here is an order to admit you to Mademoiselle Boreski, and to see her in private. Go to her at once. Bring me word that she abandons this wrongful charge against me, and you can both leave the country to-night. You can then surrender the documents. You will understand my wish for haste."

"I must see M. Siegel also," I said; "and have an order for his release."

With another effort he wrote me the necessary authority.

"Now, excuse me, I am not well;" he sighed heavily, and his head fell forward on his hands. "Please ring that bell for me," he murmured.

I touched it and went out, leaving him still in that pose of abject broken weakness.

CHAPTER XXVII

A LAST MOVE

MY interview had been so successful and the Prince's submission so complete that it never occurred to me to look for still further treachery from him.

I had carried everything before me so triumphantly; had secured Helga's freedom, and was on my way to take her the good news; she and I would leave the country; Siegel would be cleared from all trouble; and on every point I had forced from the Prince just those conditions which I chose to impose.

So overcome was my opponent, so prostrated, that only with a great effort had he been able to keep up to the end. And if I was inclined to be conceited over my victory it must be remembered that I had been pitted against a man of wide influence, drastic power, and very high position.

It did occur to me, indeed, as I was driving to the prison, that the Prince had not given me the order for Helga's release, and that he had worded his phrase peculiarly.

"Bring me her consent," he had said; but this appeared no more than the ordinary caution he would employ, seeing that he was not likely to set her at liberty without some such pledge. What he had really had in mind, however, I was to learn later.

At the prison no hesitation was shown about complying with his order. I was shown into a bare room with a small table and a couple of chairs—a place just one remove from an ordinary cell; and after I had waited some few minutes Helga was brought to me.

She was very pale, but a flush of surprise, and I think delight, swept over her face at seeing me. She just put her hands into mine as I stretched them out to her and left them there while I gazed into her eyes.

"You are very pale, dearest," I said at length. It was the first time I had ever used such a term of endearment, and her eyes and a smile noticed it.

"I am so glad," she answered, with sweet inconsequence. "But I don't in the least know how you have done it. It must be some new American method."

"This is the American method," I whispered, and drew her to me till her face was close to mine, and then I held her in a passionate embrace while I pressed my lips to hers.

"I have been so anxious for you," she murmured, putting her

arms about my neck. "I did not care for myself. I am so glad." And then of her own volition she kissed me again, and let her head fall on my shoulder with a sigh.

For a while I had no need for words, and just stood lost in the delight of her new tenderness and witching mood of love.

"You caught me so weak," she said at length, "in the joy of seeing you safe. Now satisfy my curiosity. I am only a woman, you see."

"I have come from Prince Kalkov to tell you you are free, sweetheart."

At the mention of the name, she started and would have drawn away from me had I let her.

"From him? But you have been a prisoner?"

"No, never in any real danger of being one."

"You are free now?" she cried, looking at me curiously.

"Yes, of course."

She laughed then, and backed out of my arms.

"Then my sympathy was wasted; and my remorse——"

"It was a very sweet remorse, Helga," I said, as she left the sentence unfinished.

"I thought you had been arrested, and charged with Vastic's murder; that I had brought you to ruin and shame. Oh, it was unendurable."

"And if you had known?" I asked, with a glance she read. "Was it only remorse?"

"One does strange things on—on impulse. I have suffered so, and it was such a relief."

"The gates of relief are still open," and I spread out my arms.

"I mean to see you," she cried, with a flash of the eyes and a blush.

"And I mean—to feel——"

"Come, let us be sensible and talk."

"I think we have been very sensible without talking."

"They will not let us be long together," she continued, ignoring my words and looks and sitting down.

"That will depend on you, Helga."

"On me? How?"

"You have but to say one word, and we shall be always together."

"Another American method? They are very elastic," she laughed.

"They are very thorough."

"How did you escape? Please tell me everything."

"Yes. I have come to do that. All is well now. Siegel was caught

189

at Kovna instead of me. I got through with the papers, returned, put them in safe keeping in the capital, tried to see the Emperor, and saw Kalkov instead; and when he realized what had happened, he agreed to release you, in order that you and I might leave Russia together."

"You bewilder me," she said.

"I will give you the details;" and I told her at some length all that had passed since we had parted in the train.

The story did not produce the effect upon her I wished. My note was one of jubilant congratulation; but I saw a look of thoughtful doubt settle gradually upon her face, and it hardened when I spoke of Kalkov's condition that she should abandon her war against him.

"Did he tell you he had seen me? You have not mentioned it," she said.

"No; not a word."

"He came here—here to this prison—to this very room."

"For what?"

"To threaten me first, and then to offer me your and my liberty. He swore to me that you had been arrested, and that all the papers had been found upon you; that you were charged with Vastic's murder, and that he could secure your conviction—and then he offered me liberty."

"On what condition?"

"Practically the same as you have mentioned. You have done well for me, my friend, but the Prince is too tortuous for straight-minded men to deal with him."

I began to feel about as cheap as a five-cent piece. He had failed with Helga, and then made a show of submission to me in order to use me to influence her. It was not a pleasant reflection.

"What did you say to him?"

"That so long as a breath remained in my body and a pulse in my heart I would spend that breath and exhaust the pulse to vindicate my father's memory and revenge him."

I had no answer to make; and sat chewing the cud of this new reverse. Helga saw how hard I was hit, how keen my disappointment, and tried gently to soften the blow.

"No honest man can deal with the Prince," she said; and added with a smile: "You have secured the papers by a magnificent stroke and we shall win now. It was for you I was troubled."

"It's good of you to soften the fall, but it hurts a bit all the same." My smile was a very rueful one. "If it was mere revenge I should urge you to give it up; but it's your father's memory, and I can't."

"He strove hard. He seemed to know he could make me feel

more keenly striking at you than at me; and when he said the papers were in his hands I was very near despair."

"I can understand. Well, we'll see it through to the end."

"Not you," she cried eagerly. "You must take no part. I——"

She stopped, meeting my look.

"You forget," I said lightly. "It is I who have the papers now."

"I cannot speak nor think lightly of it where you are concerned," was her earnest reply. "You must see the danger is real."

"I need no more evidence than your presence here. Yet you do not give in. If you are troubled for me, do you think I am indifferent about you? Helga!"

"No, no, I don't think that. Oh, you know," and she stretched out her hand to me. "But this purpose is my life. It is greater than all else. Yes," she cried in answer to my look, "greater even than that."

"Then I am jealous of it, Helga; so jealous that I will destroy it— or it shall destroy me. There is nothing to me greater than my love."

"It can never be," she said slowly, shaking her head sadly. "It would be cruel for me to give you hope, much as I would wish—ah, God! how much!"

"I will find a way," I declared firmly.

"There is one by which you can help." She spoke suddenly after a pause.

"What is that?"

"You are free; use your freedom to get the papers out of the country to a place of safety. Then from that vantage ground you can help me."

"It is ingenious," I said with a smile. "You mean I should be safe."

"If I know you are safe I shall be happier. I told you once I was stronger when you were away. I should be stronger now."

"But I am not going. I will not leave you here. The papers are absolutely safe in Marvyn's hands."

"You do not yet know the Prince. While the papers are in Russia he will leave no stone unturned to find them."

"But they are not in Russia. Where the Stars and Stripes fly over the Embassy it is American territory; even he is powerless."

"He will find a way. Even now I believe he has some scheme. He may have sent you here in order to search your room. He will have your movements to-day traced, and find out where you have been."

"So much the better. He will not get much satisfaction at either Embassy. He can but prove the truth of what I told him and feel the iron pressure all the closer."

"But what can you do if you remain in Petersburg?"

"I shall be with you."

She answered with a gesture that the place was a prison.

"Near you, then. I cannot go away—unless we go together."

"A kindness that is almost cruel," she sighed, and then a silence fell between us.

It was an impasse. The Prince was not likely to let her get out of his grasp unless she promised to forego her purpose; that was certain. Equally certain it was in that she would not yield. I could not ask her to abandon the work of clearing her father's memory. She had lived all her life for that one object; and knowing her so well as I now did, I felt she would cling to it to the end in the very face of death itself.

"It is an almost hopeless outlook for you," she said, breaking the long silence and speaking my own thought.

"But we have to find the way, and we shall;" and then, as if in answer to my wish, a view of the matter which had not struck me flashed upon me.

"You have thought of something," she said, reading my face.

"It may not please you. It is a compromise."

"A compromise? How? I see none."

"Well, I will put it. You have a double motive in this fight with the Prince—to clear your father's memory, and to punish Kalkov. Let me see him and tell him if he will right your father's name you will leave him alone."

"Let him continue to prosper on his infamy? You ask this?"

"If you cannot tear down the stones of this place, will you help yourself by dashing your head against the walls? As we stand, we are helpless."

"I can punish him, and all Russia."

"Will that help in the really greater object?"

"You are tempting me to be untrue to my whole life."

"I am showing you how possibly you may gain your end."

"But the proofs of his baseness will get to the Emperor."

"So we hope. But even if they do, are you sure of the Emperor? He told me that the Duchess Stephanie had seen the Emperor and poisoned his ear with the tale that you are a Nihilist. Do you think Kalkov is not cunning enough to meet a charge from such a source? It is not those papers the Prince fears, it is the complication with the Powers. If you were free to press your claim for justice, it might be otherwise: but as we are, we are desperately weak."

"It is like treachery to my father," she said vehemently.

"If it were so in reality I should not press it, Helga. But I do;" and I went on to urge it, using every consideration that occurred to me. Indeed the more I thought of it, the more was I convinced that it offered the only solution to an impossible position.

That she should be anxious to punish the man who had dealt so cruel a blow at her father, and was now pursuing her so relentlessly was natural enough; in truth I would have been glad to take a strong hand in the work. But he was old and a year or two more of unmerited honours for him weighed but little against the disastrous consequences to both of us.

The one consideration that began to tell at last with Helga, however, was the fact that her father's reputation might be righted if she gave in to me, and would probably not be if she were to remain in prison or be sent to Siberia.

"But he cannot do it," she urged, when my insistence upon this point began to influence her. "To right my father is to prove the Prince's wrong-doing. He cannot do it."

"Well, there, let me try it. If he cannot we shall be only where we stand now. I have sufficient faith in his craftiness; but we shall still have our weapons left to us. We may gain; we cannot lose."

Her brows drawn in deep thought and her face set, she was considering her answer when the door was opened, and we had a genuine surprise.

Prince Kalkov entered.

I stood up and stared at him.

"This interview was to be private," I said quickly.

"I have come to take part in it, monsieur. I have something to say that will interest you both, and probably affect your decision."

"I do not welcome the intrusion," I declared.

"And I have nothing to say to my gaoler," said Helga.

I thrust one of the two chairs over to him, and pulling the small table towards me, sat down on it between him and Helga.

"You omitted to tell me to-day that you had already seen mademoiselle, and that she had refused your offer."

"It was not necessary—then. Now, however, it is different. I will be frank with you. I sent you here that I might have your rooms at the hotel searched, and your movements to-day ascertained."

"Mademoiselle, knowing you, had already told me that was probably your object. I assured her that you would gain nothing, unless you called at a certain Embassy."

"And you were right, monsieur," he answered, quite unmoved. "I admit your caution and admire it. It has confirmed my opinion of your strength in this."

"Well?"

"What I said to you before, I repeat now—those papers must be returned to my hands, at any cost."

"There are two sets of papers," I reminded him.

193

"Those affecting me you can retain. I can protect myself from any charges and slanders founded upon mistake."

"Mistake!" exclaimed Helga bitterly.

"I said mistake, mademoiselle; and I am going to prove to you before I leave that what I say is true. But first, you are here together, and I invite you to say on what terms the other papers shall be placed in my hands."

"You had my answer to-day," said Helga.

"I do not accept that answer, mademoiselle."

"I have no other."

"I am here in no spirit of hostility, neither to make or to hear recriminations. I wish the important papers to be recovered with the least disturbance and trouble to all concerned."

"That is a threat," I put in.

"It is not so intended, M. Denver. You have acted cleverly, but you have not exhausted the resources at my command. If no terms are made now, it will leave me no option but to have you arrested, charged with treason and conspiracy in regard to these papers, and then I can use my influence with your Ambassador to secure that the papers lodged with Mr. Marvyn shall be held inviolate and then returned eventually to me. It is for you to make your choice, whether to stand by mademoiselle's answer or to make better terms with me."

Here was a fresh turn indeed, and when I glanced at Helga I saw she had turned pale, and that, like myself, she was at loss how to parry it.

CHAPTER XXVIII

LOVE WILL HAVE ITS WAY

PRINCE KALKOV was an opponent with whom it was dangerous to hesitate and fatal to appear disconcerted, so I shook myself up as quickly as I could, and answered with a smile.

"That's a very plausible story, your Highness, but if you can do all this, why are you here? It's not for your health, is it; or from any newly-born affection or solicitude for us?"

"No, I have made no such pretence," he said drily.

"Then why?"

"Because it will be less troublesome to recover the papers directly through you than indirectly from Mr. Marvyn. I merely wish you to see that they will be recovered, one way or the other."

"Then I think you'd better go to work indirectly, Prince," I said in a very deliberate tone. "If I don't accept implicitly the explanation you've just given me, don't blame me. You must set it down against that knack of yours to say one thing and mean another. Yes, I think on the whole it had better be indirectly. I see a little flaw in your plan."

"Had we not better avoid personalities and insults, M. Denver?"

"You mean about your little knacks. Is that an insult? I thought it was a canon of European diplomacy according to Talleyrand—that language is given us to conceal our thoughts. I meant it as an explanation, not an insult."

"You prefer to meet these charges?"

"Oh, yes. I don't see any difficulty in them. As for the murder charge, I happen to have at command the evidence of the man who was with Vastic at the time, and he can prove I acted in self-defence."

"The testimony of a fugitive Nihilist," he rapped out.

"True, but still testimony; and as I'm an American, it will have to be a fair and open trial. There is also Mademoiselle Helga's evidence. Yes, on the whole, I'm disposed to take that risk. As to the treason business, do you really think you'd better prove that? It was your idea that I should play the part of Emperor, and you furnished me with forged documents and other lies to get those papers back; and as you're making it an international matter, it would make rather an awkward story. Still, do as you like. But you haven't frightened me. I don't think there's a bullet in the cartridge. Go right ahead anyway, pull the trigger, and we'll see."

"I can do what I have said, nevertheless, monsieur."

"Possibly you think so—possibly, I say. But I don't agree with you. You see, my father is not only a rich man, but has a heap of influence at the White House. If I remember, too, he has a bit of a grievance against Russia; and he'd make things hum a lot if you monkey with me. I hadn't thought of bringing him into it, but I believe it would be the best thing. Helga and I were trying to think of the best way out when you came, and I'm hanged if I don't think you've given me just the cue I wanted."

"You think, perhaps, he could save the mademoiselle?"

"One thing at a time, and for the moment we're talking about my case. Yes—" I spoke with intentional slowness, as if thinking it out—"yes, I shall cable him to hurry over. I wonder I never thought

195

of it. If I can't get to the Emperor, he can, right away; and if he don't make it an international affair inside two shakes, then I don't know my own father. That treason charge was just a lovely thought of yours, Prince."

The Prince rose. I had turned the tables on him at his own bluff, but like a good player he kept his end up.

"We do not allow prisoners to have the use of our telegraphs, monsieur," he said nastily.

"The Embassy can send it in cypher. Same thing," I replied unconcerned. "The worse you make things for me, the bigger the fuss when it does get out."

He turned from me to Helga.

"You will go back to your cell, and you and M. Denver will not meet again, mademoiselle," he declared, like the bully he was.

"I am quite ready," she answered, not flinching a hair's breadth; "now that I have heard what is to happen;" and she rose and met his look steadily.

And we stood thus a space in silence. Both sides recognized that the situation was just bluff. I had shown him the rottenness of his position; and he knew that, despite my easy words, I was anxious to get the thing arranged without any of the trouble I had outlined. And yet neither was willing to take the first step down.

Then I offered him a bridge.

"Is this worth while, Prince?" I asked very quietly.

"What do you mean?"

"I have shown you my hand, and you can see it's a strong one. Why not take the card you've been keeping up your sleeve. You have one, you know."

"Do you mean you are willing to submit to me?"

"No, indeed, I don't. I've shown you I can set you at defiance and face the worst you can do, with absolute confidence that I shall win. But I'm willing to listen to what you came to say. You haven't given us the proof that Helga's charge against you in regard to her father is mistaken. What's the proof?"

"I can prove it by the man most concerned."

Helga went white to the lips.

"Name," I asked curtly.

"By her own father—Prince Lavalski. He is still living—in Siberia."

"My God, my poor father!" cried Helga, falling into a chair and covering her face with her hands. I crossed and laid my hand on her shoulder.

"Courage, Helga, courage. This may be good news, dearest."

"It is not good news, monsieur, but the worst for his daughter," continued the Prince, relentlessly. "You have forced me to tell you. His life was spared against his wish when his offences were proved; and it is by his own desire that he has remained in Siberia, dead to all who knew him."

"It is a lie, a base lie, a lie of lies," cried Helga, with sudden passion. "He is dead, and you—you, Prince Kalkov, are his murderer."

"You are ungenerous, even for an enemy, mademoiselle," replied the Prince, with a bow that was not without courtesy and dignity. "Had you come to me openly years ago, I would have told you the truth."

"It is false, and you know it. You tried to wreak your malevolence on me. You know I speak the truth, just as you know you were afraid I should tear the mask from your life and ruin you in the eyes of your Emperor. How can you be so base?"

"The full truth of your father's offences was and is known to but two men in the Empire, mademoiselle. The Emperor himself is one, and I am the other. I had and have nothing to fear from any disclosure or inquiry."

"God, that such villainy should prosper!" she cried again, with passionate vehemence.

"What I have told you is the truth, and I offer you the means to prove my words."

"What means?" I asked.

"I will not dishonour my father by even listening further," exclaimed Helga.

"Mademoiselle Helga can communicate with her father, or you, monsieur, can go to him," said Kalkov, disregarding her protest, and turning to me.

"Yes," she said scornfully. "And you would get one of your pliant tools to answer my letters or personate my dead father. I know you and your methods too well, monsieur."

"I understand your anger, mademoiselle, and pass over your taunts. I have offered you the proof I promised. I have now said my last word, monsieur," he added, turning to me.

"Can I bring the Prince back with me?" I asked.

"Certainly, if he will come. But he will not."

"No, for then I should see the deception," said Helga, with scorn; and then with a change to eagerness, "Can I go to him?"

"No; that is impossible."

"Why?" I asked.

"There are limits to my powers. I cannot send armed escorts to Siberia and back to satisfy the doubts of all our prisoners."

"I can go alone," declared Helga.

197

"And return—here?" with a significant lift of the eyebrows.

"Do you think I would break my pledged word?" asked Helga indignantly.

"I have no doubt you would endeavour to keep it. But it is a risk I should not feel entitled to take. I repeat I cannot provide an escort for any prisoner for such a distance."

"I would escort her," I broke in quickly.

He turned and looked at me coldly and steadily, as he replied deliberately:

"You are not her husband yet, monsieur. And if you were," he added, after pausing, "what greater security should I have for her return?"

"You want no more than these papers, I suppose, if she did not return?"

"If she can persuade her father to return, that will be better still. We are ready to bury the past."

"Your objection then is not to mademoiselle's going to find him, but only lest, having found him, she should still use these documents?"

"You have stated it precisely. We must be absolutely secured on that point."

"Leave me to find the way then. Give me an hour and either return here or I will see you at the palace."

"I will return," he said drily; "for if you do not decide I shall take the other course." With that threat he went away.

It was a curious situation that he left behind him. Helga had not said a word since his pointed sentence in reply to my offer to take her to her father, and I could not of course guess what she thought. But I knew my own mind very clearly; and that is always a circumstance in a two-sided discussion. At the same time I was not a little embarrassed.

Helga was the first to speak.

"Can it be true, do you think? Or is it only another of his schemes?"

"It differs a good deal from any others—at least in one point."

"I don't believe it. I won't. I am sure it is false. My father was the soul of honour and loyalty."

"You would at any rate see him!"

"Ah, my God, what would I not do to see him," she cried.

But I wished to get her away from this strenuous mood, so I said with a smile:

"Even comply with his suggested condition?"

"I was not thinking of that. How can you?"

"It would be a long honeymoon trip."

She shook her head as if my tone jarred.

"Can't you see all it means to me?"

"I know what it means to me."

"Don't!" she exclaimed, impatiently. "Be serious."

"I think we've been serious long enough. Believe me, I know all that this portentous news must be to you. Pray God it is true that your father is alive. But there are some anxieties we can face better with a bright face. So smile to me, and say you'll go with me to find and bring him back."

I held out my hands.

She hung back a moment with head averted and then turned and put her hands in mine, her face smiling and her eyes dashed with tears.

"It is all so strange," she said.

"We Americans are never sticklers for forms. We'll go with a laugh, dear, whatever we are destined to find there."

"You are so good and so strong," she whispered.

"No, I am just discovering how much better and stronger I shall be with—with my wife, Helga," I whispered back.

She came to me then, with a sigh and a laugh and lots of blushes which she hid on my shoulder from my eyes as well as from the musty dingy old prison walls. Musty and dingy? Well, no. They will never be that in my memory. For the sake of that minute they will always have a halo in my thoughts; for after all it was the prison which did so much to hasten our happiness.

And so it was settled, and for the time we just lost ourselves and babbled and laughed and sighed and held hands and kissed and laughed again; for love will have his way even in a prison with all sorts of vague troubles gibbering and pranking from the other side of the bars.

And when I glanced at my watch I found we had used up the whole hour save some ten minutes.

The problem which the Prince had left us was a big one to solve in ten minutes; but we only smiled at it, for Helga had come round to my view—to meet everything with a laugh. And in that spirit we faced the prospect of the long journey to Siberia.

When the Prince came back I had no formal answer ready for him, of course. Helga was to be my wife; and I could not get any further than that. I was certainly in no fit mood to cope with him.

I suppose he saw the chaotic state of my mind; he must have been very blind if he did not; for the thought of Helga as my wife got in my way and tripped me up every moment, so that my answers to his first questions were given almost at random.

"You have my word of honour that the moment we find matters

are as you say in regard to Prince Lavalski in Siberia, the whole of these papers will be returned to you. I suppose that will satisfy you."

"A personal guarantee is at best unsubstantial," he returned rudely.

"Does it seem so to a Russian? It is not to an American."

"I have no choice, it seems. When will you start?" he asked.

"As soon as we are married."

"That can be at once—to-night or to-morrow."

"To-morrow!" exclaimed Helga, in dismay at the suddenness.

"I suppose we must wait till then if we can't manage it to-night," I said; and she laughed to me.

"It will not be an elaborate ceremony," said the Prince drily. "A prison does not lend itself to scenic effect."

"A prison," said I, surprised in my turn.

"Mademoiselle can only leave here as your wife, monsieur."

"Then I think we'll try and manage it to-night."

"No, no, to-morrow," declared Helga, quickly.

"Better to-night; we can spend to-morrow in the preparations for the long journey," I answered. "One can't go to Siberia without clothes; even on a honeymoon, you see. We could start on the following day."

"But——" her face was wrinkled in dismay.

"No 'buts,' only smiles, Helga."

"I will give the necessary instructions," said the Prince, perceiving like the shrewd old man he was that I should carry the point.

"We must have witnesses. Mr. Siegel will be one of them," I said.

"You have the order for his release," replied the Prince. "I will wait for you, monsieur," he added, and very considerately took himself off.

He had to wait, for Helga still had scruples which I had to combat. And before I had overcome them his patience was exhausted, and he sent a messenger in quest of me.

"Thank God you'll be out of here in an hour or two, dearest."

"But——"

I stopped the protest on her lips. Any lover knows how that has to be done. She laughed at my eagerness.

"Good, sweetheart. We'll meet it all with a laugh as we agreed;" and not keeping the Prince waiting more than another quarter of an hour, I left her happy, blushing, loving—and resigned.

"I have appointed ten o'clock," he said as I joined him.

"Very well." I should have said "very well" if he had named midnight or four in the morning.

200

"I wish you to understand that I shall do all I can to help you—now," he said pointedly.

"That's all right." My head was still in the clouds. In an hour or so Helga would be my wife.

"I shall wish to know where you will be."

"God bless my soul, I hadn't thought about that," I exclaimed. "We shall stay at the Imperial. Oh, and I've no clothes. They are at the Palace. You see it's a little sudden."

"My man, Pierre, is at your service, monsieur."

"I wish you'd let him get them to the Imperial; or shall I——"

"I will see to it. There is one thing, of course, M. Denver. You will make no attempt to see his Majesty."

"I've only got an hour and a half."

"I mean to-morrow, of course," he exclaimed, testily.

"No, I'd better not, I suppose."

"To-morrow, I shall have your route carefully prepared, with full instructions to all on the way to help you forward with all speed."

"Yes, I suppose you're as anxious as I am to get the thing ended and done with."

"You will find I can be as firm a friend as I can be a resolute enemy. I wish to be your friend, monsieur, for my august master's sake."

"You've done pretty well as an enemy, Prince; let's hope the future will show us the other side."

"Then for the present, good-night."

"For the present?"

"I shall of course be at the ceremony."

I didn't want him there; but as I would rather be married to Helga in his presence than not married to her at all, I said nothing. Besides, I was not in a critical mood.

I was sufficiently practical to remember to go to the hotel and engage rooms, and on the way I stopped at a jeweller's store and bought a ring. And having done that I hunted up Harold Marvyn and induced him to consent to be at the wedding.

Then I drove to the prison where Frank Siegel was confined. I produced the order for his release, arranged all the preliminaries, and then told them to show me straight to the prisoner, as I wished to take the news to him myself.

"Hello, what in thunder brings you here?" he exclaimed, as I entered.

"I've brought the order for your release, old man."

His face fell, and he looked the reverse of pleased.

"I hope you're just monkeying. I don't want any release," he said in a tone of such irritation that I laughed.

"Sorry, but you've got to come. I'm going to be married in about half an hour, and I want you to be best man."

He took it so coolly that I could have kicked him.

"Of course that makes a difference. But it strikes me you're using me some, Harper. Who's the——"

"You know. Met her in the train."

"Oh, the Nihilist. Sounds all right. Where?"

"In the prison."

"Gee; that'll make good copy."

And that seemed its best recommendation in his eyes.

"You take it very lightly," I said, with a smile.

"Well, you see, it's your marriage, not mine."

And with that we left the cell.

CHAPTER XXIX

A LAST PRECAUTION

IT was a quaint ceremony, our marriage.

The clock was close on the stroke of ten when Siegel and I reached the prison where Marvyn was already waiting for us in the room in which Helga and I had seen each other. He shook hands with Siegel and congratulated him.

"On getting in or getting out?"

"Both," replied Marvyn, and they laughed.

"This is a queer show," said Siegel.

"Denver was never conventional," returned Marvyn with a shrug of the shoulders.

"How do they tie them up over here? Greek Church?" queried Siegel.

"Yes," nodded Marvyn. "Depends on the religion."

"Through soon?" and Siegel glanced at his watch. "I want a bath."

"A few minutes. By the way, Denver, to make the thing regular—I thought I'd better ask Hoskyns, the Embassy chaplain, to come along."

"Thank you, I hadn't thought of that," I said.

"Will you come to the chapel, monsieur?" asked a warder entering at that moment.

He led us through the corridors to the dimly-lighted gloomy chapel where Helga in charge of a female warder was waiting near the chaplain.

"Odd looking Joshua," murmured Siegel, glancing at the priest's quaint robes.

Marvyn, who did things with official decorum, took no notice and when we reached the altar rails Siegel and Helga shook hands and he said something which made her smile. Then I introduced Marvyn who was obviously struck by her beauty.

"She's very lovely," he whispered to me as we took our places.

"Yes, she'll make 'em hustle around in New York," added Siegel who overheard him.

The ceremony was in Russian and very brief. The priest spoke in a kind of droning chant and his deep voice rolled around the empty building and came back from the dark recesses behind the heavy pillars with a hollow echo more striking than cheerful.

I knew enough of the ritual to do the right thing at the right moment and when it all came to a rather abrupt and unexpected end, I heard Siegel, whose modernity was quite unaffected by the weird strangeness of the scene, exclaim in a quite audible tone, "First Half," as if it had been a football match.

Marvyn saw to the completion of the legal formalities and then Helga slipped her hand in my arm and I led her away down the cold gaunt aisle.

I was too happy and proud to think of anything except my dear beautiful wife until on passing one of the plain sturdy pillars I felt her start, and glancing round saw Prince Kalkov step from its shadow. He did not speak to us, but joined the two men.

"He said he would be present; I had forgotten," I whispered to Helga. "It doesn't matter."

"I wonder why he has hurried us so," she said. "We shall soon know."

When we reached the little room we found Mr. Hoskyns, the American chaplain, waiting for us, and Marvyn who came in alone introduced him.

"Where's Siegel?" I asked.

"Trying to interview Prince Kalkov," he replied with a dry smile.

Siegel came in time for the second ceremony which was even shorter than that in the chapel, and when the signing was finished and the others had congratulated us, Helga got ready to leave.

"That should be a good double knot," said Siegel. "Do you suppose I can go back to my cell?"

"I've engaged a room for you at the Imperial," I told him. "You'll all come round with us?"

But the chaplain excused himself and Marvyn pleaded a pressing engagement.

"I should like to come, Denver," he said, drawing me aside. "I want a word with you very particularly. Come and see me first thing in the morning at the Embassy, will you? It's about those things."

"What about them?"

"I want you to take them away. And as you're all right now, I suppose it won't matter."

"Anything to do with Kalkov?" I whispered.

He nodded.

"Indirectly, I'll tell you in the morning. You needn't worry," he added, noticing my look.

I promised to see him in the morning, and then Siegel, declaring he must have a word or two with Marvyn, persisted in going away with him.

I led Helga to the carriage and Prince Kalkov met us by the door of the prison.

"I shall see you to-morrow, monsieur?"

"Yes, assuredly. We shall be at the Imperial."

"I will come to you there in the afternoon at three o'clock. May I wish your wife and you all happiness?"

Helga said nothing; she would not even look at him, and I felt the pressure of her hand on my arm tighten.

"We ought to have it, Prince. We have had to fight hard to get even thus far," I said. "Good-night."

"Good-night."

He bared his head and bowed to Helga, and with a smile drew aside for us to pass.

Helga shivered slightly and whispered—

"I am very foolish; but I am still afraid of him."

"It's something to know he fears us also," I answered. "We have forced him to open these gates for you and you are now the wife of an American citizen. So we have the laugh on him."

"For a time," she said thoughtfully.

"No, for all our time. The Stars and Stripes will see to that. Besides, you agreed to meet even our marriage with a laugh;" and then we began to keep the agreement and to put the Prince and all his wiles out of our thoughts.

At breakfast on the following morning Helga was in excellent spirits as we discussed the prospects of our long journey and planned the day's work of preparation for it. There were a hundred things to do and innumerable purchases to make, and Helga with paper and pencil laughed gaily as the list she made grew until its length was formidable.

"There is one nut we have still to crack," I said. "What to do with the papers," and I told her what Marvyn had said to me on the previous night. I had not told her before not wishing to kindle her inflammable anxiety.

"The Prince's hand is in it, of course, and not for any good," was her comment.

"That's the best of dealing with such a man—you can always gamble on it that he means some kind of trouble."

"I think we may tear this up," she said, and held up the list we had made so carefully.

"Tear it up? But you—oh, you think we shan't be allowed to go, after all?"

"I don't know what I think, but I am sure there is treachery somewhere."

I was not in a suspicious mood, however. The world had become very bright to me and I thought Helga was too much under the influence of her former feelings. One can't shake oneself free in a dozen hours from the trammels of such a life of danger and vigilance as she had lived for years. She seemed to read my thought.

"You think I am fanciful, Harper," she said with a smile. "I hope so; but the Prince does nothing without an object and his real object is so rarely that which he lets you see."

"I am more confident than ever," I said.

"Probably he is reckoning on that, dear—to recover the papers, hoping we shall make some false step."

"I believe you're right, but——"

I paused, for it had not dawned upon me until then all that the abandonment of the journey might mean to Helga.

"I have been very thoughtless, my dear, but I see now what you mean."

She smiled gently and sadly.

"I almost hope he is not alive. He was incapable of any such crimes as the Prince hinted, and if he has had to endure the life in the mines for all these years, it would be worse than death to him. Better death than a broken heart such as his would be. You would say so if you had known him."

"Were it my own father's case I would rather he were dead, Helga. I know the pain of such a thought to you. The cruelty of Kalkov in raising a false hope is just dastardly, and to do it for some fresh crafty purpose makes it diabolical."

"What we have to do is to thwart the purpose; for, depend on it, we are in as great danger from him as ever. I think I begin to see it now."

"Show me."

"He knows that the papers will be in either your hands or mine and accordingly has hurried our marriage."

"I don't think we'll blame him for that," I interposed, and drew a glance of love from her.

"Then he put out the bait for this long journey for us together-"

"But he first opposed your going and wanted me to go alone."

"Yes, knowing it would be useless for you to go by yourself. He was merely working round to his end. He can of course deal more easily with us together. Then, see his next step. He waits until we are married and pledged to go to Siberia, and then contrives that the papers are to be suddenly forced back into our possession. Mr. Marvyn is to give them to you this morning, we are to start to-night or to-morrow; and he reckons he can watch us so closely after you get them and until we start that he will learn what you do with them."

"I meant to take them with us."

Helga thought a moment and shook her head.

"Very likely he has meant that too, but I doubt if he would take such a risk. If I read him aright, he will look for his opportunity at the first convenient moment after you leave the Embassy this morning. You will have the papers with you and an arrest and a search would give him all he wants. You see it now?"

"And see also that if it had not been for your sharp woman's wit I should have tumbled into his trap again. You are wonderful, Helga."

"There is nothing wonderful in such a guess. I know him. The question is what to do with the papers?"

"They shall go to New York," I said promptly.

"But how?"

As if to suggest an answer to her question Frank Siegel came hurrying into the room saying as he shook hands—

"Can give you just five minutes; been cabled for, and am off for home in an hour. Going to join our people in New York."

Helga and I exchanged looks.

"Leaving 'Frisco?"

"Yes," he nodded. "Same people, same papers, different place, that's all, except that it's better."

"I'm glad. Hope we shall follow you soon."

"Siberia off then?" he asked, in a matter of fact tone.

"Don't know yet. By the way, could you take something to my father for me?"

"Those papers?"

"You're very quick, M. Siegel," laughed Helga.

"My dear Mrs. Denver, I'd do anything in the world to oblige you; but this is a large order. Can't risk another arrest just now. What's up, Harper?"

"I want those papers got safely to New York."

"I can do better than take 'em; tell you how to get 'em over safely. They wouldn't be safe with me."

"How do you mean?"

"Why, get Marvyn to send 'em as Embassy business."

"Great Scott, I never thought of it," I exclaimed.

"Good-bye, Mrs. Denver. You'll like New York, and we shall have times together. Better than Siberia. Good-bye, Harper. Thanks for that chance in the prison. Glad now I got out so soon. This cable's urgent. Good-bye and good luck," and he was gone.

"American methods are a little breathless, Harper," said Helga, with a laugh. "Do you all cut knots as easily?"

"He's cut this one anyway," and then we discussed how I should proceed. We decided to act just as though we were really going away, and to make a show of preparing for the journey. And at Helga's suggestion we put up a little scheme of our own to frustrate any plan which the Prince might have formed.

Helga was to go to see after her own matters and we decided not to meet until an hour before the time Prince Kalkov had appointed to call. Then we were to lunch in our own rooms and not leave them until he arrived.

The reason for this was of course that his spies might be able to trace our movements very easily, and lead the Prince to believe that what he sought would be found with us in the hotel.

I was to call first at the Foreign Embassy to arrange matters there; then to see Marvyn, and on leaving him to drive round to various stores to purchase what I needed for the journey, and to do everything as though I had not a suspicion of treachery.

I was on the point of starting when it occurred to me that Marvyn might prove very reluctant to adopt Siegel's suggestion. In his official capacity he might be placed in a very awkward and embarrassing position, and would very probably shrink from having any more official dealings with documents about which these representations had been made.

I had no desire to get him into trouble and I therefore resolved to mislead him. Accordingly I made up a dummy set of papers

207

closely resembling those I had left with him, and I took them with me in readiness.

It turned out to be a very fortunate precaution.

Before anything was said on the subject I opened my fire.

"This jaunt to Siberia is a pretty big thing, Marvyn, and as one never knows what is going to happen I think I ought to send some papers I have with me home to my father: my will and some other things. They are very important—some of them, and as my relations with the authorities here have been peculiar, and letters have a knack of getting opened, I want you to send them over under official cover. I suppose there'll be no difficulty."

"You don't mean the—those I have."

"I mean these," I said, and took them out of my pocket.

"Oh, that will be all right," he answered in a tone of relief, and held out his hand for them. "They can go at once if you like. It happens we're sending off a special despatch to Washington about the China crisis. We've had a messenger out with important despatches from the President, and he's going back with our reply to-day. Give them to me and I'll see to it."

"I have a line or two to add to my father first. And now about the important papers. I want you to keep them till I get back from this journey."

"Don't ask me, Denver. As I told you, I'd do anything in my power for you, but this is really impossible. Exactly what has happened I don't know and was told not to ask, but I have to give my word that I've returned the things to you."

I assumed a little indignation of course and argued the point, urging my father's position and the extreme inconvenience to me in having to take such documents to Siberia, and then very reluctantly gave way and took the packets from him.

He left me then to finish the supposed letter to my father and all I had to do was to change the envelopes and I slipped the dummies into envelopes I had brought with me, endorsed precisely like the genuine ones, and I put the genuine ones into an envelope addressed to my father.

"I wish you could have sent these as well," I said, in a rueful tone to Marvyn when he brought me an official wrapping; and I pointed to the two carefully addressed dummies.

"I wish I could, but you'll understand how it is."

"It's very awkward," I replied, and put them in my pocket. "By the way, things being as they are, it's not worth while to speak of this."

"My dear Denver, silence is the very A.B.C. of our work," he answered.

There was nothing more to do, and after a word or two about our journey I pleaded the many preparations I had to make, thanked him for all he had done and bade him good-bye.

As I left the building I looked round for the Prince's agents, speculating when the arrest which Helga had prophesied would be made.

CHAPTER XXX

THE PRINCE OUTWITTED

IF Helga was right, I might expect to be stopped very soon, and I was rather surprised that I was allowed even to reach the carriage without interruption.

Had Prince Kalkov taken that prompt step, he might or might not have been able to intercept the papers after finding they were not on me, but certainly things would have gone very differently.

If the Prince did not discover the trick of the dummies until the Embassy messenger had left Petersburg, the chances in my favour would be vastly increased.

To my surprise no attempt at all was made to interfere with me. I presume I was closely watched, but it was done so cleverly that I saw no signs of it. It was not my cue to show any anxiety about it, and I drove from store to store making a few purchases and many inquiries, until the time came for me to return to the hotel to Helga. She was surprised to see me. Over lunch I told her my news, and we discussed the position.

"He feels so sure, Harper, that he has put it off. But it will come before the day is out."

"The papers are well away by this time," I laughed, "so he can do his worst."

"He means to. I have seen M. Boreski. He had heard of my arrest and release, and he came to my house when I was there."

"I thought he was out of Russia."

"The Duchess Stephanie has patched everything up with her family. So he told me. He is to get back his Polish title, with a pardon for his old conspiracy, and compensation for his lost estates."

"They must be glad that she is married."

"I think it is they are rather afraid of what she might do next. It was a strange meeting;" and she smiled. "He is not really a strong man: I mean he likes some one to lean on. He seemed afraid lest the fact of his coming to me should be known, and yet felt bound to come to warn me. He is very conscious of his new dignity."

"To warn you?"

"Yes, about this journey to Siberia. The Duchess had heard of it and told him—she must be in close consultation with Kalkov after all; probably working hand and glove with him to recover the papers. The intention is that I shall be kept there as a prisoner—if we ever reach there, that is. M. Boreski warned me strongly against going."

"Did he know anything about your father?"

"No; on that point the Prince appears to have kept absolute secrecy."

"It all seems to fit in. It will be interesting to see what he does next."

"I have seen some one else who is most anxious to see you," said Helga with a bright smile. "A most earnest admirer."

"To see me?"

"Will be another American citizen, I think, but first wishes to go to Siberia with us."

"That's easy to guess, Helga. He is a good fellow. You mean Ivan?"

"Yes," she nodded. "He used to be devoted to me alone."

"Did you tell him?"

"About what?" This with an air of supreme innocence.

"That you're no longer alone, and that his devotion has now to be divided?"

"Yes; and actually he wasn't surprised; but, oh, so ridiculously pleased."

"Ridiculously?"

She answered with a glance and a smile, and then said—

"I think he is the most faithful servant that ever lived."

"You'll find his equal in America."

"What a wonderful country your America is!" she said.

"You'll say that in earnest when you've been there a while;" and with this mixture of banter and gravity we covered our real anxieties while we waited for Prince Kalkov to come.

He was punctual. The clock was on the stroke of three when he was announced.

"You are to the moment, Prince," I said.

"I said three o'clock, monsieur."

"You are not looking well."

In truth, he was looking very ill. His face was drawn and careworn and absolutely colourless, his eyes tired, and his whole expression suggestive of a strained effort to rally an already overtaxed strength. The events of the previous day had shaken him severely; and I remembered his illness.

"I am an old man, monsieur, and not well. My heart is treacherous," he said as he sank into a chair.

It was not exactly a happy phrase, and I caught Helga's fleeting glance of surprise.

"A treacherous heart is an ugly life companion," I answered gravely. "May I suggest a glass of cognac? You have been overtaxing your strength, Prince," I said as I handed it to him.

It seemed to give him some energy, and as he put down the glass, he said in a less weary tone—

"You are packing?"

"There is a lot to do, of course. You have brought the papers and so on for our journey?"

"No."

The monosyllable was more like his old sharp abrupt manner.

"No? Oh well, we can wait a day longer if you prefer it," I answered with a sort of indulgent indifference. "When one is ill, of course, the preparation of such things is troublesome. When may we expect them?"

"I have had news that alters the matter."

"Indeed. Not bad news for us, I trust." This with quick anxiety.

"I have heard that Prince Lavalski is dead, monsieur."

"Dead!" cried Helga, and turned away.

"When did he die?" I asked.

"I do not know." It was a very lame story, and I think he felt it, although he did his best to make it impressive. "It has greatly disturbed me. I ought to have been informed of it at the time, but it has been left to reach me after long delay through official reports."

"It is very serious."

After this from me we were all silent for a time, and Helga went through to the adjoining room.

"It is tragic that you did not know this yesterday, Prince," I added at length. "To have roused my wife's hope only to kill it to-day is to inflict a very cruel blow."

"What will you do now, monsieur?"

"I find it impossible to answer off hand. Of course this proposed journey will now be useless."

"Quite," he declared bluntly. "That is why I brought nothing with me."

211

I threw up my hands as if the situation baffled me.

"Poor Helga!" I sighed.

"Will you go to your own country, monsieur?" he asked.

"If I can induce my wife to go, yes. But——" I paused.

"You will do most wisely to go."

"No doubt. But——" and I pulled up again as if in the most desperate perplexity.

"You have paused twice on that word, monsieur," he exclaimed irritably.

"You see this news puts us back to where we were before, and my wife is still resolved to clear her father's memory. And so am I."

"You will do most wisely if you go, I repeat."

"I do not think she will go until that is done. I should not, and I should not counsel her to do so, either."

"I am not accustomed to speak without full meaning, monsieur, and again I advise you to leave Russia."

"And if we do not take the advice?"

His answer was a gesture from which I might deduce what I pleased. It was all very subtly and cleverly acted; as cleverly as if the situation had arisen quite unexpectedly.

He had so manœuvred that the papers were, as he believed, now within his reach. He felt that he could compel us to give them up or have them taken from us, and then deal with us as he pleased. He was probably calculating that I must be discussing the new situation embarrassed by a knowledge of this power of his; and I therefore began to manifest some slight uneasiness.

"I wish to be your friend," he said at length.

"I am sure of that. You have given me a striking proof—I mean in my marriage. We were scarcely friendly before that," I added with a forced and somewhat nervous laugh. "But I feel rather embarrassed."

"It is a wife's duty to obey her husband."

"Naturally; but this marriage of ours was for a special purpose, you see; and we were agreed upon it."

"If you care for your wife's safety, to say nothing of your own, you will take my advice, monsieur, and leave the country with her."

"It is all so unexpected." I spoke in the manner of one taken unawares. "I will take a day to consider what to do."

"No, you must decide now," he replied firmly; thinking no doubt, as I intended he should, that I wished to use the interval to get rid of the papers.

"In a matter of such importance one must have time," I protested with a spice of indignation. "It is only reasonable." I was growing manifestly more and more uneasy, and he perceived it. "It means so much."

"It means—everything to you both, so far as your future is concerned."

"I must have time," I repeated, and began to pace the room.

"I can grant none."

"But it does not rest with you to either grant or refuse it," I retorted, as if now attempting to put a bolder face on things.

"As to that, we shall see."

He was very confident; his voice and manner showed that; and I am sure that he enjoyed my apparent embarrassment. His sharp eyes followed me as I strode up and down the room.

"Come back this evening, and you shall have our decision."

"I must know at once."

"It is unreasonable, unjust, impossible," I cried with growing anger. "I will not stand your dictation in such a matter. I can't decide now, and I won't!"

"I shall not leave the room without your decision."

"Then I will;" and I walked to the door.

"You cannot leave, monsieur."

I turned on him in time to catch a look of extreme exultation in his eyes. He guessed I had the papers on me and wished to get away with them. I promptly rubbed it in by saying very angrily—

"You shall not insult me, monsieur. If you wish to make my wife a prisoner, you can do so; she will remain; but you have no right to detain me. It is monstrous."

"You cannot leave the room, M. Denver; my men are outside."

I was now in great fear; the start I gave showed him this.

"Do you dare to make me, an American citizen, a prisoner in my own rooms? You shall answer for this, monsieur," I exclaimed with great heat, and flung the door open.

He had spoken truly. A half-dozen men were stationed at the doors of our rooms. I shut the door again angrily.

"I shall appeal to my Ambassador."

"Have you not carried this far enough?" he asked menacingly. I had come to the same conclusion—although our reasons differed no doubt. "You have no alternative now but to accept my conditions," he added.

I affected to think, and then called Helga.

"Helga, Prince Kalkov orders us to leave Russia, and because I will not consent immediately, and will not advise you to take no further steps to clear your father's memory, he threatens to have us arrested."

"It is like his Highness," she said contemptuously.

"What answer shall we give him?"

"Let him do as he will."

"M. Denver has not quite explained my position. It is that you are free to leave Russia and go to the United States, if you hand to me the papers of which you obtained possession."

"I do not make conditions with you, Prince Kalkov," answered Helga with splendid scorn.

"You are right, madame. It is I who make them, you who obey them," he cried, rising, his voice trembling with anger under the lash of her words and look. "I will have no more of this; my patience is exhausted. Will you give them up, monsieur, and go?"

He was not pretty in his anger, but I ventured on one more little tonic for it. I burst into a laugh.

"Oh, the papers you want? Why didn't you say so? I haven't them; so I can't give them to you."

"It is false, monsieur, it is false. You are lying!" he exclaimed in a flame of passion, his eyes blazing. Then his rage seemed to burst out like a long smouldering volcano, which, breaking at length through the thin restraining crust, pours out its flood of white hot lava. "I know the truth. I have heard from your Embassy. They were given to you to-day. I know where you have been since. I have watched you here, and I know they are upon your person now." I started back and, as if involuntarily, put my hand to my breast pocket. He smiled cunningly. "Yes, I understand that gesture. Come, monsieur, I have outplayed you; give them me, and even now you can go."

"With your treacherous heart, Prince, you should guard against such passion as this."

"Silence, monsieur," he said, half beside himself with anger. "Give them to me, give them to me!" and he came toward me, his hand outstretched and trembling violently. He looked the very incarnation of triumphant and unbridled fury.

"I have told your Highness I have not them," I said, drawing back.

I might as well have spoken to a whirlwind.

He answered me with a wild storm of invective, cursing me for a liar and a villain and a hundred other things, and ending with threats as unrestrained as his anathemas.

"Give them up and go. Go where you will, and take your wife with you. We have no room even in our gaols for either American scum like you or Nihilist devils like her! Give them to me, I say. I have waited and schemed for this triumph; and do you think I will let you rob me of it? Give them me, give them me."

His manner was so threatening that I half thought he would throw himself on me and attempt to drag the papers from me.

"You are not yourself. You had better call your men," I said.

Helga, pale and shrinking before his outbreak, drew behind me.

"By God! You dare to lie to me still!" he exclaimed, and hurrying to the door, brought in a couple of men. "Now, I give you a last chance. Will you give them me?"

"I have told you I have nothing to give you."

The apparent obstinacy added fuel to his ungovernable rage.

"Search the dog," he said savagely between his set teeth; "and if he resists, use force."

He watched me as the men approached, his eyes scintillating with anger and his hands clenching and unclenching with spasmodic tension.

"I shall not resist; I only protest, monsieur," I said.

"Search the dog!" he exclaimed again, his voice choked with passion.

I made no resistance, of course; I had nothing to gain by doing so; and when the men took from my breast pocket the large envelope the Prince's face lighted with triumph, and rushing at the man who held it, he tore it from his grasp, and then fell back with it into a chair as if exhausted with the effort.

He gave one glance at the writing on the envelope and looked up at me.

"Liar! I knew it." The growl of a beast gloating over its prey secured after infinite labour—but secured.

While he was enjoying this moment of supposed triumph over us, the men who had searched me stood hesitating and waiting for further orders.

It was some moments before he could rally his reserved strength and master his rage sufficiently to speak to us again.

"Even now I can be merciful. Will you go to America?" He looked at us both and tapped one of the packets.

"No," I answered firmly.

"Choose, you"—and he pointed a trembling hand at Helga—"between the mines and abandoning this."

"I will go to the mines—if you can send me there," she answered without a shade of hesitation. Her quickness seemed to rekindle his rage.

"This man and woman are under arrest," he said to the men by me. "Remain outside the door." As they went out, he sat glaring at us and fingering the packets.

"What next?" I asked.

215

"You shall answer for your crime, and may thank your God I do not send you with your wife to the mines at once."

"I don't thank God; I thank my wife's and my precautions."

"You dared to pit yourself against me; and can see the result. Failure!" He all but hissed the word at us as he shook the packet in triumph.

"What you hold there is the proof of your failure, not mine. You had better open it."

He had been so certain that for the moment he only laughed; but on meeting my look, doubt and anxiety began to steal over his face.

"The papers you seek are across the frontier; you have nothing there but blank sheets."

"It is a lie, another damnable lie! I was at the Embassy to-day."

"You forget; I was there and saw Mr. Marvyn—last night."

"My God!"

His whole soul seemed to speak in that one cry of dismay; and for a moment he looked at the packet like a dazed man, afraid to open it and learn the truth. Then with shaking frenzied fingers he tore at the seals.

Helga clung to my arm.

The paper was tough and resisted his efforts for a time, thus accentuating his excitement and suspense.

At last he opened it and stared at the blank sheets.

Then he turned on me such a look of baffled rage as I had never seen on a man's face before.

He strove to speak, and failed; and the sheets fluttered down to the ground from his nerveless fingers.

Then he sprang up and staggered toward me, stopped suddenly, uttered a loud inarticulate cry, and pressing his hand to his heart, fell prone almost at my feet.

"He is ill," said Helga, speaking for the first time, and bending over him.

"Probably dying," I murmured; and seeing the crisis, I went to the door and called his men.

"The Prince is very ill; you had better let some one go for a doctor."

CHAPTER XXXI

AT THE ELEVENTH HOUR

IT was instantly clear that we had to face a situation fraught with many awkward complications.

We were under arrest by Prince Kalkov's orders, and his men left us in no doubt that both Helga and I were suspected of having caused in some way the sudden collapse.

Two of them stood by the doors to prevent our leaving, and the others lifted the Prince and laid him on a couch; and one of these three—he who had searched me and appeared to be the chief of them—said very curtly:

"I have sent for doctors and my chief; you will, of course, remain here."

"You mean we are under arrest?" I asked.

"Those were the Prince's orders—before this occurred."

"You will find he is suffering from heart trouble, I expect; and pending the doctor's arrival you had better loose the clothes about his neck, open the window to give him air, and let him take a glass of brandy."

"Perhaps he has had some of that already," he returned, his eye falling on the empty glass. He spoke with the knowing air of a man who suspects, and he seized the glass and put it beyond my reach.

"Do not forget I told you how to revive him, even if you are such a fool as your words suggest," I answered contemptuously. "It was from that decanter there the brandy was poured; you had better seize that as well."

The doctors were first to arrive, followed quickly by a police official, and shortly after by Pierre, the Prince's confidential man.

The official spoke a few words to the doctors, and then turned to me.

Fortunately for us he was a very different stamp of man from his subordinate, and addressed me courteously.

"This is a very embarrassing position, monsieur. I understand that the Prince gave instructions for your arrest and detention."

"We are of course at your disposal. I would first assure you that Prince Kalkov's seizure is the result of illness merely, for which we are in no way responsible."

"You wish to make a statement?"

"Not yet. I am an American citizen, my name is Harper C.

Denver, and this lady is my wife. I wish to go at once to the American Embassy—on vitally urgent business."

"I fear I cannot permit that."

"I have also the honour to enjoy the friendship of His Majesty the Emperor, as the Prince's man there, Pierre, can tell you. I was His Majesty's guest at the Palace recently."

He was impressed by this; but after a moment's thought shook his head and repeated he could not grant my request.

"My purpose in going there touches all this very closely, and every moment of delay is important. May I suggest that you put a question to the man Pierre, to confirm what I told you?"

He drew Pierre aside, and they spoke together a moment.

"We must get the real papers back by hook or crook," I whispered to Helga.

The official returned, looking very grave.

"He tells me you were a Palace guest, monsieur, but adds that for some days you and the Prince have been on extremely hostile terms."

"My wife will remain here, and I am quite content that you and any number of your men should accompany me. I assure you that my visit is of extreme interest to his Majesty."

He thought this over, and at length assented.

"We must accompany you, as you are——"

"Come, then. That is all I ask," I broke in. "I shall make no attempt to shirk any responsibility in all this."

We drove to the Embassy; he and one of his men with me inside the carriage; and we were shown at once to Marvyn, who looked in astonishment at my companions, recognizing the chief.

"I am under arrest, Marvyn, that's all. I am not going to Siberia after all, and want you to stop those papers. Wire to your man, wherever he is, and——"

"He hasn't gone yet. Something turned up to delay him."

"Then get back the packet and bring it along with you to the Imperial, and just see to things. Prince Kalkov was with us, and has had a seizure of some sort, and my wife and I are under arrest."

He went away and returned soon, carrying the packet.

"If those are M. Denver's papers, I must ask that they be given to me," said the official immediately.

I hadn't thought of this.

"You can see for yourself that they bear the Embassy's seals, M. Drougoff, and are in my possession," replied Marvyn, with a readiness for which I blessed him. "I am acting, of course, officially."

We drove back to the hotel, and on the way I told Marvyn pretty well how the case stood, withholding for the moment, however, the fact that I had deceived him in the morning.

The Prince had been removed from the room, and Helga was alone there under guard. She was not in the least disconcerted by the fresh development, and had had tea served in anticipation of my return.

"What is the charge against M. Denver, M. Drougoff?" asked Marvyn.

"At the present I am not informed. Prince Kalkov had ordered it; and there is now of course, the fact of his Highness's—seizure." He hesitated for the word.

"You will allow us to consult in private?"

"Certainly, M. Marvyn. I am indeed rather at a loss what to do except that M. Denver must remain under arrest."

We sat down then to Helga's tea-table.

"I must explain one thing," I began at once. "I misled you this morning about those papers. Those are the real things—what I brought away with me were shams."

"Do you mean to say—" he began, but I interposed.

"Listen to me a moment, and be angry afterwards if you like. The liberty, and probably life, of us both were at stake. Kalkov had planned to force the things into my hands; and as soon as he thought you had given them to me, he dogged every movement of mine after leaving you this morning, and came here to get them by force. All this pretence for a journey to Siberia was just a lie; and we got wind of it in time."

"Why didn't you tell me?"

"I had no proofs, my dear fellow. I wished you to be able to pass your word that you had given them back to me—you did hand them me, remember, and I gave them back under the different cover. I deceived you intentionally, I know—but more than my life was at stake," and I glanced across to Helga.

"It might have been a gravely compromising matter for me, Denver," he said, seriously.

"I should have taken the consequences of my act, of course, and my father would have exhausted every resource to put things right. But you see now what would have happened if I had had the papers here. The dummies were taken from me by force, and I was put under arrest; and my wife also."

"I am sure Mr. Marvyn will see it as we do," said Helga.

"I wish to," he replied. "And was it the discovery of the—that he'd been tricked—caused this collapse?" I nodded, and he whistled: "Phew, that's a circumstance. What are you going to do?"

"There's only one thing. I must see the Czar, and you must hold on to those papers like grim death till I can take them to him."

"But with this indefinite charge hanging over you——"

"My dear fellow, it's got to be done; and done at once, before the Prince gets up enough strength to interfere. The Emperor will see me, I know; and your people must arrange it. It's absolutely essential. I'm done, if I don't get to him."

"But you see——"

"There's a most plausible reason for the audience, Mr. Marvyn," interposed Helga quickly. "His Majesty will be most anxious to know at first hand the facts about Prince Kalkov's illness; and we alone can tell him."

"Splendid, Helga, splendid," I said; and Marvyn agreed. "Get my name to him somehow; any old way'll do; and I'll answer for the rest."

"I'll go and see about it at once," he declared. "Meanwhile, what's to happen to you?"

"Short of cutting our heads off, I don't care," I replied, as we rose. "Don't worry about that;" and I hurried him away.

"Now, M. Drougoff, we are at your disposal," I said to the police agent as soon as Marvyn had gone. "What are you going to do with us? I may tell you the American Embassy people are working energetically in the affair, and I am sure to receive very soon a summons to wait upon his Majesty."

"My people tell me that a very serious charge is hanging over you both—I mean apart altogether from this."

"They tell you wrong, then. My wife was charged in some Nihilist practices and imprisoned by order of Prince Kalkov; but the Prince himself ordered her release from the prison last night, and was present when she came away with me."

"But yourself?"

"I have never been charged, and, as I say, was with Prince Kalkov yesterday when my wife was released."

"It is a very extraordinary complication. What is behind it?"

"There is a good deal behind, of course; but the Prince himself can best explain it, when he is well enough. At present I am only concerned to know whether you wish to put us under lock and key. We are quite ready."

He was manifestly perplexed what to do.

"I cannot release you, monsieur; you will see that?"

"It's only for an hour or two at the worst," and I went back to the tea-table.

"I will send and inquire how the Prince is."

"It's a question whether he recovers in time to stop the interview with the Czar," said Helga to me.

"No, he can't stop it now."

After a few minutes the messenger returned, and M. Drougoff crossed to us.

"His Highness is much better, monsieur; he is rallying fast, and the doctors say that in an hour probably, or at most two, I may be able to see him and take instructions. In the meantime it will be most convenient for matters to remain as they are. I do not wish to trouble your charming wife and you unnecessarily."

"Very well, I am much obliged to you," I answered. "We can do nothing but wait," I said to Helga, when he had gone back to his seat. "Wait, that is, and hope he won't get well too soon."

"I thought he was worse," she replied.

"I wish with all my heart he was," I agreed.

Wishing was of no use, however; and there we sat waiting for a time that seemed interminable, each trying to prevent the other from seeing how real and harassing was the anxiety of the suspense and each conscious of, and smiling, at the other's efforts.

Helga was very brave, very calm, and very cheerful; and only in little signs and gestures—a start, a glance, a movement of the features or hands—could I see how the strain tried her.

Much less than an hour of this exhausted my patience, however.

"I wish whatever's going to happen first would happen and be done with it," I exclaimed. "I feel like a man staked on a volcano top, uncertain whether it's going to explode and blow me up, or give way and let me through into the lava."

"You'd make a bad conspirator, Harper," said Helga, smiling. "They have to endure this kind of thing for days, weeks and months."

"We should manage it quicker in the States."

"Those wonderful States again. Tell me a lot about them. My new country," she added sweetly.

"There are no Kalkovs in them, for one thing, and—what's this, I wonder," I broke off, as a man came in and spoke to M. Drougoff.

It was nothing, or apparently nothing, for the man went out again, and his superior sank again into the condition of watchful inactivity, the result I concluded of many years' training in spy work.

"I wish to Heaven Marvyn would send us word what's doing. He might know one would be anxious."

"He can scarcely have done anything yet. He has been gone barely an hour," said Helga gently.

"I told him he'd have to hustle."

"But he does not know the Prince is getting better."

"If he doesn't hurry up as if he did know it, he's—well, he's an ass, and my father ought never to have got him into the diplomatic service. Yes, laugh away, I know I'm an idiot; but it helps a heap to blame the other fellow;" and I laughed, too.

And so the minutes dragged until something did happen.

Another message was brought to Drougoff, and this time he got up and approached us.

"The Prince is well enough to receive me, monsieur."

"Thank God for that," I exclaimed, almost as heartily as if he had told me we were both free. Anything was better than suspense.

He went away, leaving the man to take his place.

"How is the Prince?" I asked him.

"Nearly recovered, monsieur. Weak, but that is all."

"He's won the race, I'm afraid, Helga. We may as well get ready. Where will he send us, I wonder. We must manage somehow to leave word for Marvyn."

"They won't let us do that. We must stop here to the last possible moment. Think of everything you can to use up time."

"Bully for you. You always have some good notion."

M. Drougoff was not absent long, and looked very troubled when he entered.

"My instructions are, I deeply regret to say, monsieur, to remove you at once."

"Where?"

He named two different prisons.

"The charges?" I asked next.

"I am not instructed to mention them, monsieur."

"Then I am not going," I said firmly.

"Pray consider, monsieur. Resistance will be quite useless."

"I have considered, I assure you; and I shall resist. If your instructions are to kill me or maim me, you may obey them, if you wish. But I do not move from here alive, and as I am a citizen of the United States, my death may be a circumstance."

"Let me persuade you, monsieur."

"You can try if you like;" and try he did for over a quarter of an hour of invaluable time, at the end of which he was in despair, and I was as obdurate as ever.

"When Mr. Marvyn returns and advises me to go, I'll go; but until then I refuse point blank. You are too courteous a man to make a good butcher, I am sure, and I can put up an excellent fight at need."

"I must obey my orders, monsieur," he replied tersely.

222

"And as an American citizen, I refuse to budge without knowing the charge against me, and until my Embassy's people are here."

"I am deeply sorry, but I have no alternative;" and he rose.

Then Helga came to the rescue with a suggestion.

"Had you not better return to the Prince with our decision? My husband is a foreigner, and a friend of His Majesty; and the situation is altogether unusual."

"It is useless," he persisted.

"Very well, then," I said; "we'll clear the decks. I was getting ready for a long journey, monsieur, and have arms here. If there is blood-shed, the responsibility will not be mine. I am innocent of any offence, and you may rely on it I will not be taken alive."

This was very unexpected, I could see, and he hesitated.

"I will acquaint his Highness," he said after a pause, and left us again.

"Do you mean to fight, Harper," asked Helga, anxiously.

"Not I. We've nothing to fight with," I said, smiling; "but we've gained twenty minutes and more. I wish Marvyn would come."

"You took me in. I thought you were in earnest," she replied, in a tone of intense relief.

M. Drougoff was away longer than even I had hoped; and when he returned he had a surprise for us.

"His Highness himself is coming, monsieur," he announced, shortly.

"I don't see that he can do any good, but that's his matter," I said; and then we all stood in silence.

The shuffling of many feet was heard, the door was thrown wide open, and the indomitable old man was carried in lying on an improvised litter, with two doctors at his side.

They set him down in the middle of the room, and the bearers drew away.

"I have come to see my orders obeyed," he said, with a glance at Drougoff, and then at Helga and myself. His voice was weak, but his manner implacably stern.

"Then you have come to see an ugly fight," said I, as firmly as though I meant resisting to the last.

"Arrest them both, Drougoff. You have my authority for using any force necessary."

"What is the charge against us?" I demanded.

"Do your duty, you, Drougoff," he said, viciously.

M. Drougoff signed to his men.

"Go forward, Helga. You can waste a little time yet," I whispered.

She did splendidly again. She clung to me for a moment as if overcome, and then with passionate distress bade me good-bye.

The men held aloof during this; and when she went to them she contrived very cleverly to get rid of a little more time.

But the way was clear at length, and Drougoff stepped towards me.

I drew back and put my hand in my pocket.

"You will come no further, monsieur, or your life will be the forfeit."

He stopped abruptly.

"Let your men fire if he resists," said the relentless old man.

Drougoff gave the necessary orders, and for a tense moment I looked along the barrels of three levelled revolvers.

"Come, monsieur," said Drougoff.

I burst into a laugh.

"Yes, I will. I have no firearms;" and I pulled my empty hand from my pocket.

Then at last came the proof that I had not blustered in vain.

Harold Marvyn came hurrying in, accompanied by a man I recognized as the officer whom I had seen the previous day in the ante-room of the Emperor.

"I am glad to see your Highness is so far recovered," said Marvyn; "but what does this mean?"

"That two dangerous Nihilists are on their way to prison, monsieur," came the reply, sharp and stern.

Marvyn's indignation at the tone showed in his face.

"The Emperor has commanded Mr. Denver's immediate presence at the Palace, your Highness. This is an outrage upon an American citizen."

"Outrage or no outrage, they are going to prison, monsieur."

"Colonel Vilda," said Marvyn, turning to him.

"I have the Emperor's commands, your Highness. They are peremptory, and I must obey them."

"And the woman?" The old bully's tone was worthy of him.

"Madame Denver is to accompany her husband to the Palace, to be in readiness should his Majesty require to see her."

"She is a dangerous Nihilist, Colonel."

"They are his Majesty's commands, your Highness."

"I am at your service, Colonel," I said.

"We have a carriage waiting, M. Denver."

He offered his arm to Helga, and I followed with Marvyn, and went out without even casting a glance at Kalkov; but I saw the two doctors bend over him anxiously.

"You had to hustle, Marvyn."

"Some," he nodded.

"It was a near thing."

"So it looked."

And with that and a laugh of relief we got into the carriage.

CHAPTER XXXII

THE END

HELGA was waiting for me with a look of eager anxiety when I came out to her from my interview with the Emperor.

"Well?" she asked, as she came to me.

"Yes, it is all well," I answered smiling. "All well, all the best it could be—for us. Not for the Prince," I added drily.

"And my father?"

"Justice will be done to his memory, my dear, full justice. You were right in the kernel of your plans—to get to the Czar."

"I was certain of that," she said.

"If you could have got to him all this would never have happened. I never saw a man more moved. I left all the papers with him and he's going to study them himself, and then see you. Never a breath of the truth has ever been allowed to reach him."

"My dear father," she murmured. "At last," and she sighed.

"Old Kalkov has had things his own way and has had a fine past; but I don't envy him his future."

Marvyn entered the ante-room then.

"How have things gone, Denver?"

"Couldn't have gone better, thanks to you."

"By gorm, I'm glad," he exclaimed with a sigh of relief. "The ice was so thin I was afraid we should be through."

"It will bear every one except Kalkov, and it'll put his light out. You may gamble on that."

"It was a big risk to carry," he said, thinking of himself.

I smiled.

"You should have had half an hour of ours," I suggested.

"Yes, I know," he answered with a quaint smile. "But one's official responsibilities make such a difference, Denver."

225

"True, but even unofficially one can have a sort of sneaking regard for one's life and liberty."

"I shall never forget your help, Mr. Marvyn," said Helga, sweetly, as she gave him her hand.

"I would take the risk again for such a smile, Mrs. Denver."

"Now you're talking," said I. "It's very pretty of you, but I hope we shan't have to ask for it; although we may still need the Embassy's protection, if the Emperor carries out his threats."

"How's that?"

"He seems to contemplate putting an end to Mrs. Denver."

"Harper?" cried Helga.

"It's true—as true as it is staggering."

"No spoke in the wheels I hope?"

This from Marvyn.

"He threatens," I said, looking very grave.

"Then why are your eyes laughing, Harper?" cried Helga.

"It'll be no laughing matter if we find our marriage annulled."

"That's only putting the riddle a different way;" and Helga slipped her arm into mine and clasped her hands on it.

"What is it?" asked Marvyn, seriously.

I had before observed his keen scent for trouble from afar. The serious side of things always appealed first to him.

"He threatens," I repeated.

"Haven't we had enough problems lately?" and Helga wrinkled her brows in half comical perplexity. "But I can wait quite calmly."

"He wants to make out that as the daughter of a prince and his friend, you ought to be considered a kind of Imperial ward to whose marriage his consent was necessary; so that——"

Helga interrupted me with a laugh.

"I knew it was nonsense."

"I don't see that under the circumstances such a claim could be maintained," declared Marvyn gravely.

"And further that Helga cannot be Mrs. Denver."

"Who am I then?"

"He talks about making reparation of everything and giving you your father's title."

"But I can't be a Prince, surely!"

"You would of course be Princess," said Marvyn, in the same dry official manner.

"Mr. Denver's Princess! What an odd mixture!"

"I think it would be rather the Princess's Mr. Denver," said I.

"And what did you say, Harper?"

"Oh, that as to the material compensation we could talk, but that about the title we'd go back to the hotel and discuss it. Will you come with us, Marvyn?"

He excused himself on the plea of business and left us, and Helga and I were just going when Colonel Vilda came to summon her to an audience with the Emperor. She was to go alone.

"I congratulate you, Mr. Denver," he said to me when he returned from ushering her into the presence.

"I've been doing that to myself very heartily, Colonel, I can assure you."

"The Princess will make a brilliant figure in the Court."

"Which Princess, Colonel, and which Court?"

"The Princess Lavalski," he answered, smiling.

"We have no Court in the States, Colonel."

"But you will not take her from us in the very moment of our finding her again!"

"You've managed to get along pretty well without her so far, I fancy."

"But, my dear monsieur! She's so charming, so beautiful, so wealthy—the world will be at her feet."

"It'll have to be the western hemisphere of it then, I think."

"Ah, but it would be a crime to take her away."

"I shan't take her away, Colonel—but somehow I have an idea she won't much care to stop."

"But it is too bad;" and he laughed and spread his hands.

There came a little commotion at the door then, and when it was opened, Prince Kalkov was carried in seated in a chair.

"Let His Majesty know that I crave an immediate audience with him, Colonel Vilda, on urgent matters of State," he said.

"His Majesty is engaged, your Highness."

"I am accustomed to be obeyed, Colonel Vilda," returned Kalkov austerely.

The Colonel drew himself up at the tone, paused and then bowed.

"I will take your Highness' message," he said, and left us.

"You have seen the Emperor, monsieur?" said the Prince to me.

"Yes."

"What passed between you?" he demanded, with much of his customary arrogant insistence.

"It was a confidential interview, monsieur."

"If it concerned me I have a right to know."

"I must ask you to excuse my saying anything. You and I began as friends, then we had a pretty sharp burst as antagonists; now if you please we must be neutrals—I have nothing further to say to you."

227

"I have yet to see his Majesty, monsieur." Even now he was ready to threaten me in his indomitable doggedness.

I took no notice, and presently Colonel Vilda returned.

"His Majesty is unable to see your Highness," he announced.

"I will not take that answer," declared the Prince vehemently. "The matters are too urgent and vitally affect his Majesty himself, for me to take it. I have been his loyal adviser and faithful minister for many years. I am not to be thrown aside on the bare word of hirelings and traitors." He was fast losing self-control in his passion when he checked himself and said: "Give my humble greetings to his Majesty, tell him I am ill and perhaps dying, and solicit most earnestly that he will see me. Say it may be the last time on earth I may ever speak to him."

"His Majesty was very decided," said the Colonel.

"His Majesty does not know either how ill I am or how urgent my business. Should I be here like this, if it were not?"

Colonel Vilda went in again and this time the interval before his return passed in silence.

When he returned, Helga was with him. I saw she had been weeping and that the tears were still in her eyes.

"They are tears of joy and gratitude, Harper," she whispered, taking my arm and then started as she saw Prince Kalkov.

"His Majesty deeply regrets to hear of your Highness's illness," said the Colonel, "and he counsels your immediate return to your house, where he will communicate with you."

The old man listened with frowning brows and unmoved firmness.

"It is not true," he declared doggedly.

"It is as I say, your Highness; and his Majesty further bids me say that as your health has broken down, he will immediately relieve you of all your official duties."

"He cannot mean this—and without ever seeing me," he cried.

"His Majesty is too overcome by news which has reached him to-day, to be able to endure the strain of an interview with your Highness, and has retired to his private apartments."

"My God! after all my years of service."

"Come, Harper," whispered Helga; and we hurried out glad to escape the sight of our enemy's overthrow.

On the way to the hotel she told me all the Emperor had said to her; the regrets he had expressed; the sorrow he felt; the promises he made; and the hopes he had expressed for her future happiness.

"As a Princess?" I asked; "or as——"

She glanced and smiled and ran on into the hotel, leaving me unanswered.

At the hotel Ivan was waiting, anxious concerning our journey to Siberia, and overjoyed at seeing us together again.

"Has your Highness any commands?" I asked Helga.

"Harper!"

"Well, has Mrs. Denver any wishes?"

"We are not going to Siberia, Ivan," she said to him. "Everything has come right."

The great burly fellow laughed with the delight of a child.

"I could cry with pleasure, mademoiselle," he said.

"Hullo, that's still a third title for you—mademoiselle," I laughed.

She would not hear me.

"But we are going on a long journey, Ivan, all the same," she said, in a very matter of fact unconcerned tone.

"Where?" I asked.

"To New York, of course; where else should Mrs. Denver go, indeed?"

"Bully for you," I cried and then—but Ivan was in the room; so I turned him out first and told him to go and pack, as we should start as soon as possible.

And we did.

www.ingramcontent.com/pod-product-compliance
Lightning Source LLC
Chambersburg PA
CBHW032043240626
47154CB00003B/1057